GREEN-EYED
LADY

WITHDRAWN

CHUCK GREAVES

was born in Levittown, New York. He is an honors graduate of both the University of Southern California and Boston College Law School and spent twenty-five years as a trial lawyer in Los Angeles. *Hush Money*, his first novel, was named by SouthWest Writers as the Best Mystery/Suspense/Thriller/Adventure Novel of 2010 and won SWW's Storyteller Award. He lives in the American Southwest.

GREEN-EYED LADY

CHUCK GREAVES

WORLDWIDE®

TORONTO • NEW YORK • LONDON
AMSTERDAM • PARIS • SYDNEY • HAMBURG
STOCKHOLM • ATHENS • TOKYO • MILAN
MADRID • WARSAW • BUDAPEST • AUCKLAND

Recycling programs
for this product may
not exist in your area.

ISBN-13: 978-0-373-28223-4

Green-Eyed Lady

Copyright © 2013 by Charles J. Greaves

A Worldwide Library Suspense/December 2016

First published by Thomas Dunne Books for Minotaur Books, an imprint of St. Martin's Press.

"Green- Eyed Lady"
Words and Music by Jerry Corbetta, J.C. Phillips, and David Riordan
(c) 1970 (Renewed) CLARIDGE MUSIC COMPANY, A Division of MPL Music Publishing, Inc.
All Rights Reserved
Reprinted by Permission of Hal Leonard Corporation

This is a work of fiction. Names, characters, places and incidents are either the product of the author's imagination or are used fictitiously, and any resemblance to actual persons, living or dead, business establishments, events or locales is entirely coincidental.

This edition published by arrangement with Harlequin Books S.A.

® and TM are trademarks of the publisher. Trademarks indicated with ® are registered in the United States Patent and Trademark Office, the Canadian Intellectual Property Office and in other countries.

www.Harlequin.com

Printed in U.S.A.

This book is for the late Don Mike Anthony,
my dear friend and mentor,
who loved crime fiction,
golden retrievers, the law, and a glass of good wine,
although not necessarily in that order.

Politics is supposed to be the second-oldest profession. I have come to realize that it bears a very close resemblance to the first.
—Ronald Reagan

PROLOGUE

EVEN NOW, in vivid hindsight, he could not recall which he'd noticed first: her crumpled shape on the blacktop or her voice echoing across the nearly empty parking lot. A cry of anguish, he'd thought at the time. A cry for help.

She was already to her feet by the time he'd reached her. There was a rip in her hose at the knee; that much he remembered, and a dislodged crocodile pump at which she'd stabbed, hopping, with the nylon dagger of her foot.

"Are you all right?" he'd asked her, breathless, lamenting this banality even as he uttered it.

She'd been leaning forward then, with one hand braced on the big Mercedes and her auburn hair hanging like a theater curtain, partially obscuring her face.

"Did you see him?" she'd asked as she straightened. Her eyes, he'd noticed then in the sodium lamplight, were green. Not blue green or hazel, but the bright, mossy tincture of verdigris on an old copper lantern.

"See who?"

"That man." She'd waved vaguely toward the traffic on Hollywood Boulevard. "My purse."

He remembered that he'd stepped in the direction she indicated, frowning into the darkness and the strolling tourists and the flaring headlights, a histrionic gesture.

"Never mind." She'd sighed, brushing at her hip. Her

skirt was tight and it rode up her thighs as she twisted to inspect behind her. "You've been very kind."

They'd stood in silence, both regarding the car.

"Keys?"

She'd moved her head side to side. "In the purse. Along with my phone."

"I have a phone," he'd offered, reaching into his suit jacket, but she'd ignored this, gazing instead toward the hills that stood in dark repose above the bright lights of the city.

"Not to mention my auto club card, my credit cards, all my cash," she'd said then, more to herself than to him. "Shit!"

"Shall I call the police?"

"The police? What would they do?" She'd straightened her skirt, wriggling at the hips. "Fill out forms? File them in a drawer?"

"My office is just down the street" is what he'd said next, when actually he'd been thinking, we could both use a drink. Musso and Frank is just around the corner. They make a killer martini.

She'd fixed him with the eyes then, emerald cold and probing, as if reading his private thoughts.

"Perhaps you could call me a cab. That would be very kind of you."

"Do you live nearby? I'd be happy to drive you."

"No, thank you. I couldn't impose."

"Don't be silly." He'd smiled his campaign smile then, the hundred-watt dazzler that showed his dimples to best advantage. "It would be no bother at all."

HE'D PEGGED HER for forty, over twenty-five years his junior. Taut and tanned. Gym membership, yoga classes, maybe a beach house on the weekend. Two diamond studs, a Cartier wristwatch, and no rings, but a woman with that face and that body had to have been married. Divorced, probably. A messy divorce, with Beverly Hills lawyers and a big battle over the prenup.

"Have I met you somewhere before?" she'd asked him as they merged with the eastbound traffic.

"Warren Burkett," he'd replied, and to his surprise, she'd shown no sign of recognition. A promising development.

He'd offered his hand, and she'd hesitated before taking it.

"Bridget Rose."

"Green Oak, you said?"

"Do you know the Observatory? It's just to the west. Miles out of your way, I'm sure."

"Why? Do I look like I live on the wrong side of the tracks?"

She'd flashed her own smile then, white in the oncoming lights.

"Not at all. You look very prosperous. And very trustworthy." She'd smoothed her skirt with her palms, her eyes drifting to the neon storefronts. "That must come in handy, whatever your line of work."

THE HOUSE WAS back from the road, the driveway dark and curving. Huge, in the sweep of the headlights. Faux Georgian in style. He'd parked his Jaguar under the porte cochere, and there she'd turned again to face him, offering her hand.

"I can't thank you enough. You've been so very helpful."

"Scout's oath," he'd told her, smiling again, holding

her hand a moment too long. "On my honor to do my best to help a lady in distress."

"'Honor.' I haven't heard that word for a long time," she'd said, opening the car door, her long legs swinging onto the gravel, her sudden absence manifest in the plastic glare of the Jag's dome light. He'd moved his hand to where she'd sat, the leather warm yet to his touch.

His car idling in the darkness, he'd leaned across the console to watch as she mounted the steps, paused, then turned, fists on hips, speaking words he couldn't hear until he killed the engine and opened his own door and stood hopefully amid the cricket song and the wash of city lights that ran for endless miles below them.

"My house keys!"

HER FOOTSTEPS HAD crunched on the broken glass as she crossed the foyer to key in the security code.

"Won't your husband be upset?" he'd asked her then, trying to sound casual as he unwound the handkerchief from his fist. To which she'd replied by tossing her jacket onto a chair back and striding into the gloom. Her heels *klack-klack-klacking* on the polished hardwood, fading until the metered ticking of a grandfather clock was the mansion's only sound.

He'd stood in the darkened foyer until a light appeared, and she'd returned in silhouette, moving toward the staircase.

"There's ice in the freezer," she'd told him. "And a bar just over there. I'll have a Scotch, if you're not in too great a hurry."

She'd not been gone a minute when the telephone rang, and he'd heard her voice upstairs in quiet conversation. He'd fumbled for a table lamp, and loosened his tie, and taken down a pair of cut tumblers from a shelf behind the bar. Then, in the stainless-steel vastness of the kitchen, he'd found the ice.

When she'd returned downstairs to find him in the living room, it was not, as he'd vaguely hoped, in some filmy negligee, but in the very same clothes she'd been wearing before. Except, he'd noticed, that her legs were bare.

"Here," he'd offered, but she'd only gestured, and so he'd set her drink on the table.

She'd worked the room lights then, adjusting the dimmers, and then she'd moved to the stereo cabinet. A classical radio station.

"There," she'd said, turning at last to face him. "Isn't that better?"

The room's appointments were tasteful, and expensive, and thus of a piece with their owner. There was a piano in the corner, black and gleaming, and a matched pair of Chinese vases that flanked the marble fireplace. Above the mantel hung a painting in a heavy gilt frame: two women in a garden setting, playing at croquet.

She'd stood before the painting, her gaze uplifted, and he'd moved to stand beside her.

"Do you know art?" she'd asked him.

"Impressionist?"

"It's a Morisot. From the Bonhams auction in 2007."

"It's very beautiful."

She'd slipped her arm inside his, her eyes still on the painting. "I collect beautiful things," she'd told him then. "Beautiful things that make me happy."

She'd begun to undress him right there in the living room: his jacket, his tie, his belt. Then, after he'd stepped out of his trousers, she'd led him by the hand, as a mother might lead a child, back through the foyer and up the stairs. His brain was swimming, the *klack-klack* of her heels a measured counterpoint to the wild beating of his heart.

Inside the master suite, she'd turned him around and pushed him roughly onto the bed, standing over him as she tossed her hair and worked the buttons of her blouse.

"I'm going to use the bathroom," she'd said, more than a little breathless. "I won't be a minute."

Had he been thinking clearly, the fact that she'd exited through the hallway door would have been his first clue, and that she'd stooped to retrieve her torn panty-hose from the floor. But at that particular moment, his thinking had been anything but clear.

The next clue, however, could not be missed—even by a naked man in a strange bed whose imagination was not, he was mortified to recall, the only aspect of his arousal—coming, as it did, in the form of two LAPD officers bursting through the bedroom door with their guns drawn.

"Christ!" one of them had said, lowering his weapon. "Holy shit."

By the time the detectives had arrived, the crime scene investigators had all but finished lifting prints from the table lamp, the freezer, the crystal glasses. Nothing, he'd noticed, from the light switch or the stereo or the alarm console. The detectives had parked their Crown Victoria under the empty porte cochere, and they'd beckoned him into the living room, where nothing hung over the mantel.

"I don't suppose we could find a way to keep the press out of this?" he'd asked them, tempering the panic in his voice.

The detectives shared a glance as they opened their notebooks. They'd clicked their pens and crossed their legs, their faces hard and impassive.

"No, I suppose not." He'd smiled weakly. "Perhaps I'd better call a lawyer."

ONE

"THERE'S NO FOOL like an old fool."

So concluded Warren Burkett, the former mayor of Los Angeles and, of more immediate significance, the Democratic Party's nominee for a U.S. Senate seat whose occupant would be determined in three short weeks, on the first Tuesday in November.

Burkett stood at the window with his back to my law partner, Marta "Mayday" Suarez, who'd been typing on her laptop as our silver-haired visitor spun his remarkable tale. Now he pinched the blinds to scan the street below, where a trio of TV news vans hugged the curb and where paparazzi on foot and on sleek Japanese motorbikes flanked a black Lincoln Town Car on whose fender a driver leaned, arms folded, the vulturous shadow of a circling news helicopter darkening the whole chaotic scene.

"The *Times* said that your car was recovered in Pasadena." I lifted the newspaper from my desk for his inspection. The banner headline read: BURKETT HELD IN THEFT PROBE.

He returned to his chair and sat. When he resumed his story, Mayday resumed her typing.

"It was parked at my house, on South San Rafael. *Inside* the gates. The keys were in the ignition. No fingerprints, apparently, and no clue as to how it got there. And no missing painting, of course."

Mayday and I shared a glance. "Was there a remote controller for the gate?"

He nodded. "On the visor."

I rescanned the *Times* article. "Who else knew your schedule that day? If she was waiting for you outside the restaurant, then she had to have known you'd be there, and that you'd probably be alone."

He considered this. "That's a hell of a good question. Harwood, of course. A few others in the campaign. Plus Kaneta, and some of his people. We were drinking sake. You ever drink sake?"

"Not on purpose."

"It's like warm cat piss." He shook his head sadly. "The things you put up with in a campaign, you don't want to know."

There was a knock at the door, and the aforementioned Harwood, Burkett's body man, leaned his crew cut into my office, tapping his wristwatch with a finger. Burkett nodded and waved him off.

"Where was I?"

"Back at the restaurant."

"Oh, yeah. It's called the Geisha House, which doesn't help any. Sounds like a goddamn brothel."

"Geisha House," Mayday read from her laptop. "'Sushi and sashimi with a contemporary spin.'"

"That's the place." Burkett, who'd been nervously jiggling his foot, stood again and crossed to the window, again pinching the blinds. He was silent for a moment, seemingly lost in thought.

"It's like keeping pet rats," he finally said. "The press, I mean. They're kind of cute, and you can play with 'em when you want to, but God forbid you stumble and can't get up. Because the next thing you know, they're eating your entrails for breakfast."

"What about the Mercedes?" I asked him. "In the parking lot?"

"I don't know anything about that. I suppose they're checking. Do you know these detectives?"

I nodded. "Madden is smart, and a straight shooter. Alvarez is something of a cowboy."

"Something of an asshole," Burkett corrected. He moved again toward the desk, but then he stopped and pivoted, pacing now like a caged animal. "That article say anything about the house on Green Oak?"

I laid the paper flat. There were four *Times* reporters covering the story. Not to mention stringers from every daily newspaper, broadcast station, cable channel, radio outlet, Internet site, and political bathrobe blog in America.

"The house belongs to a cardiac surgeon and his wife. The Bloomfields. Seems they're on vacation in Europe."

Burkett grunted. "Here's what I don't get. Was this a honey trap or was it a robbery?"

"Sex," Mayday said. "The robbery makes no sense, and if you'll pardon my saying so, you do have something of a reputation."

He stiffened slightly, looking from me to Mayday and back again. Then he resumed his pacing. "All right. So the painting was what? An impulse? Her fee?"

I refolded the paper. "What was the name she gave you? Rose something?"

"Bridget Rose."

"Mean anything to you?"

Burkett shook his head. Mayday, still fingering her keyboard, sat up straight.

"'Bridget Rose Dugdale,'" she read. "She was an Irish debutante turned IRA soldier. She has her own Wikipedia page. Millionaire's daughter. Oxford educated. In 1974 she and an accomplice hijacked a helicopter and used it to bomb a police station in Northern Ireland. Uh-oh."

"What?"

Mayday looked up from her screen. "It says here that she also took part in a major art heist. Home-invasion style. The thieves made off with nineteen Old Masters paintings, including a Gainsborough, a Goya, and a Vermeer. Also in 1974."

"How old is this person?"

"She'd be around seventy-five now. Not our green-eyed lady."

Another knock. This time Harwood came all the way in, with my secretary, Bernadette, trailing behind him.

"We have NBC at noon," the big man said. "I'm sorry, but you made me promise."

Burkett nodded, checking his watch. "Okay, Bill. Thirty seconds more."

After the door had closed again, Burkett got down to cases. He wanted to hire the law firm of MacTaggart and Suarez to defend him in the criminal case. He'd pay our standard hourly rates, which he'd double if we could get the charges kicked by Election Day. He'd pay a bonus if we could find the woman and have her indicted. A double bonus if we accomplished *that* before Election Day. And if we proved that Larry Archer was behind it all, he'd make me the next attorney general.

I think he was kidding about the attorney general.

I stood as he offered his hand. "I don't have to tell you what's at stake, MacTaggart. Nothing less than the integrity of our political process. If that hoodlum uses a stunt like this to win the election…" He shook his head ominously, leaving the thought unfinished.

"One last question," I said to his back as he reached for the door handle. He stopped and turned to face us.

"Why me? You must know dozens of downtown lawyers, all with bigger reputations than mine."

For the first time that morning, Warren Burkett smiled.

"Hell, I know more lawyers than O. J. Simpson. But Russ Dinsmoor told me once that if he were ever in trouble, you're the guy he'd hire, and that's all I needed to know."

THE FIRST ELECTION that I could personally recall was the presidential contest of 1988, when Ronald Reagan's vice president faced off against Michael Dukakis, then the governor of Massachusetts. I was twelve years old at the time, and I can still remember sitting in a topless bar in Boyle Heights with my uncle Louis, watching the debate on television. This was instead of sitting in Dodger Stadium watching Orel Hershiser face down the Giants, since Uncle Louis, my mother's cheerfully dissolute older brother, had been to babysitting what Bernie Madoff was to retirement planning. This was September, still two months from Election Day, and I'd asked Uncle Louis which candidate he thought would win.

He'd lit another cigarette and considered the proposition.

"Kid," he'd finally told me, "the only way Bush loses

this election is if they catch him in bed with a dead girl. Or a live boy."

The same could have been said of Warren Burkett the day before yesterday. Larry Archer, his Republican opponent, had been trailing anywhere from eight to ten points in all the major polls, which meant that, on the list of people with a motive to implicate Burkett in a lurid sex scandal, the billionaire developer's name stood out like a black swan in winter.

"It's just too obvious. Even for a blunt instrument like Archer."

Mayday looked up from her Cobb salad, hold the bacon, hold the turkey, and olive oil and balsamic on the side. We were sitting in our usual booth at the Only Place in Town, a homey neighborhood eatery in the sleepy suburban village of Sierra Madre, California.

The Only Place was not, as its name suggested, Sierra Madre's only restaurant. There was Lucky Baldwin's Pub for draft beer and finger food, and Corfu for Mediterranean fine dining, and the Buccaneer Bar for tequila shots and a knife fight. It was, however, the only spot from which we could keep an eye on the front door to the office while Bernie performed her midday shopping ritual.

Our booth looked onto the street, which, thronged with press and gawkers just an hour earlier, had returned to its somnolent normalcy. Only a few reporters had lingered in the wake of Burkett's departure—to snap photos of us and elicit our "no comments" as we'd emerged from the office for lunch—and now they, too, were gone.

The restaurant's player piano segued to "A Bicycle Built for Two," and I realized that, amid the burble of voices and the clinking of silverware and the ring of the cash register, I was feeling the old adrenaline again.

It was only three months before that I'd salvaged both Mayday and our secretary, the inimitable Bernadette Catalano, from the smoldering wreckage of my old law firm, Pasadena's storied Henley and Hargrove, which had imploded following an ethics scandal and the deaths of its two senior partners, one of whom, the aforementioned Russell H. Dinsmoor, had been my closest friend and mentor.

I'd spent the months that followed adrift on a metaphorical life raft, recovering from Russ's death—an event I could have prevented—and from an awkwardly ended romance with what I'd thought was the girl of my dreams. I'd kept myself busy by providing grand jury testimony, and settling Russ's estate, and saving my own skin with the State Bar of California. I'd moved into the home I inherited from Russ, and plunged into an epic bender, and resurfaced somehow inspired to begin working again. I'd tracked down Mayday just as she was about to sign on with a downtown L.A. megafirm. And when Bernie answered our classified ad for a secretary, the circle was aptly complete.

"Plus, there's the art connection," Mayday said, jarring me from my reverie.

"What art connection?"

She wiped her hands and opened her omnipresent laptop. She tickled the keyboard then turned the screen around to face me. On display was a page from the Web site of MOCA, the Los Angeles Museum of Contemporary Art.

"So?"

"So, look at the board of trustees. The chair, to be specific."

There were smiling headshots running in a vertical column on the left side of the screen, and there were two reasons why Angela G. Archer's photo stood out from the others. First, she appeared to be a dozen years younger than any of her board colleagues. Second, she was the only museum trustee who, by dint of her hair and makeup, could have passed for one of the *Real Housewives of New Jersey*.

"*That's* Larry Archer's wife?"

Mayday nodded.

"Sheeh."

She adjusted the screen. "It does seem a little clumsy. Either Archer is none too bright, or someone is out to make him look like the worst sort of political opportunist."

"Or both."

Mayday's fork paused, her eyes drifting into the street outside. "There's something nefarious about a scandal with the potential to ruin two political careers at once. It's almost Machiavellian."

I gathered my Big Cheese sandwich in both hands. It was a Machiavellian combination of bacon, tomato, and melted cheddar on fried cheese toast, slathered in mayonnaise and garnished with a generous stack of onion rings. Mayday winced as I took a bite.

"The painting," I said with my mouth full. "What do we know about the artist?"

"Berthe Morisot," she replied, working the keyboard with one hand. "The most famous of the female French impressionists. She was a student of Èdouard Manet, and she married Manet's brother, Eugène, in 1874. Some say she continued to love both men."

"Scandalous."

"Quite."

"So Morisot married Manet's brother in 1874, and Bridget Rose Dugdale heisted art in 1974. Coincidence?"

Mayday frowned. "That's a bit of a stretch."

"Maybe, but don't forget, somebody chose that specific alias, and that specific house, wherein hung that specific painting. What do you suppose it's worth?"

"That would depend—on the size, and on the provenance. Millions, certainly."

"But very hard to fence."

"Almost impossible, given the publicity."

"Which makes the crime all the more interesting."

THE NEWSPAPERS I'D requested from Bernie were waiting on my desk. They included *The New York Times, USA Today,* and *The Wall Street Journal.* According to *The Times,* Larry Archer was a fascist cretin and an existential threat to American democracy. According to *The Journal,* Warren Burkett was a closet Socialist who kept a harem of female interns on speed dial. According to *USA Today,* Jessica Simpson lost twenty pounds on an all-grapefruit diet.

There was one thing, however, on which all the papers agreed: With the Senate divided more or less evenly between Democrats and Republicans, this election was crucial in determining the course of our nation's future.

Having heretofore followed the campaign with only limited interest, I had some catching up to do. Archer,

I knew, was a Las Vegas transplant who'd made his outsized fortune as the founder and CEO of Archer Properties, a residential construction behemoth whose projects stretched from sea to shining sea. It built massive, ant farm subdivisions with amenities that ranged, depending on location, from golf courses to ski resorts to hotel casinos. Archer was early onto the Tea Party bandwagon, and his politics ran strongly to the antitax, antiunion, antiregulation orthodoxy that has come to define the party of Abraham Lincoln and Oliver Wendell Holmes.

There had been a small kerfuffle early in the campaign over Archer's stock holdings in several corporations that were donors to his cause. This was assuaged, to Archer's satisfaction at least, by placing his assets into a blind trust managed by his wife's brother, one Anthony "Tony Gags" Gagliano, whose position at Archer Properties seemed to be vice president of Union Affairs and Cement.

According to Warren Burkett, one of L.A.'s most popular mayors, his return to elective politics had been a matter of selfless duty, both to party and country, coming as it did after the unexpected illness of the Senate's Democratic incumbent, for whom no heir apparent had been groomed. Burkett was drafted by acclamation when his only credible challenger, a firebrand Bay Area congresswoman, had aborted her primary campaign following a particularly unfortunate incident at the Dinah Shore golf tournament in Palm Springs involving a hot tub, a WNBA point guard, and a tabloid photographer.

None of the news articles mentioned Angela G. Archer or her art world connections. Those that mentioned Bobbi Burkett, my client's wife of forty-plus years, described her in terms that ranged from "long-suffering" (*The Journal*) to "stalwart" (*The Times*) to "generously proportioned" (*USA Today*).

IT WAS ALMOST five by the time Mayday called in. I had asked her to find out what she could about Toshiko Kaneta, the sake-swilling campaign donor whom Burkett had been prospecting on the night he'd met his green-eyed muse.

"Dead end" were the first words she spoke into her cell phone. "I think he's clean."

"Why?"

"Half intuition, half evidence. Or lack of evidence."

"I'm listening."

"First of all, he's a model citizen. Not even a parking ticket in the United States, and he's lived here for ten years. He manages U.S. operations for a Japanese electronics manufacturer called IchiDyne, one word, capital *I,* capital *D.* They make specialty products for hospitals and research laboratories, including Lawrence Livermore, which means he'd have a high federal security clearance."

"So what was he doing with Burkett?"

"IchiDyne spreads a lot of money among the political class. They've donated over a hundred grand in this election cycle alone, split more or less equally between Republicans and Democrats. Nothing unusual about Kaneta meeting with a candidate this close to Election Day."

There was a knock on my door as Mayday spoke, and Bernie entered with a package that she carried as though holding a saucer of nitroglycerin, setting it gingerly on my desk. The box was brown cardboard, and the printed label bore my name only, with no address or postage or tracking label. Below my name were the printed words FRAGILE/DO NOT SHAKE. I pantomimed a question, and Bernie mouthed the word "messenger."

I extracted the letter opener from my drawer.

"Okay, I'm still listening," I said to Mayday.

"Second, I tracked down the manager who was working at Geisha House on Monday night. He recognized Burkett, so he paid close attention to their party. He said that after Burkett left, Kaneta and his people stayed for another hour. They ordered two more rounds of sake, had a jolly old time, and then paid with a company credit card."

"So?"

"So, this is the intuition part. As in, how would you expect a person to behave if he'd just set in motion a million-dollar art heist? Would he be nervous or relaxed? Would he be furtive or obvious? Would he linger or bolt? Would he cover his tracks or leave a clear paper trail?"

The box was thin and square and fairly lightweight. The brown paper tape cut easily, revealing a bed of cotton wadding inside.

"Okay, Marta, good work. Call it a day, and I'll see you in the morning."

I don't know what I was expecting when I parted the cotton, but what I saw was something both oddly familiar and completely surprising. I lifted it from the box and set it carefully on my blotter.

It was an old-fashioned Etch-A-Sketch, the classic children's toy with its red plastic frame and its round white dials. There was a message on the screen, carefully scribed in thin black lines onto the graphite-gray background. The message read:

KEEP YOUR
EYE ON
THE BALL

TWO

ELECTION DAY MINUS TWENTY.

When I entered the courtroom, I saw that my client—a pale, balding CPA named Max Drescher—was not alone. There were, in fact, a dozen or so men sitting with him in the spectator section, all of them white, all of them middle-aged or older, many indifferent to conventional standards of personal grooming. Most of them wan and furtive and badly dressed, in the cardigan-and-flannel-shirt fashion of men who live alone and who don't get out very often, and for whom a Wednesday morning sojourn to the federal courthouse amounts to a kind of grand adventure.

Max rose when he saw me, and the others followed his lead. I beckoned him with a finger as I moved to the rear of the courtroom.

"Hello, Mr. MacTaggart. Great day to start a revolution!"

At five feet six inches in shoe lifts, his pale eyes blinking behind Coke-bottle lenses, Max made for an unlikely revolutionary. The fact was, however, that Maxwell Drescher had not paid his federal income taxes in over a decade, this despite earning a sizable income not only from his accounting practice, but also from Libertarians for Tax Revolt, an organization he'd founded and whose membership dues he'd used to self-publish a series of antitax, antigovernment manifestos with titles like *The Big Tax Hoax* and *You Don't Owe the Government a Dime!* Between his books, his Web site, and a busy schedule of how-to seminars, Max proudly admitted to having achieved precisely that with which the government had charged him, namely, inciting thousands of otherwise law-abiding citizens to file fraudulent tax returns.

"We're just entering a plea today, Max. I'm afraid your fan club will be disappointed."

He extracted a folded paper from his pocket. "Can't I read a statement at least? I worked on it all night."

"As long as it consists solely of the words "not" and "guilty."

Max looked crestfallen. "Not even about the capitation clause?"

"We'll save that for later," I assured him, placing a hand on his shoulder. "We'll spring it on them when they least expect it."

As U.S. district judge Cynthia Manville took the bench and called up the matter of *United States versus Drescher,* Max and I moved to the defense table, while the assistant U.S. attorney assigned to the case—an efficient young woman in a tight ponytail—stood to recite the preliminaries.

"Does the defendant waive reading of the indictment?" the judge asked.

As I stepped to the lectern, I heard a hissing sound behind me. I half-turned to see one of Max's acolytes out of his seat and leaning over the railing.

"The flag!" he whispered, pointing in short jabs. "The flag!"

"Is there a problem, Mr. MacTaggart?"

"Uh, no, Your Honor. I was just—"

Before I could finish, Max Drescher was on his feet.

"Your Honor, any hearing conducted under a maritime flag of war is patently unconstitutional, and therefore void ab initio. I object to these proceedings on those grounds alone, while expressly preserving all of my other objections."

There was an audible stirring behind me, and a collective murmur of approval.

"Mr. MacTaggart, would you like a moment with your client?"

"Uh, that shouldn't be necessary, Your Honor. We're prepared to waive reading of the indictment and to enter a plea of not guilty."

"Very well." The judge lowered her reading glasses and made a calendar note. "Is time waived?"

"Yes, Your Honor."

"Then trial is set for March the twelfth. The people will give notice." She turned her attention to Max, who stood with arms folded, his face fairly glowing with revolutionary zeal. "Mr. Drescher, conspiracy to defraud the U.S. government is a very serious charge. You have an excellent attorney. In the future, I suggest you listen to his advice."

Max nodded tightly. "I will, Your Honor."

"And the flag stays, gold fringe and all."

Max shrugged, showing his palms.

"The clerk will call the next matter."

Out in the hallway, it looked like the fishing boat scene from *One Flew over the Cuckoo's Nest* as Max's devotees crowded around him, grinning and slapping his back. I was invited to join them for coffee, but I demurred.

"I have a date with the D.A. at ten," I told them,

checking my wristwatch, "and as Max will tell you, it's rarely a good idea to keep the government waiting."

TOM SLEWZYSKI HAD come a long way in the years since my short and somewhat rocky tenure as a deputy public defender, when he and I had locked our young stags' horns over matters great and small. Now, as the duly elected district attorney for the County of Los Angeles, Slew oversaw a far-flung bureaucracy that included over a thousand assistant district attorneys, three hundred criminal investigators, and roughly eight hundred support staff. It was, as his Web site proudly boasted, the largest local prosecutorial agency in America.

I was scanned, wanded, patted down, and carded before being escorted on the elevator up to Slew's inner sanctum, a plush corner office atop the criminal courts building on Temple Street, where the man himself sat with his feet up, working a rubber band between his thumb and forefinger. He wore a crisp white shirt and a bright red tie with matching suspenders, all in the classic Stephen Colbert mode—a Republican politician modeling a comedian who parodied Republican politicians, the scene presenting a veritable Ouroboros of unwitting caricature. On a sofa to his left sat the hulking figures of LAPD Robbery-Homicide detectives Mike Madden and Chico Alvarez.

Nobody rose to herald my arrival.

"As I live and breathe, if it isn't Jack MacTaggart. Friend of the friendless and defender of the downtrodden." The D.A. held up the morning's *Times,* in whose front-page, above-the-fold story my name appeared. "So, tell me, how does it feel to finally run with the big dogs?"

There were many reasons for Slew to dislike me, including my criminal defense background, my voter registration, and the string of courtroom losses I'd stapled to his early résumé. But none of these fully accounted for the sneer in his voice or the smirk he shared with his LAPD buddies. The simple fact was that Tom Slew-zyski's animosity toward me was personal.

"I'll let you know," I told him, helping myself, unbidden, to one of the empty client chairs. "As soon as I spot one."

He sat upright in his swivel chair, tossing the newspaper aside. "Warren Burkett," he said, shuffling some files on his desk, "has been a very naughty boy. Breaking and entering. Burglary. Grand larceny. Good thing we nabbed him before he jacked off on the sheets, or we'd have had to charge him with unlawful discharge."

Chico Alvarez thought that was hilarious.

"You know what I'm thinking, Mac?" Slew continued. "I'm thinking maybe I'll try this case myself."

"Great. The odds of acquittal just doubled."

The district attorney's face darkened. "I know why you're here, and you're wasting your time. There'll be no plea on this one. No special deal for the big-shot defendant. Did you notice that statue downstairs, of the lady with the blindfold? Equal justice under law. That's what Warren Burkett can expect from this office."

Now *that* was funny, only now nobody was laughing.

"Do you really believe that a man in the middle of a U.S. Senate contest, himself a multimillionaire, would take time out from his campaign schedule to commit a residential burglary? And then climb into bed with his clothes off to wait for the police?"

Slewzyski spread his hands. "Yet those appear to be the facts."

"You'll be laughed out of the courtroom, Slew, and not for the first time."

"Oh, yeah? Let me tell you something I've learned in politics, MacTaggart." He leaned back again and returned his feet to the desk. "There's winning battles, and there's winning the war. Let me give you an example. Let's say, for instance, that you're right and that this case gets tossed at the prelim. Just for argument's sake. That's losing a battle. But let's say that happens *after* the election, after Californians have gone to the polls to choose between a candidate with a spotless record and a candidate with a string of felony charges pending against him. That, my friend, is winning the war."

"There's only one problem with that so-called strategy, Slew. I just checked at the clerk's window. You couldn't wait to get your bullshit charges in the newspaper. You've already filed."

"So?"

"So we're not waiving time. We'll plead tomorrow, and you'll have ten days to convene a preliminary hearing."

Slew's grin faded ever so slightly.

"That's your prerogative," he said, "but without this alleged green-eyed lady, your boy's still facing a solid B and E, and you and I both know he's not walking from that."

I turned to the two detectives, who sat like spectators at a tennis match.

"Do you mean to tell me that these crack investigators won't be able to locate the key witness in time for the hearing?"

"They'll get to it as soon as they can, MacTaggart, but with the four open homicides they're already working, it may take them a few days." He turned to Alvarez. "Like, maybe eleven."

I shook my head as I stood and made for the door.

"If Burkett had kept his dick in his pants," the D.A. said to my back, his voice rising, "he wouldn't be in this mess. You think about that."

I stopped with my hand on the doorknob, turning again to face them.

"Here's something for you to think about. It's called motive. As in, who would have a motive to frame my client this close to the election? As in, who would have the art world connections to move a famous painting? And as in, which candidate do you think will come out of this with the most egg on his face?"

THE SIERRA MADRE Police Department is headquartered in a concrete-block building wedged between City Hall and the volunteer firehouse, just a few blocks west of the law offices of MacTaggart and Suarez. Today, with the sun dissolving the late-morning haze and the sycamore trees throwing cool shadows onto the tidy village sidewalks, it made for a lovely stroll.

With fifteen sworn officers serving ten thousand residents within a city limit of three square miles, the SMPD more closely resembled the police department of Andy Griffith's Mayberry than the one in Los Angeles, a mere twenty-five miles to the south. And it even had an officer named Fife.

Regan Fife, a golden-girl blond with a Coppertone tan and a Doublemint smile, greeted me in the small vestibule lobby. Petite and athletic, she wore her uniform snug, which only served to heighten the overall impression of a prep school lacrosse star who'd kept herself in game shape. If God were a twenty-five-year-old woman, I thought as I followed her swaying ponytail through the security door and down a back corridor, She'd have Regan Fife's ass.

The corridor was narrow and lined with posters and bulletin boards, and it delivered us to a small interview room at the back of the station, the door to which was overhung by a caged bulb that glowed red when Officer Fife stepped inside and snapped on the lights.

"This used to be a darkroom," she explained.

"And now so cheery."

"Can I offer you some coffee?"

"Black would be lovely, thank you."

She closed the door behind her, leaving me alone in what amounted to an eight-by-ten cell with four white walls and two wooden chairs, only one of which was on wheels. I sat in the other and set my package on the table. The table was made of a white laminate material with rounded corners and beveled edges, and it was, I noted, securely bolted to the floor. All that was missing were the bare swinging bulb and the two-way mirror.

"That was quite a little gathering you folks had yesterday," Regan said when she returned, a foam cup in each hand. "Next time, give us a heads-up and we'll arrange traffic control."

"Next time, just send in the dogs and water cannon."

She set my cup on the table next to the package, and when she closed the door again, the ringing of phones and the muffled clatter of keyboards from down the hallway gave way to a soundproofed silence.

"So," she said as she sat and sipped from her own cup, "what can I help you with today?"

Mayday and I had first met Officer Fife around a month earlier, at the Only Place, where we'd first exchanged pleasantries, then business cards, and then stolen glances across the crowded dining room. Later, up front at the cash register, I'd wooed her with my boyish charm and witty banter. Yes, that was a Glock G-23 she wore on her hip. No, she'd never had to shoot a jaywalker. Yes, she was sure the bullet wasn't buttoned in her shirt pocket.

Today, as I'd told her over the phone on my drive back from L.A., I was hoping to take our relationship to the next level.

"You guys have access to the IAFIS, right?"

Her eyes narrowed at the mention of the FBI's national fingerprint database.

"Yes."

"So, for example, if I'd been printed by the State Bar, you could access my records, right?"

"I guess so. Hypothetically."

"And if I had a client who'd been booked on Monday night in L.A., you could access those records as well? Hypothetically speaking?"

She leaned back in her chair. "Are we talking about Warren Burkett now?"

I opened the box and removed the Etch-A-Sketch from the cotton batting, setting it carefully on the table. We both looked at the now-blank screen.

"I think I'm getting the picture," Regan said. "You suspect someone of breaking into your toy chest."

"And to prove it, I need to know if there are any fingerprints on this thing besides my own. Which should be on record."

"Or Warren Burkett's?"

I shrugged. "You never know who to trust with your toys."

She glanced over her shoulder at the door.

"Maybe. But not right now. How soon do you need it?"

"Anytime between now and when you and I have dinner tomorrow night."

"Ahh," she said. "The next level."

"At first I was thinking Big Cheeses at the Only Place, but now I'm leaning toward Pasadena. How do you feel about the Arroyo Chop House?"

"How about Sushi Roku?"

"Do they serve sake?"

"Of course."

"Oh, boy. It's a date."

THE L.A. OFFICE of Bonhams Auctioneers is on Sunset Boulevard, just east of Fairfax. I found a parking spot on the street and waited on the sidewalk out front for Mayday's arrival.

There wasn't much in the way of foot traffic on a Wednesday afternoon, so I killed time checking messages on my phone. I had both personal and business e-mail accounts, one private and one public, and the latter showed seventeen new messages, all from media outlets.

Tom Slewzyski had been right about one thing: The big dogs were running now, and they were making a hell of a racket.

Mayday's silver Lexus trolled the curb line, honked

once, then turned the corner and accelerated north onto Stanley. I waited until she'd made her way back, power-walking in her gray power suit, before slipping the phone into my jacket.

"Sorry! I got hung up at the County Recorder."

"What've you got?"

She shifted her bag to the other shoulder and unzipped a side pouch on her computer case. From it, she produced two photocopied pages.

"Farmers insured the mortgage," she told me as I read. "In 2001."

"Well done."

"That doesn't mean they insured the contents. Or that they're insured at all."

"Don't worry," I told her, folding the page into my pocket. "Nobody hangs a priceless painting over their mantel without some kind of insurance."

I held the heavy glass door as she passed under my arm, then followed her into a large, airy space with hardwood floors and spotlighted paintings on pristine white walls. The room was hushed and air-conditioned, and felt more like a museum or a high-end art gallery than the office lobby it was. A few browsers with catalogues shuffled from painting to painting, leaning in to inspect the brushwork, while a huge central case displayed things like jewel-encrusted eggs and leatherbound books and old Indian pottery behind glass.

Beside the display case stood a uniformed guard with a sidearm, an earbud, and fingerless black gloves. He followed us with his eyes as we approached the front counter, where an elegant woman stepped forward and smiled as she folded her hands on the glass.

"Good afternoon." Her look was appraising. "How might I be of assistance?"

I drew a business card from my pocket with two fingers. "Jack MacTaggart and Marta Suarez. We're here in the matter of the Bloomfield robbery. You may have read about it in the newspapers. A Morisot, unfortunately. We're making inquiries in respect of Farmers Insurance."

I'd chosen my words carefully, not that it mattered, because as soon as I'd said "Bloomfield," she'd reached for the telephone, her smile frozen in place.

"Mr. Laurent? A gentleman to see you, and a lady. They're attorneys, from Farmers Insurance. Yes, about Dr. Bloomfield.

"Our director of impressionist and modern art will be right with you," she said as she set down the receiver. "May I offer you some water? Or a glass of wine?"

"Do you have any sake?" I asked her.

"No, I'm afraid not."

"Nothing for me, then."

Laurent, when he descended the staircase at the rear of the lobby, was wearing a navy cashmere suit paired with a cream-colored shirt and a periwinkle tie that appeared, at first glance, to be speckled with dollar signs. It wasn't until he got closer that I saw they were actually little carousel horses. He extended a hand.

"Marcel Laurent, at your service." The Frenchman dipped his head as we shook. He was fortysomething, and lean, and had the grip of a dead codfish. "Madame." I thought he was going to kiss Mayday's hand, but he only bowed again. "Please." He indicated a path to the staircase, and fell into stride beside us.

In terms of its size and streetscape view, Laurent's

office was somewhat less impressive than I'd expected. That is, if you ignored the Claude Monet winter haystack painting adorning the wall behind his desk. He made a show of squaring some papers and setting them aside, weighting them with a carved ivory figurine.

"I cannot tell you how upset we were to learn of Dr. Bloomfield's loss," he began. "Please convey to him our most sincere condolences."

"According to the preliminary claim report," I said, unfolding the page Mayday had cribbed from the County Recorder, "the painting was purchased here at auction in 2007. We were wondering if you had a record of that transaction, and a photo of the painting itself."

"Surely Dr. Bloomfield has a transparency?"

"Dr. and Mrs. Bloomfield are still abroad, I'm afraid."

The Frenchman pursed his lips, rearranging our two business cards on his blotter with a manicured finger. "Tell me, how is my old friend Mr. Haverland? Still working himself to the bone, as you Americans say?"

Our eyes met, and held, and I made a quick decision.

"I don't know any Mr. Haverland."

"Ah, so stupid," the Frenchman said, relaxing back into his chair. "I was thinking of State Farm." He lifted his receiver. "Paul? Please bring me the May 2007 impressionist book. Right away. Thank you."

Paul, when he arrived, was a mop-haired college boy who, judging by his aquiline nose and oddly patrician air, might have been Laurent's son. The book he delivered was a white three-ring binder through which the older man paged with practiced authority.

"Here it is," he said, turning the book to face us. "Lot Five-zero-seven, three-six-four. *The Croquet Party.*"

Inside the plastic sleeve were several pages of forms, plus a color photo of the painting. In the photo, two women in outsized hats were standing in a garden setting holding wooden mallets. They were surrounded by flowers in pastel shades of pink and blue, and in the grass at their feet lay a striped wooden ball.

"What was the gavel price?" Mayday asked him.

The Frenchman turned the book and, with a short sniff to make clear his disdain for matters *de l'argent*, said, "Two million four, U.S."

I broke the silence that followed. "Can we get a copy of the photo, please? And the sales documentation."

He nodded to the kid, who'd been standing at attention by the door. The kid took the book and left.

"I hope you'll forgive me, but this is a very important question, Mr. Laurent. Who would have had access to Dr. Bloomfield's identity—to his name and address? Or to the fact that he'd purchased this painting at auction?"

The Frenchman stiffened. "I can assure you that Bonhams is renowned for its discretion, Mr. MacTaggart, and for its commitment to client privacy and confidentiality."

"Yes, I'm sure that's the case, but what if I told you that the thief targeted this specific painting, and identified it as having come from this particular auction?"

"I'd say to you that this is impossible. Unless…"

"Yes?"

"Well. Unless Dr. or Mrs. Bloomfield told others, who told others. You know how these things go, but I can assure you that the information did not come from us."

"How many of your employees have access to these auction records?"

"Only a few. All trusted, all carefully vetted. All bonded and insured."

"Do you have a list of names?"

He thought for a moment, then slid open a drawer and extracted a typewritten roster of telephone extensions. He uncapped a gold fountain pen and placed check marks next to half a dozen names on the list.

"Here," he said. "You may keep this."

I examined the names. "I don't see any Paul."

Laurent's mouth tightened as he retrieved the list. He checked off another name.

When the kid returned, he set a large white envelope bearing the blue Bonhams logo on Laurent's desk. The Frenchman slid it in my direction, and I gathered it up along with the phone list as I stood.

"Thank you for your cooperation, Mr. Laurent. Let me assure you that we'll do everything in our power to see that the painting is returned and the thief apprehended, and that the Bonhams name stays out of the press, of course."

At this, the Frenchman brightened.

"Yes, exactly so." He rounded the desk to pump our hands. "Thank you, Monsieur. And you, Madame. Please do not hesitate to call on us again." With that, he led us out into the hallway, where I'm reasonably sure he failed to notice Mayday as she swept our business cards into her purse.

THREE

BOVARD AUDITORIUM, a stately redbrick edifice at the heart of the USC campus, tonight was floodlit and teeming with activity. News vans were shoehorned along both sides of the narrow frontage road, where police and event staff in yellow windbreakers directed traffic, checked media credentials, and prepared for the crowds that were soon to follow.

All of which I observed from the relative quiet of a fountain about a hundred yards opposite the building, in front of the main campus library. There in semidarkness, I slid my phone from my pocket and saw that there were twelve new e-mails, all from reporters on deadline, all requesting comment on what the press had apparently dubbed the Goldilocks Affair.

Hearing the *klack-klack* of rapid heels on the sidewalk, I turned to see Mayday emerging from the darkness. She hadn't changed from this afternoon, and she still carried her purse and her laptop, only now the shoulder straps were crossed like Zapata's bandoliers.

"What's so funny?"

"Nothing. Did you bring the contract?"

She patted the computer case. "Bernie wasn't too happy about staying late."

"You don't say."

"They released the mug shot this afternoon. Have you seen it yet?"

"How bad?"

"Well, it's not Nick Nolte. I'd put it somewhere between Mel Gibson and Paris Hilton. Dazed, but still oddly poised."

"Not too warm, not too cold."

She followed my eyes to the hubbub across the way.

"What are you going to tell him about taking the Fifth?"

"Whatever we tell him, do you think he'll listen?"

"He's in a difficult spot."

"Self-inflicted, some would be quick to point out."

Mayday read her watch. "Tell me something. What makes a man like Warren Burkett behave the way he does with women?"

"I don't know. The same thing that drives him to seek public office, I guess. Some odd combination of insecurity and hubris. Apparently, it's endemic to the species."

We crossed the road together, through the news vans and the portable klieg lights and the growing crush of bodies near the front of the building. There was a will-call table set up in the alcove, at which we presented our photo IDs and were issued laminated passes on lanyards. The passes featured side-by-side photos of Burkett and Archer, like a pair of aging middleweights, with the Bovard Auditorium tower looming large in the background. Across the bottom, each pass read ALL ACCESS.

As we shuffled toward the entrance doors with their portable metal detectors, a familiar voice cut through the clamor behind us.

"Jack! Jack! Wait up!"

Terina Webb of *Channel 9 Action News* elbowed her way through the crowd. She was coifed and camera ready in a dark business suit, her blond hair lacquered to a high sheen, and she carried a remote microphone.

"You haven't returned any of my messages!" she said, clamping hold of my arm. "I thought we were friends!"

Terina Webb's definition of a friend was any news source who'd return her calls on deadline. In Burkett's pet rat simile, she met all the criteria: She was nice to look at, occasionally fun to play with, and would eat her young for a story.

"Hi, I'm Terina," she said to Mayday. "You must be Marta Suarez."

"Nice to—"

"Now, Jack, I have a camera just over there, and it won't take but ten seconds to put your handsome face in front of half a million viewers who are just *dying* to hear your client's side of the story. Plus, it'll be great exposure for your new law practice. Right, Marta? You tell him."

She'd been physically pulling me away from the building, and she would have dragged me clear across the lawn had I not finally set my feet.

"Come on, Terina, you know I can't comment. Unless of course you've got something juicy you'd like to trade?"

We'd been noticed by now, and people were crowding around us, with someone throwing a spotlight in my face. Terina pulled me closer to whisper.

"The D.A.'s called a press conference for tomorrow morning at the courthouse. Word is he's got some kind of surveillance photo of Burkett with a woman."

There was another, louder commotion out by the road, and a brightening halo of lights. The spotlight on my face swung away to where Larry Archer stood in front of a portable blue backdrop. He held a folded sheet of paper, and microphones were being set up before him in a large and hasty bouquet. Terina let loose my arm and literally ran in the candidate's direction.

"Fame, alas, is fleeting," I said to Mayday.

"And fleet. Even in heels."

WARREN BURKETT SAT before a lighted mirror with tissues sprouting from his shirt collar as a woman applied his stage makeup. Standing behind the candidate was a fat, disheveled man in a worn tweed jacket, reading to him from a thick three-ring binder. The monologue consisted of one-line talking points on a wide range of topics, from the federal deficit ("no larger than we want, but no smaller than we need") to immigration reform ("show me a thirty-foot wall, and I'll show you a forty-foot ladder") to homeland security ("projecting American values abroad is our best defense against terrorism at home").

The fat man, Scott Tully, had been introduced to us as Burkett's chief campaign strategist. In the darkened chair beside the candidate sat Bill Harwood, the candidate's ubiquitous body man, his arms folded and his eyes watching the door. By now I was figuring Harwood for ex-Secret Service, since he had both the look and the presence, which is to say, clean cut, unobtrusive, and vaguely menacing.

As the makeup woman applied the final strokes of suntan-in-a-bottle, Tully came to the last item in his briefing binder, a subject he introduced with the euphemism "recent negative developments." At that, all eyes turned to Marta and me. I cleared my throat, and we all waited for the makeup woman to finish packing up her case.

"I met with Tom Slewzyski this morning," I told them as the door closed behind her, "and he made two things perfectly clear. First, he's determined to prosecute this thing, and he might even do it himself. Second, he has no intention of helping us find either the woman or the painting until after the preliminary hearing."

Burkett grunted. He began plucking the tissues from his collar. "When's the hearing?"

"You said you wanted this thing resolved before Election Day."

"I do."

"Good. If we plead tomorrow, they'll have to hold the prelim within ten days."

"Christ!" Tully erupted, turning a circle. "The last thing we need is a televised perp walk the day after the debate!"

"The last thing we need," Burkett told him calmly, "is a slow bleed that lasts until Election Day."

I nodded to Mayday, and she handed me the items from her case.

"We also visited Bonhams' auction house." I passed the color photo of the missing Morisot to Burkett. "Look familiar?"

He tilted it to the light. "That's the one."

"They claim that only a half-dozen employees have access to the auction records, but I'd put the number at double that, plus maybe the cleaning staff and building maintenance, and God knows who else."

Burkett grunted again as he returned the photo. He seemed unnaturally calm for a man who was about to walk onstage for a nationally televised political debate in which the first question was likely to be "So, seen any good art lately?"

Tully was pacing now, studying me as he walked. "You're the so-called expert. What are the odds they can make this bullshit stick?"

"All they have at this point are the cops, but at a preliminary hearing, that's all they'll need." I turned to Burkett. "Chances are good you'll be bound over for trial, on a charge of breaking and entering."

"Shit!" Tully slammed his book to the floor, and we all jumped. Except Harwood.

"Have you seen the overnight polls? We're down five today in Gallup! Down twelve in Fox News!" The fat man ran a hand through his thinning hair. "This can't be happening to me."

There was a rap at the dressing room door, and a girl with headphones and a clipboard stepped in to announce, "Ten minutes."

Burkett swiveled back to the mirror, adjusting his tie. "If I plead tomorrow, when will the trial be held?"

"We can request an expedited trial setting after the prelim. Then it's up to the court."

"What about the girl? Any leads?"

I looked at Mayday. "We heard a rumor that Slewzyski's called a press conference for tomorrow morning. They apparently have a surveillance photo of the two of you together."

Burkett stopped his preening and eyed me in the mirror. "Is that good or bad?"

"It depends. If she can be identified from the photo, then it's good. If not, I'd call it a wash."

"But she's my alibi!"

"Or your accomplice."

While he chewed on that, I continued. "In any event, I don't think releasing the photo has anything to do with the criminal case. I'd say it's more about the political impact of publishing a picture of you alone with an attractive woman who isn't your wife three weeks before the election."

"You're goddamn right it is," Tully said.

Burkett nodded. "Tom Slewzyski is a shrewd politician. He knows which way the wind blows, and right now it blows toward Archer. We need to find that girl."

I checked my watch. "I know that. I also know you don't want to hear this right now, but I have to say it. You have the right to remain silent, and to make the D.A. prove his case with witnesses and physical evidence. If you go out there tonight and answer questions about the incident, then whatever you say will definitely be used against you in court."

Again Burkett nodded. "I understand."

"Okay then, last item." I handed him our fee agreement, complete with bonus clauses. "I need to get your autograph on this."

MAYDAY AND I were ushered to a reserved seating area toward the front of the auditorium, which by now had filled to buzzing capacity with spectators and media and, up front where we were seated, the friends and families of the candidates.

I recognized Bobbi Burkett from her photos. She sat in the front row with a younger woman who, similarly plus-sized, I guessed was their daughter. Directly across the center aisle, I recognized the big hair and striking profile of Angela Archer, who was seated next to a thick-necked goombah tugging at his collar with a finger. To her left sat a conspicuously odd couple consisting of a lizard-faced greaser in an electric-blue zoot suit and a Japanese girl who looked like a blown-up anime cartoon doll.

Mayday tapped my knee, nodding toward the media section, stage right. There Terina Webb stood on her seat, hand to brow like an Indian scout, scanning the rows behind her.

The house lights dimmed, and to restrained applause, an aged gentleman shuffled onto the stage. I recognized him from public television, which I've had occasion to glimpse while clicking from *CBS Sports* to *ABC Sports* with my TV remote. The old newsman steadied himself by a little desk at the center of the stage, from which he thanked us all for attending, reminded us to refrain from applause or other displays of partisanship, and exhorted us to vote in three weeks' time for the candidate of our choice.

Then, as the stage lights brightened and the moderator settled in with his back to the audience, three cameras rolled into position. The large video monitors on either side of the stage flashed ON THE AIR as the guy behind the center camera touched a hand to his headphones, nodded once, then counted down on his fingers, pointing at last to the moderator.

The light on his camera blinked red.

"Good evening, ladies and gentlemen, and welcome to tonight's live broadcast from the campus of the University of Southern California of this third and final debate between Larry Archer and Warren Burkett, the Republican and Democratic candidates, respectively, for the United States Senate seat from California. I'm Howard Leland of PBS *NewsHour,* and I'll be your host and moderator for this evening's event. Due to the extraordinary level of interest in this particular contest, tonight's debate is being broadcast live on PBS stations nationwide, as well as on most network and cable news outlets."

Here he paused for effect, or maybe to check his defibrillator. The guy was around ninety years old.

"The questions I'll be asking tonight are mine alone and have not been shared with the candidates or their campaigns. Each candidate will have two minutes to respond to each question, and each response will be followed by a one-minute rebuttal. So, without further ado, let's welcome to the stage businessman Larry Archer and the former mayor of Los Angeles, Warren Burkett."

The APPLAUSE message flashed, and the audience obliged lustily as the candidates appeared from opposite wings and strode to their respective lecterns. I watched Bobbi Burkett, who stood and clapped with the appropriate level of enthusiasm as her husband, ever the savvy pol, crossed to Archer's lectern to offer his hand in bipartisan friendship. Archer looked like he was being handed a subpoena.

"Good evening, gentlemen," Leland continued once the applause had quieted. "As determined by prior coin toss, we begin tonight's debate with a question for Mr. Archer." He consulted his notes. "Sir, you've come out publicly as a strong opponent of a woman's right to choose—"

"As prolife. Please."

This brought applause from up in the balcony.

"Or prolife, as you would have it. My question, sir, is in two parts. First, whether your position extends to cases of rape or incest, and to those in which the life of the mother is in clear and imminent danger. Secondly, whether there are any circumstances under which you would vote to confirm a Supreme Court nominee whose record suggested anything but unstinting opposition to the Court's *Roe v. Wade* decision."

Archer looked across the stage toward Burkett. His eyes twinkled in the overhead lights.

"I know that my opponent has a personal interest in keeping the government out of women's bedrooms."

This was met with an equal measure of laugher and scattered groans, to which Archer raised a hand.

"Because if the government stayed out of women's bedrooms, then Mr. Burkett wouldn't have been arrested in one on Monday night. Be that as it may, my position on the sanctity of human life is clear, and has been clear throughout this campaign, but just for the record, I'll state it again: Every life is sacred. Period, with no exceptions. And if another left-wing baby-killing activist judge gets onto the Supreme Court, it'll be over my dead body."

More applause, and a few loud whoops from the balcony, where they might have been selling beer.

"Mr. Burkett?"

"It's difficult for me to believe that in this day and age, in which a woman's right to make decisions regarding her own reproductive health has been the law of the land for forty years, we still have fanatics who long for the good old days when our sisters and daughters suffered and died at the hands of back-alley abortion providers. Invariably, these fanatics are male, and white, and past the age at which this personal, gut-wrenching decision is anything but hypothetical. In Mr. Archer's case, I suspect it involves a purely political calculus, in which he hopes to gain a few more votes and a few more campaign dollars from a constituency that thinks nothing of using the political process to advance its so-called Christian agenda. Whatever one's position on this issue, though, and whatever motivates that position, be it passion or politics, can't we at least all agree that it's a subject that's too damned serious to be joked about?"

The applause that followed was loud, and sustained, and included contributions, I noted, both from Bobbi Burkett and Mayday. I checked my watch: fifty-eight seconds.

"Now to you, Mr. Burkett…"

So the evening went. However difficult the issue— from Middle East policy to offshore oil drilling to Wall Street regulation—Archer would find a way to reduce it to a neat bumper sticker, pandering to a public that longed for simplicity and certainty in an increasingly complex world. Burkett, in contrast, would launch into a nuanced dissertation on pros and cons, costs and benefits. I was reminded of Bertrand Russell, who said that the whole problem with the world is that fools and fanatics are always so certain of themselves, and wiser people so full of doubts.

Two grueling hours later, each candidate was given sixty seconds in which to deliver a closing argument.

"On November the fifth," Archer began, "the voters of California will be faced with a clear choice. They can elect a liberal, big-government career politician who, not incidentally, will be entering a plea in criminal court tomorrow morning, or they can elect an outsider who's a proven job creator and a man they know will take a chain saw to the deadwood in Washington. I invite every Californian to join me tonight in ending the nanny state, in ending the welfare state, and in returning the Golden State to its once and future glory. God bless you all, and God bless the United States of America!"

There followed prolonged applause, punctuated by a two-fingered whistle from Angela Archer's general direction.

"Mr. Burkett?"

"Thank you, Howard, and thank you to everyone here at USC who worked so hard to make this event possible. There isn't very much on which Mr. Archer and I agree, but there is one point, and I think it's an important one. Never in the history of this state have voters been faced with a starker choice between two candidates and two political philosophies. At a time when the richest one percent controls forty percent of our nation's wealth, one candidate proposes tax cuts for the rich and Medicare and Social Security cuts for the rest. At a time when climate change threatens endangered species and fragile ecologies, one candidate proposes to abolish the EPA and eliminate even the most basic protections for the air we breathe and the water we drink. And at a time when our nation pays over a billion dollars per day for foreign oil, often to repressive and dictatorial regimes, one candidate promises to cut all subsidies and incentives to develop clean, renewable energy here at home."

At this point, Burkett paused and looked across the stage at his opponent.

"Yes, Larry, it's true, I'm not a perfect messenger. There are times when I've disappointed my family, and disappointed myself, but I challenge you and your billionaire casino backers and your millionaire Wall Street cronies to name one instance in which I've disappointed my constituents, or betrayed a trust, or abandoned a principle in which I believe."

"Time, Mr. Mayor."

"Time indeed, Howard. Time for Californians to reject the politics of division and distraction, and to focus on what's really at stake on November fifth. For them, for their children, and for all of California. Thank you and good evening."

Half the audience was on its feet, cheering wildly, drowning out the moderator's sign-off. Then, as the credits rolled on the video screens, the candidates' families were allowed up onto the stage. I watched as the women both did that dewy-eyed, stand-by-your-man thing that political wives seem to have down pat. Then, with both candidates grinning and pointing into the audience as the stage lights finally dimmed, I watched Bobbi Burkett step out of the spotlight, her smile fading, and trudge back down to her seat.

BACK IN THE now-crowded dressing room, spirits were notably higher. A newly animated Scott Tully was bounding around, slapping backs and pumping hands, while Burkett's wife and daughter posed for a photographer. Then the door opened, and the candidate entered, and everybody in the little room clapped. He was followed by Harwood, who stopped and scanned the crowd with stone-faced impassivity.

"Mr. MacTaggart?"

Bobbi Burkett approached us, a wineglass in her hand.

"Yes. And this is my partner, Miss Suarez."

"Delighted." She shook our hands in turn. "I just

wanted to say hello to the man who's going to keep Warren out of jail."

"We'll certainly do our best."

"I hope you can appreciate now what's at stake in this election. Not just for Warren, but for the entire country."

"Yes, ma'am, I believe I can."

"Good," she said, patting my arm as she moved back to her husband. "We're all counting on you."

Mayday and I lingered a while longer, watching the people who came and went. Many were staffers, but there were also local pols and a few national media figures. After a half hour or so, we made our move to leave. Then I noticed something that, for reasons I couldn't explain at the time, stopped me at the door.

It was the sound technician, finally removing the lapel microphone from Warren Burkett's jacket. First he traced the wire into the candidate's shirtfront, then circled behind to remove a radio transmitter from the candidate's belt.

"Mr. Mayor!" I called over the heads of the milling guests. I pointed to the corner of the room, where Mayday and I retired and waited until Burkett joined us, shaking hands and touching shoulders along the way.

Just as Harwood completed the huddle, I ducked my head for privacy.

"Didn't you tell us that our green-eyed friend"—here I glanced about and lowered my voice even further—"unbuckled your belt herself?"

Burkett's brow furrowed. "Is this really the place—"

"Did the police impound your belt?"

"Why would they?"

"Did they check it for latent fingerprints?"

He visibly brightened, finally catching my drift.

"No, now that you mention it."

"And have you worn that particular belt since Monday night?"

"By God, I don't believe I have."

"Okay then, listen carefully. Go home tonight and put your hands in a pair of socks. Handle the belt from the middle, not the ends, and put it into a large Ziploc baggie. And when you bring it to the courthouse tomorrow, hand it directly to me and nobody else. Understood?"

He nodded. "Understood."

"Good. It's the criminal courts building on Temple Street. Let's meet in the fifth-floor restroom at exactly eight fifteen."

FOUR

THE AUDITORIUM WAS a sea of empty seats, vast and darkly crimson, quiet but for the *clang* and *crash* of the TV crew onstage breaking down the set. A tight gaggle of dignitaries lingered at the front of the orchestra section, and as Mayday and I made our way down to the center aisle, we were blocked by the human rhino who'd been Angela Archer's seating companion. He'd lost the necktie, and his shirt was open to reveal a mat of graying chest hair through which a gold chain snaked like a python.

"Hey," he said.

Since I was now a well-informed consumer of political news and commentary, I took a chance on his identity.

"You must be Tony."

"My sister would like a word with you" is what he said next, although it came out more like *my sista would like a woid witch youse.*

"Troglodyte," I said as I tried to slide by, but again he blocked my path.

"Maybe you didn't hear me so good."

"Maybe it was the elocution."

"The what? What did you call me?" he said, crowding me now, his chest swelling, and I could see where this was heading.

"Okay, sure," I told him. "I've always wanted to meet your sister."

He wasn't certain how to take that, but he extended a thick arm to the side, much in the way that Marcel Laurent, the unctuous Frenchman, had done for us at Bonhams. Only there was a certain *je ne sais quoi* lost in the translation.

Angela Archer, Tony's little sister, was looking up with feigned adoration at a balding bloviator whom I recognized as one of the talking heads from Fox News. Angela was slender and impeccably attired in a simple beige dress. The guy was tall and loud and seemed more than a little annoyed when Angela's attention started to wander coincident with my approach.

"You'll excuse us for just a moment," she told the guy, squeezing his hand as she hooked her arm into mine.

"So," she said, leading me toward the front of the stage, "I understand you're the man who's been hired to defend poor Mr. Burkett."

"You hear good," I told her in a parody of her brother's patois, which she didn't seem to notice.

"I also understand you've developed an interest in impressionist art, and in those who might wish to collect it."

She really did hear good. I stopped and turned to face her.

"As an arts patron yourself, I'm sure you're equally concerned about the theft of a priceless painting, whatever the circumstances."

"My taste," she said, plucking lint from my lapel, "runs more to the nontraditional. To the alternative, you might say."

"Your taste in art."

"Of course. What else are we talking about?"

She tugged on both lapels then, stepping back like a haberdasher to admire the fit of my suit.

"This is all very interesting, Mrs. Archer. But I've had a long day, and I'm very tired, and my dog is waiting up for me at home."

"A boy and his dog. How sweet." She stepped closer again, as if to take me into her confidence. "If you'd like to learn more about the L.A. art scene, which you might find quite helpful in representing Mr. Burkett, we're having a little party tonight."

"We?"

She nodded toward the empty seats, and I saw that two of them, deep in the purple shadows, were still occupied: by Lizard Face, and his Japanese doll.

"Here," Angela said, palming something from her purse and slipping it into my breast pocket. "Come by in an hour. You won't regret it, I promise."

A flutter arose onstage, and we both looked up to see Larry Archer strutting forth from his dressing room. He had Tom Slewzyski in tow, and trailing both of them were LAPD detectives Mike Madden and Chico Alvarez.

Angela patted my pocket as she returned to join her husband, and I stood apart from the group as they all played kissy-face. Alvarez was the only one to acknowledge my presence, which he did by forming a gun with his thumb and finger and squeezing off a shot.

"What was that about?" Mayday wanted to know.

I removed the business card from my pocket. Above the address appeared *ricky rio/streetscrapes* in a slanting, customized font.

"I'm not sure, exactly. But I think I've just been propositioned."

WITH AN HOUR to kill, I stopped at the Pantry Café for
some pie and a cup of coffee. The fabled downtown
eatery was open twenty-four hours a day, seven days a
week, three hundred and sixty-five days a year, Christmas and New Year's included, thereby providing in-
somniac Angelinos with unlimited opportunities for
gastrointestinal discomfort. While it was not true, as
some city guidebooks claimed, that all the Pantry's
waiters were former convicts, it was absolutely true
that many of the cooks could be indicted for attempted
murder.

It was approaching midnight, and Mayday had gra-
ciously agreed to stop by Sycamore Lane to look in on
Sam, who, although having both a new dog door and an
enormous backyard at his disposal, was no doubt concerned as to the whereabouts of his personal attorney.
Sam was half golden retriever and half truant officer,
and staying out past curfew was a disciplinary offense.
Sam had entered my life three years earlier, when I'd
found him wandering, shivering and frightened, on the
shoulder of the Golden State Freeway. I figured he'd
been dumped there, or had maybe fallen from the bed
of a pickup. Once I got to know him better, I realized
he'd probably been out directing traffic.

The pie finally arrived, and a refill on the coffee. I
watched through the plate glass as the bums and the
hustlers and the street kids came and went like rev-
enants on the cracked and dirty sidewalk, all of them
prowling, all of them searching for that golden opportunity they believed was waiting for them around the next
corner, always the next corner, in the City of Angels.

I fished out the business card and set it on the table.

The address I recognized as the Brewery, a warehouse complex turned artists' collective off Main Street, just north of the railyard, in one of L.A.'s grittier neighborhoods. What I couldn't recognize was the motive behind the invitation. Maybe Larry Archer, in the best Don Corleone tradition, wanted his friends close and his enemies closer. Or maybe they were hoping I'd have a few drinks and trip over my tongue.

Then again, maybe they were just friendly folks from out of town who liked to throw a good party.

The Mercedes was parked in an all-night lot on Ninth, and I had to bang on the little plywood booth to wake up the attendant. The car was a near classic—a 1973 450SL convertible—and one of the few items of the late Russ Dinsmoor's personal property I hadn't inherited. Instead, I'd had to track the car down and buy it from the Pasadena branch of the American Heart Association, to whom Russ had generously bequeathed it. They'd been more than happy to part with it for a mere 20 percent over Blue Book, lending new meaning to their slogan "Blood: It's in You to Give."

The gate to the Brewery parking lot was open when I arrived, the building itself dark and forbidding, with a smokestack rising above it like an extended middle finger aimed at the sparkling downtown skyline across the river. It was, in fact, a complex of several disparate buildings, some in brick, some sheathed in corrugated tin, all of them divided by courtyards and alleys and all of them connected by elevated steel walkways. It took me a while to find an entrance, and longer still to find a directory telling me that Ricky Rio's loft was number 14, in the old ironworks building.

When I finally found the right stairway, the percussive thump of a hip-hop tune led me straight to a metal door at the end of the hallway. It was the door on which the number 14 had been spray-painted in bulbous cartoon digits.

I knocked and waited, and then let myself in.

A hundred or more people were crowded into a cavernous, two-story space overhung by a cantilevered balcony. Some were dancing, and some were crowding the portable bars at opposite ends of the room, but most were clustered in groups of three or five, their heads bent in shouted conversation. Two of the room's walls were old warehouse brick, and these were brightly embellished with spray-painted words and images and punctuated by twisted sculptural eruptions of welded pipe and rusted scrap metal.

A row of spectators peered down from the balcony, where a shirtless, sweating DJ in dark shades and headphones worked a pair of old-school turntables. The dancers on the floor below formed a large vortex at the room's center, bathed as they were in the soft tans and pinks of a projected video image that swept the room in searchlight fashion, and it was only as the image passed over the room's white walls that I recognized it as a pornographic film: a graphic, close-in shot of enormous thrusting genitalia.

I made my way to the bar, sidling through the crowd, and just as I reached it, the room lights dimmed and the porno flick was replaced by the swirling pinpoints of a lighted disco ball. The dancers whooped, and the hip-hop smoothly segued into an ear-splitting remix of a Top 40 hit from the early seventies, the lyrics to which froze me where I stood.

Green-eyed lady, lovely lady
Strolling slowly towards the sun
Green-eyed lady, ocean lady
Soothing every raging wave that comes

"Sir?"

"Huh?"

"I said, what would you like?"

The bartender was a college kid in a bow tie and vest who maybe used his nose ring as a bottle opener. I pointed to the tub of ice on the floor behind him.

"Got any Bud?"

"Sorry, just the Stella."

I felt a hand on my back, and I turned around into the upturned visage of Angela Archer.

"So glad you could make it!" she shouted over the music. "Things were starting to get boring!"

The candidate's wife had teased her dark tresses into an Amy Winehouse beehive that threatened to topple her over backward. She'd doubled down on the eyeshadow, the effect of which was a sort of Cleopatra-in-rehab look, and she'd traded her cocktail dress for a white vinyl mini emblazoned with cartoon faces and word balloons, as though she'd been wrapped in a page from the Sunday funnies.

"Aren't those the Fox News boys over in the mosh pit?"

She waved a dismissive hand. To me she said, "They've all gone home to bed," and to the bartender she said, "Double Grey Goose, rocks."

Drink in hand, she guided me by the arm across the dance floor and over to the circular staircase leading to the balcony. "Follow me," she said, and the view as

I climbed, while definitely not unpleasant, was surprisingly liberal for the wife of a neoconservative.

It was incrementally quieter up above, and we stood together in a corner of what must have been the sleeping loft when not playing host to a pharmaceutical swap meet. A skinny kid in a black turtleneck and Clark Kent eyeglasses came over to offer us some white lines on a mirror, but Angela waved him off. She had, I noticed then, more rings than fingers.

"You like to live dangerously," I told her. "I could have made a bundle just then with my cell phone camera."

She raised her glass. "Vodka's still legal, thank goodness, and Tony would have shoved the phone up your ass. Sideways."

I followed her eyes as they scanned the floor below us. "I didn't see your husband downstairs. Or Tony, for that matter."

"My dear husband is spending the night at the Intercontinental, where he's hosting a donor breakfast in the morning." She swirled her ice and sipped again. "Oilmen. Texans, I think, with big hats and big wallets. But Tony's around here somewhere."

Maybe up on the roof, I thought, swatting at biplanes.

"Tell me something. What motivates a man like Larry Archer to run for the U.S. Senate? He must have better things to do than sit in committee meetings all day and discuss soybean subsidies."

"My husband is a salesman," Angela said, nodding to someone below. I leaned over to see Lizard Face moving toward the stairs. "When the housing bubble burst, he ran out of product to sell. So he began selling himself."

"Sounds like he'll be right at home in Washington."

Angela turned from the railing. "There's someone I'd like you to meet. Ricky Rio is one of the hottest artists in L.A."

"Is this his work?" I nodded toward the walls, which were pulsing now in the staccato flash of a strobe light. "Or was the place vandalized while he was out?"

"Please don't be conventional, Mr. MacTaggart. I'm drowning in conventional."

To my unenlightened sensibilities, graffiti is vandalism, pure and simple, and stems from the same base instinct that impels Sam to pee on fire hydrants. My definition of art has always been pretty simple: If I can reproduce it, then it isn't art. Looking around at the ten-foot cartoon letters and the tattoo-style renderings of bleeding hearts and winged skulls that adorned the throbbing walls, I saw very little that I couldn't reproduce.

"Ricky Rio is a national treasure," Angela continued, "right up there with Haring and Basquiat. I'm sure you've seen his work around town, but you probably didn't realize it was his."

I knew enough about so-called Street Art to understand that the huge sprayed and stenciled images of people and slogans that appeared overnight on the sides of buildings or on blank billboards, particularly downtown and along the freeways, were part of a running contest between a handful of L.A. graffiti crews who'd graduated from tagging busses and train cars to enjoying the rarified realm of gallery shows and museum exhibitions. But before they could cash in on the big bucks, they first had to make their reputations on the street, where cops, rival artists, street gangs, and gravity all conspired to bring them down to earth.

Rio arrived with an entourage consisting of three other guys, one of whom had a video camera on his shoulder, plus the Japanese anime girl. He, too, had changed since the debate, and now wore a black T-shirt and tight black jeans. The T-shirt read CART IS NOT A RHYME. The girl was dressed as before, in a plaid miniskirt and white knee-high stockings. Her hair was in twin ponytails streaked with pink, and the pink matched both her lipstick and her two-tone platform shoes. She was over six feet tall, skinny as Olive Oyl, and must have had something surgical done to her eyes, which seemed half again larger than normal.

"Ricky, this is Jack MacTaggart," Angela said, anointing me with her vodka glass. "Jack was just admiring your work."

Lizard Face more closely resembled Ian McShane than Edward James Almos, although both could have read for the part. I put his age at just short of fifty. His hair was long and black, and his face was deeply pocked by an epic case of boyhood acne. He was around five feet nine, and generally slender, but powerful in his tattooed upper body. His most striking feature by far, however, was his eyes: ice blue and world weary, as though they'd witnessed more pain and sorrow than one tortured soul could endure.

He didn't offer a hand, but the girl pressed her palms together and bowed. "*Konbanwa,*" she said, giggling. "I am Legs. And this is Mouse and this is Benny and this is K-Jaw."

The song changed again as the strobe light faded, and suddenly it was my own twenty-foot video image that was projected onto the wall. There were boos from the crowd below us.

"Jack is Mr. Burkett's lawyer," Angela explained to Ricky. "He's been looking for a painting."

"Sorry, man. I don't do paintings." Rio leaned his tattooed forearms on the balcony railing and spoke into the void. "Paintings have boundaries. People who buy paintings cut holes in their walls to see beauty outside. People with boundaries. But all they see is a square, you know? Squares for squares. They need to lose the walls and go outside for themselves. That's where the beauty is."

And here, I thought, is where the bullshit is. I was suddenly very tired.

"The painting I was looking for is old, and French."

"Like Brigitte Bardot," he said. "Like ennui."

"Like Berthe Morisot," I told him, my enormous mouth moving silently on the wall.

He fished a pack from his pocket and lit up a Marlboro. Legs blew out the match, then clapped her hands and giggled.

"I know what you're talking about," Ricky said, his eyes again sweeping the crowd. "I watch the news. Do you watch the news?"

"Sometimes."

He nodded. "I saw you on the news. With a Latina chick. She was cute."

"I'm told that the painting I'm looking for would be very difficult to fence."

He turned again and fixed me with those sad, sad eyes.

"Fence? What are you, Joe Friday? That painting will never be seen again, man. Not in our lifetime. It's on a rich man's wall, and a poor man's conscience. If I were you I'd forget all about it."

Angela stepped closer and put a hand on Ricky's shoulder. "We're doing an exhibition at MOCA next month. StreetScrapes, a Ricky Rio retrospective. The preview party is Sunday afternoon. If you'd like, I'll leave your name at the door."

"Oh, boy," I told them.

"Bring the girl," Ricky suggested, returning to his vigil. "She's cute."

"Thanks, I'll do that. She's my law partner. I think she knows a lot about art."

I left them up there on the balcony and squeezed my way back through the crowd, stopping at the filthy bathroom on the way out. Then, as I weaved my way toward the exit, a large and familiar presence blocked my progress.

"Hey," he said.

Tony Gags had lost his suit jacket, but he still wore his shirt with the open collar, damp now with perspiration. He'd either been dancing or burying bodies out in the alley.

The music changed again, and the disco ball started to twirl. I moved to my right, but Tony moved to block me. To my left, the same. I smiled at him, and he smiled back. Then I hit him with a short right uppercut just under the rib cage.

He toppled forward to one knee, wheezing and gasping, and I stepped past him. I walked halfway to the door, and then I turned around.

People were helping Tony to his feet. I looked up toward the balcony, and there were Angela and Rio, both of them watching me. Angela raised her glass.

As I reached the door, I heard another smattering of boos. When I turned this time, I saw the twenty-foot video image of another clean-cut guy in a business suit. The guy frowned at the camera. Then, as he reached a giant hand toward the lens, the image went black.

I guess Harwood had been hoping to keep a lower profile.

FIVE

ELECTION DAY MINUS NINETEEN.

I could feel the vibe on the street as I approached the courthouse, an invisible energy that thrummed and pulsed, announcing to the attuned that there would be big game afoot this morning inside the Clara Shortridge Foltz Criminal Justice Center.

News vans, like so many vultures on a wire, lined the curb on Broadway, and as I descended the steps to the main courthouse entrance, I passed sound technicians wiring a portable lectern bearing the official seal of the district attorney of the County of Los Angeles.

Photographers surged from the lobby as I removed my keys and belt and placed them in the little plastic tub to run, along with my briefcase, through the boxy X-ray scanner. Then, as I re-outfitted myself on the other side and made my way to where Mayday waited at the elevators, a shuffling tide of reporters moved with me, their shouted questions echoing off the glass-and-concrete walls.

Mayday studied her phone as I stopped and faced the throng.

"Okay, people, listen up. All we're doing today is entering a plea of not guilty." The elevator chimed behind me, and the big steel doors slid open. "Other than that, we have nothing new to announce."

There were groans and a few residual flashes as the

doors slid closed and we found ourselves alone in hollow silence.

"Are we good?"

Mayday nodded, and I hit the button for five.

"By the way," she said, showing me the *Times* Web site on her phone, "the Bloomfields are back in town."

"Since when?"

"Last night, apparently. It says they're meeting with the district attorney this afternoon."

"Slewzyski has a busy schedule."

"And another photo op."

When the doors opened on five, we were engulfed in another, larger scrum. This time, as we'd rehearsed, Mayday climbed atop a hallway bench and turned to face the media horde. They closed ranks around her as she raised her hands for quiet. As she began to speak, I slipped away toward the restroom at the far end of the hallway.

There was a kid at the sink with a righteous shiner and a butterfly bandage on his eyebrow. A toilet flushed, and a balding lawyer emerged from a stall with his shirttail flapping and a sport coat over his arm. They chatted together as the lawyer tucked his shirt and washed, a process he concluded by admonishing his client to keep his big fucking mouth shut in front of the judge this time.

When the door had closed behind them, I set down my briefcase and faced the empty urinal. I checked my watch. It was eight twenty-five.

When the door next opened, this time to the sound of reporters clamoring in the hallway, it was Warren Burkett who ducked under Harwood's arm as the big man set his weight and shoved the door closed behind him.

Burkett straightened his tie with his free hand. "Jesus Christ" is all he said.

"Good morning."

Burkett grunted. He hefted a briefcase onto the sink and worked the double latches. The lid lifted, and he held the plastic baggie aloft. The coiled belt was brown with a silver buckle. I took possession, again noting the time, and transferred the baggie to my own briefcase, with Harwood watching me from his post at the door.

"Division Thirty is felony arraignment court," I told Burkett as he moved to use the urinal. "We'll enter and sit together in the courtroom. When our case is called, we'll both walk through the gate to the lectern on the left. When the judge asks for your plea, you'll say 'not guilty.' That's the only thing you'll say all morning, unless the judge asks you to confirm a representation I've made, and in that case you'll say, 'Yes, Your Honor.' Understood?"

Burkett flushed and moved to the sinks. "I think I can handle that."

"I'm assuming you still want a trial before the election?"

"Have you seen the polls? You're goddamn right I do."

"Okay then. My final piece of advice would be to say nothing to the press, but you're a big boy in that regard."

He studied me in the graffiti-scarred mirror as he bent to wash his hands. "Is this the judge who'll conduct the preliminary hearing?"

"No. This judge will pull a name at random off his computer. Pray for a Democrat."

"I always do," Burkett said, wadding a paper towel

and tossing it into the can. He patted his hair and flashed a practiced smile at the mirror. "Are we ready?"

"Whenever you are."

We moved to the door in tandem, and Harwood yanked it open. The collective camera flash was blinding. Burkett led the way, smiling and nodding and calling to reporters by name, while Harwood and I paused to face off in the doorway.

I said, "After you, party boy."

ARRAIGNMENT COURT WAS its usual three-ring circus of choreographed chaos. The public benches were crowded with lawyers, with those of their clients lucky enough to have made bail, and with the tight-mouthed wives and fidgeting children of the latter. As for the rest, a high Plexiglas barricade stretched along the right-hand wall, framed in wood and roofed in chain-link fencing, behind which milled a motley assortment of head-shaved and tattooed custodies in their Easter egg coveralls—navy for the general population, orange for the K-10/high powers, canary yellow for the mental patients, and sky blue for the homosexual keep-aways—all of them variously preening and scowling, slouching and pacing, each enjoying a welcome respite from the boredom and terror that was the L.A. County Men's Central Jail, the largest prison in the free world.

At the front of the courtroom, a cadre of young deputy district attorneys pored through stacks of case files, pausing to call out case names and huddle with the public defenders or private defense attorneys, many of whom then broke away to confer with their clients through the barred slot in the barricade, all of this transpiring under the watchful eyes of a dozen ham-armed sheriff's deputies. Meanwhile, the few empty seats that remained in the courtroom filled with reporters, many of them pausing to chat with the lawyers or with each other, the overall effect being not a temple of justice so much as a teeming Turkish bazaar.

Burkett stood in the aisle watching the sausage grinder of justice churn, his expression equal parts bewilderment and concern.

"Christ," he whispered. "Do we have to sit through all of this?"

"Somehow I doubt it."

Then, right on cue, the hallway doors opened and Tom Slewzyski breezed into the courtroom trailing a pair of uniformed deputies. Slew was TV ready in his navy suit and baby-blue shirt and solid maroon tie, and as he paused to regard the ordered pandemonium, the young ADAs up front nudged one other and redoubled their efforts to look busy.

Slew nodded once in our direction. He did not, I noticed, bother to sit. Within seconds of his arrival, a buzzer sounded two short bursts and the other lawyers found their seats as the clerk and the court reporter moved into position. The room fell silent. A door opened on the front wall, and the judge appeared in his robes.

"All rise," the courtroom deputy boomed. "The Superior Court for the State of California, County of Los Angeles, is now in session, the Honorable James Fenton presiding."

All sat again as the young jurist donned his reading glasses, squinted at his calendar, and announced, "*People versus Burkett,* Case No. BA-three-seven-five-zero-two-seven."

There were catcalls from behind the Plexiglas as a deputy held the gate open for my client. Slew and I stood shoulder to shoulder at the lectern to announce our appearances, with the district attorney, out of either habit or hubris, spelling his name for the court reporter. The judge looked up from his notes.

"Does the defense waive reading of the complaint?"

"We do, Your Honor."

The judge was studying Burkett as if he were some windblown rara avis that had somehow landed at his feeder.

"Has the defense received the state's discovery?"

Without turning, Slew reached a hand to a young deputy behind him, and she passed him a slender folder.

"Let the record reflect that I'm handing to Mr. Mac-Taggart a full and complete copy of the state's discovery to date," the D.A. said, giving me the folder. "Let the record also reflect that the state has, not surprisingly, received nothing in return."

The folder contained the initial incident report, a brief addendum prepared by the lead detectives, and a photocopy of a grainy photograph. Six pages in total. The photo appeared to have come from a surveillance camera mounted around fifteen feet above street level on Hollywood Boulevard. It showed a late-model Jaguar with a male driver and a female passenger barely visible through the windshield, taken just as the Jag passed under a streetlight.

"Mr. MacTaggart?" the judge prodded.

"We have nothing as yet to disclose, Your Honor. It's not exactly a document-intensive case."

"Very well, then. Mr. Burkett, how do you plead to the charges that have been filed against you?"

Burkett straightened. "Not guilty," he said, with just the proper note of indignation. Behind us, a dozen pencils scratched.

The judge made a notation of his own. "The accused has the right to have a preliminary hearing commenced within ten days. Is time waived, counsel?"

"No, Your Honor. Time is not waived."

This brought the judge's head up. He looked from me to Slew and back again.

"I see," he said. He tapped the calendar with his pencil and then half-turned to his clerk. "In that case, the matter will be set for a preliminary hearing on the earliest available date within ten days from today in Department…"

"One-twelve," said the clerk, reading from his computer.

"In Department one-twelve. That would be Judge Marquez. Is notice waived?"

"Notice waived," I replied brightly.

Slewzyski looked as if he'd swallowed a bug. "The state will give notice," he growled.

Back in the hallway, after the initial assault of camera flashes and shouted questions, Slew invited the assembled press to join him downstairs for a few prepared remarks. Mayday and I slipped out ahead of Burkett and Harwood, and the four of us rode the elevator together—and alone—thanks to an arm bar by Harwood that blocked any reporters from joining us.

"Well?" Burkett asked as the doors closed and the elevator lurched into motion.

"We could have done worse. Sylvia Marquez is a Gray Davis appointee and a former deputy public defender. She's good, but she's nobody's patsy. She'll call balls and strikes, but she might give us the corners."

Burkett grunted, reading his watch. "We're heading to Sacramento in an hour. When will the hearing take place?"

I looked to Mayday. "We'll get on her calendar as soon as we can. Expect a week at least. I'll call you as soon as we know."

"And what about the belt?"

"Don't worry." I patted my briefcase. "I know just the man for the job."

We parted company on the sidewalk, with Burkett and Harwood piling into a black Town Car. Mayday and I watched as the press corps spilled forth from the building and assembled by the lectern, where an easel had been set up with a poster-sized enlargement of the photo in my briefcase.

"Department one-twelve?" Mayday asked, and I nodded.

"See what you can do with the clerk. Explain that the future of the free world hangs in the balance."

"And then?"

"Then I was hoping you might drive out to Hollywood and pay a call on the Bloomfields."

"In respect of Farmers?"

I smiled, and she smiled in reply. Then I watched as she descended the stairs and elbowed her way through the reporters, just as Slewzyski stepped up to the microphone and tapped it with a finger.

"Nobody is above the law," he began, his amplified voice echoing into the street as I turned and started toward the parking garage.

SUSHI ROKU FRONTS a brick courtyard off a narrow alley in Old Pasadena, the Crown City's historic shopping and dining district. There were, in addition to the inside seating, four outside tables, all empty, with propane heaters to fend off the evening chill. After confirming that I was first to arrive, I asked the African American hostess to seat me at one of them. A Japanese waiter brought menus and a wine list, while a Mexican busboy filled the water glasses. The place was a regular United Nations.

Each table setting consisted of a woven-fiber mat, double-stacked plates, three small bowls—each containing a colorful dab of some paste or unguent—a tea service, and a polished black stone on which rested a set of balsa-wood chopsticks in a red paper sleeve.

It was going to be a long evening.

Regan Fife arrived on the button, her honey-blond hair luminous in the last, slanting light on the courtyard. She wore her jeans tight and faded, with her tailored black blazer hiding the off-duty weapon I assumed was holstered at the small of her back. She was taller in heels, and she seemed somehow older, radiating not only her usual wholesome athleticism, but also an air of sophistication.

She smiled as I rose to greet her, and she hung her oversized bag on the chair back.

"Sushi," she enthused. "What a great idea!"

The Japanese waiter reappeared to ask if we'd seen the wine list.

"I'll have the house sake, warm," Regan told him without looking.

"I'll have the same. Only cold. And make it a Budweiser."

"So," she said, taking up her menu, "I saw you on the six o'clock news tonight. You didn't look happy."

"That was my game face. Inside I was dancing the rhumba."

She sighed theatrically. "It must be nice to work on glamorous cases with national press coverage. All I ever do is patrol Sierra Madre. Do you have any idea how boring that is?"

"I can imagine."

"Nothing ever happens—and I mean *nothing*."

"Come now, don't exaggerate. What about that big littering bust at the Wisteria Festival?"

"Not funny."

"If it's any consolation, I spent my afternoon researching the capitation clause."

"The what?"

"Article One, Section Nine of the U.S. Constitution. Believe me, you don't want to know."

She closed her menu. "The hamachi looks good."

"Really good."

"And the ika."

I nodded. "You can't go wrong there."

"Why do I get the feeling you don't eat sushi?"

The waiter returned with our drinks. He had the telltale good looks of an aspiring actor waiting tables to pay the rent. He pulled out a cheat sheet and read us the evening's specials, or maybe it was a scene from *Seven Samurai*. Regan went with the hamachi, or whatever it was called, and a California roll. I opted for the tempura shrimp with white rice, whereupon the waiter pointed out that there was a Benji Burger on the children's menu. I gave him the stink-eye.

Officer Fife unhooked her bag from the chair back

and rummaged inside. I moved the little bamboo cen-
terpiece, and she set my cardboard package on the table.

"I tried both ultraviolet fluorescence and cyanoac-
rylate fuming," she said.

"I love when you talk like that."

"Yours are the only fingerprints I found. Looks to
me like whoever's been in your toy box was careful to
cover his tracks. Your prints are on the frame and the
screen, but there was nothing on the dials, even after
the message was written."

"Who says a message was written?"

She turned the box, so that the label FRAGILE/DO NOT
SHAKE faced me.

"Ah."

"I don't suppose you're going to tell me what this
is about?"

"Are you sure you want to know?"

"Come on. I violated a dozen federal regulations to
run these prints."

So I told her the story, or as much of the story as I
could tell without violating attorney-client privilege.
She listened attentively. The food arrived by the time
I'd finished, and she unsheathed her chopsticks while
the waiter set a knife and fork next to my plate. I ordered another beer.

"If it were my investigation," Regan said, "I'd get
an APB out to every art dealer and auction house in
the country, plus the FBI and Interpol. I'd run a search
on every art theft on the West Coast over the past ten
years. Then I'd run a background check on every employee at Bonhams. Then—"

I set the Ziploc baggie on the table.

"What's that?"

"It's the belt Burkett was wearing on the night he was arrested. The LAPD never checked it for latent prints."

"Did the woman…?"

I nodded.

"And I suppose you want me…?"

I nodded again.

She inspected the baggie, holding it aloft like a herpetological specimen.

"This is evidence tampering, you know. We could both get in trouble."

"Trust me, I'm a lawyer. Besides, I'm already in trouble. I have a preliminary hearing in less than ten days, and I need to identify the green-eyed lady, find her, and then tie her directly to the crime scene. That belt could do it, but neither the D.A. nor the LAPD will help me out. In fact, if they knew I had the belt, they'd probably try to stop me."

She was still frowning.

"Then again, I don't want to interfere with your busy patrol schedule."

I reached for the baggie, but she snatched it away.

"Not so fast. If you really think the D.A. will try to bury this, or delay it for some political reason—"

"I know he will."

"Then *that* would be evidence tampering. Not to mention obstruction of justice."

"A crime that you, a sworn law enforcement officer, could prevent before it happens."

Again she regarded the belt. "With probable cause, based upon evidence provided by a reliable source."

"Obtained within your jurisdiction."

"We're not in my jurisdiction."

"Ah, but we could be. Later tonight, for example."

"In your dreams, counselor."

Smiling, I took a folded sheet from my pocket.

"What's that?"

"Nothing. Just the address of Ricky Rio's studio. I think he lives there. Also, William Harwood's name and physical description. I figure Harwood for former law enforcement or former military. Maybe both."

She studied me for a long moment. Then she shook her head, slipping both the note and the belt into her handbag.

"I already know I'm going to regret this."

"No kidding. There's still time to order the Benji Burger."

"I'll see what I can come up with," she said, placing her bag back on the chair. "We'll deal with the jurisdictional issue later."

But before we could do so, as we lingered over our green tea ice cream, who but Marta Suarez should appear at the far end of the courtyard, in short shorts and running shoes, heading our way at a trot, I folded my napkin and stood.

"Thank goodness," she said, fanning herself with her hand. "Your phone is off, so I had to call Bernie at home. I'm sorry to interrupt, but you've got to see this."

She unslung her laptop and cleared a space on the table. I dragged another chair over.

"I was at home, reading up on the candidates, and I saw that Archer had just posted a new campaign ad on YouTube. Check this out."

She pecked at her keyboard, then turned the screen to face us.

"Hit the PLAY arrow. Watch it all the way through for context."

The subject of the ad was the environment—or, more precisely, why clean-air regulations were hurting California's business environment. In the video, Larry Archer looked all regular-guy folksy in a flannel shirt and chinos. He began by telling the camera that he was at his vacation cabin on Lake Arrowhead. He talked about his deep love of hiking and nature and killing things with firearms. Then, as he walked from his living room onto the deck, with the tall pines whispering in the background, he explained how California's continued participation in a regional cap-and-trade market for greenhouse gas emissions was actually a Communist plot to kill baby seals and foster Islamic terrorism. Or words to that effect.

Mayday rebooted the video. "Okay, now watch it again."

This time, just as Archer started to move toward the deck, Mayday froze the image. "There. Over his shoulder."

An arched doorway opened behind the candidate, and visible through it was a thin slice of wall in the room beyond. On the wall hung a painting, the lower left corner of which could be glimpsed in the upper-right corner of the frame.

There were pastel flowers in the painting, and grass, and nestled in the grass was a striped wooden ball.

SIX

ELECTION DAY MINUS EIGHTEEN.

I was listening to KNX NewsRadio as I ate my Wheaties in the kitchen, and I had the TV in the den tuned to Channel 9 *Action News* with the volume on high. Sam, unaccustomed to watching me consume media along with my breakfast, sat with a stuffed toy in his mouth and a hopeful look on his face.

There'd been no mention of the Archer campaign ad, which didn't surprise me, because no photo of the missing painting—or even its title, *The Croquet Party*—had ever been made public. Even if they had, I wondered how many viewers would have been sharp enough to spot what Mayday had spotted.

What I did know, again thanks to Mayday, was that Dr. and Mrs. Bloomfield had met with Slewzyski yesterday and had given him a transparency of the painting. This meant either that the D.A. hadn't put two and two together as yet, or that he had but was keeping the scandal under wraps.

How quickly things could change, I thought, in the fickle and fluid world of politics. Now there lay before me a universe of options, and all of them were good.

I could, for example, call Terina Webb and give her the story of a lifetime. Better yet, I could call up one of those celebrity gossip sites like *Radar* or *TMZ* and sell the scoop for enough cash to cover our office overhead for a year. Or I could take a page from the D.A.'s playbook and hold a press conference on the courthouse steps.

Taking the high road instead, as my mentor Russ Dinsmoor would have done, I could e-mail the video link to Slew, or to Detectives Madden and Alvarez, with a copy to the FBI for insurance. Speaking of insurance, I was pretty sure that Farmers would have liked to get in on the action as well.

As I said, all my options were good.

The drive from Sycamore Lane in San Marino to the office in Sierra Madre took anywhere from ten to fifteen minutes, depending on the surface street traffic, which today was Friday morning light. All hands were on deck for my 8:30 A.M. arrival, and we assembled in the office conference room.

"I've heard nothing on the news this morning," I began, which Mayday, laptop open before her, confirmed with a nod.

"Nothing on the Web," she said, "and the ad is still up on YouTube."

"Can they make it disappear?"

She shook her head. "Not completely. Plus, I've already burned a copy for safekeeping."

Bernie followed this exchange with a puzzled look. "What are you talking about?"

Mayday brought her up to speed, using the Bonhams' photo and the YouTube clip as visual aids.

"Holy shit," Bernie said when the video image froze. "That little ass-wipe's got the painting!"

"So it would appear."

"What are you gonna do about it?"

I looked to Mayday. "Partner? It was your discovery."

"I know, and I've been thinking about it all morning."

"And?"

"First of all, I think we should call our client, before he learns about it from somebody else. Plus, given everything he's got at stake, I think we should let him make the final call. Within reason, of course. There may be political angles to this that we're not even seeing."

"Bernie?"

"Me? I've got around fifty phone messages out there." She nodded toward reception. "I say let's call in the press and make popcorn."

"What about you?" Mayday asked me. "What would you propose?"

It was a good question. But there was another, possibly more urgent question that had yet to be addressed.

"Keep your eye on the ball," I reminded them. "Let's think about that for a second. Whoever sent the package had to have known what was going to appear in the campaign ad. That means the ad had to have been filmed sometime between Monday night, when the painting went missing, and Tuesday afternoon, when the package was delivered. That's a pretty tight window. It also means that somebody who'd seen the ad, or the footage from which it was to be cut, wanted to tip us off to what they'd seen. What's more, that person, whoever it is, had to have known what the stolen painting looked like."

Mayday nodded, following my logic. "Okay, let's take the last part first. The only people who knew what the painting looked like were the Bloomfields, some people at Bonhams, plus Burkett and the green-eyed lady."

"Wrong," I said. "There are thousands of art collectors and curators who would have known that painting on sight. The question is, how many knew it had been stolen on Monday night?"

"The cops knew," Bernie said.

I nodded. "And the D.A."

"And the thief."

"Or thieves."

"Wait a minute." Mayday took up a pad and pencil. "First, knew the painting on sight. Second, knew it had been stolen. Third, knew it had been filmed at Archer's cabin. Fourth, knew we'd been hired by Burkett. Fifth, wanted us to find the painting."

"Good," I said. "Now, as of Tuesday afternoon, which of those five categories contained the smallest number of identifiable actors?"

She frowned. "The third. Knew it had been filmed at Archer's cabin."

"I agree. And that's where we need to start looking."

WARREN BURKETT, once informed of our little discovery, had gleefully opted for the full-bore media reveal, and within an hour's time had arranged a press conference for 2:00 P.M., to be held at his main campaign office, on Wilshire Boulevard in Los Angeles. Mayday and I were to be in attendance, he told us, dressed for our fifteen minutes of fame. His only regret, he said in parting, was dropping our nuclear bombshell on the Archer campaign during the traditional Friday-afternoon-where-stories-go-to-die news dump.

Bernie's assignment was to have the Bonhams photo of *The Croquet Party* enlarged to poster size and mounted on a foam-core backing. Mayday's was to continue monitoring the media, and to alert us if we'd been scooped. The first of my assignments, and the one on which I'd insisted, was to call the district attorney and personally advise him that the painting had been found. The second was to plan for what we knew would follow.

Back in my office, Nerf basketball in hand, I left an urgent message with Slew's assistant, telling her that I had a major development to report in the Burkett case. The D.A. called ten minutes later, sounding more than a little peeved.

"This'd better be good, MacTaggart."

"I called you as a matter of professional courtesy, Tom. Don't kick a gift horse in the ass."

"I'm listening."

"You remember that painting the Bloomfields showed you yesterday? *The Croquet Party*?"

"How did you…? Never mind. What about it?"

"I thought you might like to know where to find the original."

The D.A., to his discredit, didn't miss a beat.

"You mean your client wants to confess and cop a plea? I already told you, no special deals for the big-shot defendant."

"You mean no deals for Democrats."

"I mean that if you know the whereabouts of that painting, you'd better report it right now or risk being charged yourself."

Confirming what I'd suspected—that he was still in the dark.

"Since when is recovering stolen property a crime, Slew? I missed that class in law school."

"Cut the bullshit, Mac."

"You cut the bullshit. Do you want the painting or not?"

There was a moment's pause while he swallowed a chunk of his ego.

"Yes, damn it, I want the painting!"

"Okay, then, but first you have to make me a promise."

"Jesus."

"You need to promise me that if I tell you where to find the painting, you and I will go pick it up together."

"I don't have to promise you shit."

"That's true, and you know what? I think I'll call the FBI instead. Goodbye."

I hung up the phone and banked a ten-foot fadeaway jumper off the glass. I was really enjoying this.

The phone rang again, and I put it on speaker. "Mac-Taggart and Suarez, how may I direct your call?"

"You asshole."

"That would be Mr. MacTaggart. Whom shall I say is calling?"

"All right, it's a deal."

"Let me hear you say it."

He sighed. "If you tell me where the painting is, you can come along with us when we retrieve it."

"Cross your heart and hope to die?"

"Don't push it, MacTaggart."

"Okay, now listen carefully. Come to Burkett's campaign headquarters on Wilshire at two o'clock this afternoon."

"And the painting will be there?"

"No, but that's when I'll tell you where to find it."

I hung up the phone before he could protest, and I retrieved the ball from the net.

"You and everybody else."

BURKETT'S CAMPAIGN WAS headquartered in an empty storefront in the 8000 block of Wilshire, just east of La Cienega. Huge BURKETT FOR SENATE posters plastered the windows, while out in the street were sound trucks, mobile radio stations, TV news vans, and brightly de-caled passenger vehicles stretching bumper to bumper for three city blocks.

Inside the building, all the desks had been shoved to the walls, leaving a wide central aisle now filled with row upon row of folding chairs, all facing the rear. That's where a podium, an empty easel, and two flat-screen television monitors stood at the ready.

By one fifty, all the chairs were occupied, while be-hind them, a row of news cameras on tripods stood backlit against the street-side windows. Late-arriving reporters were relegated to standing room, while a team of campaign volunteers bustled to and fro, wiring the podium and testing the PA system and triple-checking the video feed to the monitors.

All this I observed from behind the podium, through a crack in the door leading to the lone inner office where Scott Tully, Mayday, and I, joined by a half dozen young staffers, waited for the fun to begin. We'd been assem-bled for nearly an hour, discussing logistics, rehearsing our assigned roles, and pinching each other in disbe-lief that the gods of political momentum had deigned to jump-start the stalled Burkett bandwagon.

"Five minutes," Tully said into his cell phone, and moments later the alley door opened. Warren and Bobbi

Burkett entered the office together, both of them som-
ber, followed by the omnipresent Harwood. I saw the
black Lincoln parked outside, and imagined the scene
that had just played out in the backseat, with Burkett
entreating his wife once again to stand by her man in
the harsh glare of the klieg lights.

"Jack," Burkett said warmly, gripping my hand with
both of his. "If I win this thing, I owe it all to you."

"You'll owe it to Marta, but don't give her a big head
or she'll ask for a raise."

While the candidate turned his attention to Mayday, I
watched as his wife, so warm and convivial on Wednesday evening, stood now with her back to the room.

I returned to my viewing post in time to see Tom
Slewzyski enter from the street and pull up short in the
doorway. Trailing behind him were Madden and Alvarez. The three of them conferred briefly before moving
to a spot along the wall. Moments later, the ursine shape
of Anthony Gagliano appeared and took a position on
the opposite side of the room.

"The gang's all here," I announced over my shoulder.

"Okay," Tully said, checking his watch. "Two o'clock
on the nose. Are we ready? Warren? Let's get out there
and win an election."

When the office door opened, the room became elec-
tric. Mayday led the way, hoisting the poster onto the
easel, while Warren and Bobbi Burkett followed behind
her to stand at the side of the podium, where I, the last
to emerge, took my place at the microphones.

"Good afternoon," I began, waiting for the room
to settle. "Thank you for coming. My name is Jack
MacTaggart, and I've been retained by Mayor Burkett
in connection with certain false and reckless charges

filed against him by the District Attorney's Office. The most serious of these charges involves a painting called *The Croquet Party,* by an artist named Berthe Morisot, which was stolen from a Los Angeles residence on Monday evening. A photo of that painting you can see here to my right. The reason we're here today is to announce that the painting has finally been located."

There was a murmur from the floor, and I waited for it to subside.

"Mayor Burkett will take the podium to address this matter in a moment, but first, please indulge us while we show you a brief campaign advertisement."

There were groans.

"Hold on," I continued, showing a hand. "This isn't one of Mr. Burkett's pieces, but rather, one of Mr. Archer's. It was released yesterday evening. You can view it yourself on YouTube, but let's all take a moment now and watch it together."

The room lights dimmed, and the video monitors blinked to life, and there stood Archer in his red flannel shirt.

I watched the faces as the video played. All were turned to the monitors, including the district attorney's. Only Tony Gags kept his rhino eyes riveted on me.

"Sure, we all love the environment," the audio continued, "but we can protect it without regulations that kill jobs and hamper small business." Then the video froze.

There was a long delay while the audience processed what they were seeing. Then there were gasps, and pointed fingers, and pandemonium.

Half the reporters were on their feet, some surging for the doors and toppling chairs in their wake. Half were on their cell phones, hands over ears, barking instructions or dictating copy. Some shouted questions at Burkett, while others just stared, open-mouthed, as their heads swiveled from the picture on the easel to the image frozen on the video monitor. Slewzyski, when I saw him again, was staggering toward the door like a man who'd been pepper-sprayed.

A semblance of order had been restored to the half-empty room by the time Warren Burkett stepped to the podium, with Bobbi beaming dewily at his side. He started off with a line that I'd fed him, aimed right at the heart of the district attorney.

"I heard it said someplace recently that nobody is above the law..."

I caught up with Slew on the sidewalk, where he and Alvarez stood waiting for Madden to bring their car. In the street behind them, it looked as though someone had dropped the green flag at Le Mans, with news vans and passenger vehicles peeling off into traffic amid honking horns and screeching tires. Such was the frenzy that nobody, it seemed, had even noticed the D.A.

"I thought that went rather well," I told him cheerily.

"You lied, MacTaggart."

"Nope. I did exactly what I promised."

Alvarez stepped forward to point a finger at my chest. "You compromised a pending investigation, asshole. Half these clowns are on their way up to Arrowhead, and we don't even have a warrant!"

"A warrant?" I reached into my jacket and withdrew the folded document. "You mean one of these?"

A siren chirped at the curb, and we all turned to see the black-and-white Sierra Madre Police Department cruiser roll to a stop.

"What do you say, Tom? Care to ride along?"

Alvarez shouted something from the sidewalk as I dodged between cars and opened the passenger door.

"Last chance," I called from inside, fanning the warrant through the open window as the patrol car started to roll.

On the sidewalk, Slewzyski broke into a run.

"I DON'T KNOW who you are, young lady, but you're in big trouble."

We'd hung a right on La Cienega, and I could see the Beverly Center looming up ahead. I turned to face the D.A. through the heavy steel cage separating the backseat from the front.

"Tom Slewzyski, Regan Fife."

"Hello," Regan said.

"You're outside your jurisdiction, Officer, and you're obstructing justice. Pull to the curb right now, and that's an order!"

"I told you he can be cranky. He seems cranky, don't you think?"

"I mean it, Officer. You have no authority here."

I unfolded the search warrant and read the caption aloud: "To Any Peace Officer in Los Angeles County…"

"Arrowhead's in San Bernardino County!"

"*People v. Fleming*," I reminded him.

"Damn it!"

He had his phone out and was dialing.

"Just think of Officer Fife as a kind of referee, Tom. As long as nobody holds, clips, or jumps offside, you won't even notice her."

I consulted the side-view mirror. Alvarez and Madden were closing behind us in a white Crown Victoria, their grill lights flashing blue.

"Right on Santa Monica, then left on Highland," I told Regan.

Slewzyski twisted in his seat. "Okay, listen up," he said into his phone. "No, I'm okay. Radio ahead to the sheriff in San Bernardino and have them cordon off the street. I don't know. Wait a minute." Then to me he said, "What's the address?"

I read from the warrant. "Palisades Drive."

"Palisades Drive. No press and no through traffic, you hear me? We'll be there in under an hour."

He lowered the phone. "All right, MacTaggart. I hope to Christ you know what you're doing, because if you fuck this up, I'm gonna feed you to Chico. Both of you."

We took the Hollywood Freeway to the eastbound 134, stayed in the carpool lane, and passed a dozen news vans mired like mastodons in the tarpit of Friday afternoon traffic. Regan zoomed past the slower traffic by weaving onto the inside shoulder wherever space allowed. We were traveling Code Three, with lights and siren blazing, all but scraping against the K-rail median, with the Crown Vic right on our tail.

"You drive like a girl," I told Regan, hanging on for dear life.

"You think so?"

"Yeah. Danica Patrick."

Once Slew had settled down, he passed the hour conducting county business by telephone. By the time we'd hit the 18 and started climbing into the mountains, he'd calmed enough to appreciate that we'd actually done him a favor. Several favors, in fact, starting with solving his highest-profile case.

"How did you ever manage to notice that painting in the video?" he asked me, tucking the phone into his pocket.

"You've met Marta. She can be scary sometimes."

"Larry freaking Archer." The D.A. shook his head, his legs crossed and his arm slung over the seatback. "What the hell was he thinking?"

By the time the lake flashed into view, we were deep in the tall pines and smelling the cold mountain air. Regan had her GPS unit active, and she navigated the winding lakeside streets with one eye locked on the screen. We rounded a bend and encountered a pair of sheriff's cruisers parked nose to nose, blocking our way. We slowed to a stop, and Slew hung his creds out the rear-seat window.

"L.A. County District Attorney!" he shouted. "Close the street behind us!"

From the street side, Archer's so-called cabin looked more like a ski lodge, or maybe a small Alpine hotel, with its three stories of articulated logs punctuated by cut-glass windows and topped by a green copper roof. The deputy posted out front blew warmth into his hands, and I surrendered the warrant to Slew as we approached.

"Is anybody inside?" the D.A. asked as the deputy scanned the warrant.

"No, sir. My orders were to secure the front entrance until you arrived."

"Okay." Slew nodded to Alvarez, who rang the bell, then banged on the huge oaken door.

"Police officers executing a warrant!" the detective shouted, checking his wristwatch. After sixty seconds had passed, he turned to the D.A. "No response."

This meant that the premises could lawfully be entered, even if it meant breaking down the door—which in this case was purely hypothetical, since the door was heavier than a Bergman film festival.

That's when we all heard it.

Faint at first, masked by the high wind in the pines, the rhythmic sound grew louder and more distinctive as it neared.

"Chopper," Madden said, stepping back from the door.

The helicopter swung in low, banked a hard turn to the left, and then landed behind the house. We all hurried to the sound, down an embankment slick with pine needles, and as we circled to the rear of the property we saw the chopper resting on a lakeside pad at the end of a sloping lawn.

"Archer," I said to Regan as the little man strode forth from under the still-moving rotors. Tony Gags emerged next, crouching and trotting behind him, his knuckles all but scraping the manicured ground.

"What the hell, Tom?" Archer shouted, marching past the D.A. without slowing. Slew followed after him, waving the warrant.

"I'm afraid we need to search the house, Larry. You've seen the video?"

"Yes, I've seen the goddamn video, and I'll tell you right now it's some kind of trick." Archer fumbled with his keys, then froze when he saw me, his beady eyes narrowing into slits. "What the hell is he doing here?"

"Never mind that. Let's go inside and have a look."

Archer let loose a string of choice expletives.

"You govern in prose," I told Regan, "but you campaign in poetry."

We all entered the house off a flagstone patio that led to a carpeted game room. There was a pool table, and wall-mounted deer heads, and an old Wurlitzer jukebox that glowed in the semidarkness, casting a jaundiced light on Tony Gags's face as he followed my every move.

"We shot the piece upstairs. This way."

Archer led us up a back staircase and into a darkened great room, where he twisted a dimmer and a dozen Tiffany lamps warmed to life, bathing the room in a soft, liquid glow. There was a stone fireplace, and colorful Navajo rugs, and whatever furniture wasn't made from gnarled and polished burl wood was made from giant elk antlers.

"Here." Archer threw another switch, and the curtains slowly parted, flooding the room with a breathtaking view of the lake.

We all blinked.

"The camera was right where you're standing. I was over there, and then I moved out to the deck like this."

Archer reconstructed his movements on the video. We shared a communal look, and then we all surged as one, through the arched doorway and into the dining room beyond, where, just as in Warren Burkett's account of his night in the Bloomfield residence, the wall where the painting had hung was now completely and maddeningly blank.

SEVEN

"CURIOUSER AND CURIOUSER."

Mayday, newly arrived, followed the flight of the tennis ball to where it clanged off the KEEP DOGS ON LEASH sign, where Sam one-hopped it and returned to Regan at a run. He dropped the ball at her feet and backed a step, his tongue thick and lolling.

"Did you question Archer about the video?"

"I tried, but he didn't see the wisdom in cooperating with his opponent's lawyer. Something about hens and foxes. I heard him tell Alvarez that the shoot was arranged by Tony, but that they wouldn't discuss it in my presence. That's when Regan and I left."

Even for Lacy Park, the residents-only common in the old-money center of San Marino, it was a quiet Saturday morning, the tranquility of which was accentuated rather than broken by the park's only other visitors, a slow-motion trio of Chinese women practicing their tai chi. Officer Fife handed the ball to Sam and then returned to join us on the blanket. Sam followed her and flopped down in the shade.

"I'll let Regan tell you the rest. She had a very fruitful evening."

The day was unseasonably warm, and both women were wearing shorts: khaki cargos for Regan and pleated dress jobs for Marta. Marta wore a fitted white shirt, while Officer Fife hid her off-duty weapon under a loose linen blouse. In the Best Legs Futurity, I'd have given the nod to Regan, but only by a nose in a photo finish. She crouched and rummaged in my backpack for the water bottle, then refilled Sam's bowl as she spoke.

"I printed the belt and got a positive match. They belong to a woman named Joan Marsden. She had a disorderly conduct arrest back in 1987, and another in 1990. Both in L.A., both out of Hollywood Division. She jumped bail on the second pinch and vanished."

"Prostitution?"

Regan glanced my way. "That'd be my guess, but she falls off the radar after that. No DMV or credit or real property. No utilities, Accurint, Google, or Facebook. Nothing."

"Not very helpful," Mayday said.

"Hold on," I told her. "It gets better."

Sam ambled over to us and plopped the muddy ball into his bowl. He lapped at the water, then returned to his spot in the shade.

"Ricardo Tenorio," Regan continued, pinching the ball from the water, "better known as Ricky Rio, has more priors than Shirley MacLaine—mostly trespassing, vandalism, and parole violations—but back in the early nineties, he was busted for pandering, also by Hollywood Division, and he did a year at Corcoran. He apparently saw the light after that, and went from defiling women to defacing buildings, getting rich in the process. The Brewery loft is just his studio. He also owns homes in Silver Lake and Santa Barbara."

Mayday frowned. "From pimp to vandal to art scene entrepreneur. I guess crime pays after all."

"Art is not a crime," I told her. "And there's more."

Regan dug into the backpack for the pages she'd printed, and she handed them to Mayday.

"I found this article in a magazine called *ARTnews*. It's from 2006. It's about a special unit that the FBI formed to deal with art crimes in the wake of the Boston museum heist in 1990. Take a look."

Mayday sat cross-legged, petting Sam as she read. Meanwhile, at the far end of the lawn, the tai chi ladies had packed up their things and were heading in our direction. As they passed our blanket, one of them spoke sharply, pointing to the leash law sign.

Sam lowered his ears. Who knew the little rascal spoke Mandarin?

"Special Agent William Harwood," Mayday read aloud, "declined to comment on the extent to which his team has used informants to solve its most high-profile cases. 'Suffice it to say, we use every tool at our disposal,' he said with a knowing smile. 'Our obligation, after all, is to history.'"

THE ONLY PLACE teemed with the Saturday lunchtime crowd, so with our regular booth taken, Mayday and I opted for a sidewalk table out front, which afforded us a ringside view of the foothills looming large and lilac purple over the low boulevard storefronts. Many of the shop windows sported Halloween themes, from cotton spiderwebs to full-on graveyard spectacles, and there were even a few bulbous pods on display, a whimsical nod to *Invasion of the Body Snatchers,* the 1956 horror classic that had put sleepy Sierra Madre, as the fictive town of Santa Mira, on the cinematic map.

"Looks like the polls have flipped again," Mayday

said, refreshing her laptop screen. "Quinnipiac overnight has Burkett back on top."

"A guy could get whiplash."

"I guess voters prefer a philanderer to a thief."

"In a state like California, you'd think they'd demand both from their elected officials."

She closed the lid as the waitress brought our lemonades. "So what's our theory, now that the painting's gone missing again? Is Larry Archer a puppet, or is he the puppeteer?"

"I'll tell you one thing. He walked into that house with absolute conviction that the painting wasn't there."

"Because he knew it had already been moved."

I shrugged.

"Come on, it all fits. Archer connects to Angela, Angela connects to Rio, and Rio connects to Marsden, the green-eyed lady."

"Pimp to prostitute?"

"Don't you think?"

"I don't know. Maybe."

"You've got a better theory?"

"Regan thinks Archer was telling the truth."

Mayday nodded, then stared off into the mountains for longer than was conversationally appropriate.

"What?"

"Nothing."

"Come on, I know that look."

"It must be convenient for you, that's all. Having your own police officer."

"What's that supposed to mean?"

"You know damn well Regan didn't have permission to run those fingerprints for you, or to get you that search warrant, and now you've made her into a material witness. She's taken huge risks on your behalf."

"She's a big girl."

"Yeah, right. Ask yourself a question: Are you being fair to her? That's all I'm saying. You shouldn't lead her on if you're not interested. You're better than that."

"What makes you think I'm not interested? In case you haven't noticed, Regan's cute, she's smart, and she's extremely capable. Sam likes her, and I like her. What's not to like?"

"And you're on the rebound, and she's young, and she obviously looks up to you."

"On the rebound? Please. I've already rebounded. I lead the league in rebounding."

Mayday, who'd really liked Tara Flynn, my last girl-friend, and who, I suspect was still in touch with her, eyed me without speaking.

"What?"

"Nothing. I've said my piece."

"Good. Now can we get back to the matter at hand?"

"Sure." She opened the lid on her laptop just as my phone vibrated.

"MacTaggart."

"Mr. MacTaggart? This is Shoshanna Gold, calling from Farmers Insurance here in Los Angeles? I hope I'm not disturbing you on a Saturday afternoon?"

"Not at all." I looked at Mayday. "What can I do for my friends at Farmers?"

"Well, sir, I work with our high-value subrogation unit? In connection with the Bloomfield matter?"

She appeared to be one of those people who, like *Jeopardy* contestants, communicate only in questions.

"Go on, I'm listening."

"I had occasion to meet yesterday afternoon with a Mr. Marcel Laurent? Over at Bonhams Auctioneers on Sunset? I believe you know the gentleman of whom I'm speaking?"

"Laurent," I said. "That does ring a bell. Let me think for a moment…"

"He certainly remembers you, sir. He said he'd been only too happy to cooperate with my colleague Mr. MacTaggart from Farmers Insurance."

I held my paper placemat to the phone and crumpled it into a ball.

"I'm afraid you're breaking up, Shoshanna. I'm just entering a tunnel…"

I rang off just as Mayday found what she was looking for. It might have been my imagination, but her keystrokes seemed sharper than normal.

"According to Archer's public campaign filings," she said, "he's made payments to several different video production companies. We won't know who he used on the Arrowhead piece until the end of the next reporting period. That's ten days before the election."

"Next Friday."

"By the way, Archer's campaign treasurer? The guy who signs the FPPC reports? Anthony Gagliano."

"No shit. They let you sign those with an X in crayon?"

She leaned back in her chair, her eyes still fixed on the screen.

"Are we keeping our eye on the ball, Jack?"

"Meaning?"

"Meaning we assumed that anonymous message came from a friend who was trying to help us. Only now I'm starting to wonder."

"Go on."

"Well, for starters, who's the one being set up? First we thought it was Burkett, then it turned out to be Archer, but now, with the picture missing again—"

"Hold on," I told her. "Let's not lose sight of the fact that Burkett had a lock on this election. He had no motive to rock the boat, so it definitely started with Archer. We'll argue that Archer set Burkett up, then got caught with the picture, then made it disappear. We can expect Slew to contend that Burkett stole the picture, then used it to frame Archer, then somehow hid it somewhere."

"But, like you said, Burkett was already winning, so why would he do that?"

"That's why ours is the stronger case. Assuming there's still a case at all."

She looked up from the screen. "You think the D.A. will drop the charges?"

"It was bullshit from day one, and it's only gotten worse. The political advantage is all but gone, so why pick at a scab? If I had to guess, I'd say yes. The problem is, we're still no closer to the painting, or to the girl."

"But if we've already put the painting in Archer's possession through the video, then who cares about the girl?"

I waited while the waitress set down our lunches. A steaming Big Cheese al fresco promised a new and exciting culinary experience.

"I care, that's who, and so should you. For one thing, there's our fee agreement—and I'm referring, in case you've forgotten, to the bonus we earn for indicting the green-eyed lady before Election Day. More important, aren't you the least bit curious to find out what the hell's been going on?"

Mayday frowned as she dressed her salad. It was an elaborate ritual.

"It won't hurt my feelings if you take her," she finally said. "In case you were wondering."

"What?"

"Regan. To the museum opening. It's the least you could do to thank her."

"Will you please stop that?"

My phone vibrated again, crawling on the hard plastic table. I took up the *ARTnews* article and rolled it into a tube as I swiped the little glass screen.

"Sorry, Shoshanna! I'm still in the tunnel!"

"MacTaggart?"

"Who is this?"

"It's Madden. You'd better get over here. Chico wants to ask you a few questions."

The detective sounded as if he were outside, with voices and traffic noise in the background.

"Over where? What's going on?"

"Christ, I thought you'd have heard by now. We're at the Colorado Street Bridge."

"Heard what? I'm just eating lunch."

He said something I didn't catch, his voice muffled by a hand over his phone.

"Jack? We're under the bridge, on Arroyo Boulevard. Never mind your fucking lunch."

SPANNING THE ARROYO SECO on the city's west side, the Colorado Street Bridge once served as the main westward artery out of Pasadena, until the 134 Freeway was built in the early 1970s. Now it handles only light residential traffic, when not serving as a backdrop for films and television commercials. Arroyo Boulevard runs beneath the bridge, connecting the leafy old neighborhoods along the southern Arroyo with the Rose Bowl stadium and public golf courses to the north.

Built in 1913, the arched concrete bridge still features its original beaux arts flourishes, like iron railings and antique lanterns, and it towers some fifteen stories above the pavement. It is this unique combination of history, height, and hard landing that has earned the local landmark its more common name: Around Pasadena, it's known as Suicide Bridge.

We approached from the north, taking Rosemont down to Seco Street and turning south on Arroyo Boulevard. As we passed the Rose Bowl Aquatics Center, the road began to climb. Up ahead we saw parade barricades, and uniformed Pasadena PD officers turning cars around. I lowered the window as I slowed, shouting to be heard over the traffic noise echoing down from the freeway overhead.

"The name's MacTaggart! LAPD detectives Madden and Alvarez sent for me!"

The officer stepped away from the Mercedes. He spoke into a handheld radio, plugging his ear with a finger. Then he nodded to his partner, who moved the barricade aside.

They were all assembled behind a chain-link fence just east of the roadway. I knew it to be the parking lot of an abandoned army depot that was awaiting conversion into some sort of public park. There were a dozen or more cars, both marked and unmarked, plus a mobile crime scene laboratory. There was also a coroner's van, parked near the spot where the crowd of officers, techs, and medical examiners was thickest.

"This can't be good," I said to Mayday as we found

a shaded spot under the bridge. We crossed to the gate of the depot lot, where a PPD uniform with a clipboard eyed our casual attire. I gave him our names, and he asked for our photo IDs.

I spotted both Alvarez and Madden, the former sitting in the driver's seat of the white Crown Vic with the door open and a telephone glued to his ear, and the latter conferring with a female crime scene tech. Madden and the tech were standing next to something on the ground that was covered by a black plastic tarp.

I caught Madden's eye, and he nodded. Directly above us, ant-sized figures walked the bridge, inspecting the eight-foot spike-topped railing that the city had installed decades ago to deter would-be jumpers. Mayday lifted her eyes, following my gaze.

"Oh. My. God," she said quietly.

I looked to the west. Across the Arroyo, along the canyon's upper rim, stood the gated stone mansions of South San Rafael Avenue. These majestic aeries of the city's ultrarich included at least two notable structures: The first was the home that had served as stately Wayne Manor in the old *Batman* TV series. The second was the home of Warren Burkett.

"MacTaggart!"

Madden was waving me over.

"I think I'll wait here," Mayday said.

Madden followed my approach, watching, I thought, for any reactions to what I was about to see. Without speaking, he crouched and lifted up a corner of the tarp. He looked at my face as he yanked it all the way back.

The body was grotesquely splayed, and oddly two-dimensional. She wore a tan skirt-and-sweater set, the skirt short and fairly tight, the sweater bunched and twisted. She wore nude hose and one high-heeled shoe. She sported diamond earrings and a thin gold wristwatch and an oversized gold charm bracelet. She'd landed faceup, with the back of her skull now flattened like a blown tire.

There was surprisingly little blood, given the height of the fall, and what blood there was had formed into a tight crimson halo that almost matched the color of her dark, auburn hair.

Her eyes were wide open.

EIGHT

"LOOK FAMILIAR?"

Chico Alvarez was beside us now, working a wad of gum. He blew an enormous pink bubble.

"Never seen her before in my life."

"No, but you've heard her described. So have I. So has the whole goddamn country."

"When did it happen?"

"Last night, late. After midnight certainly. A jogger called it in this morning. It's always a fucking jogger."

Madden replaced the tarp while Alvarez turned on his heel and moved toward the Crown Vic. Madden and I followed behind him.

"Her name's Marsden. Or Mardian, take your pick. She's an art dealer. Or maybe she's a high-end madam, if you believe the talk up in Santa Barbara."

Alvarez reached into the front seat of the car and removed some folded papers. He blew another bubble as he found what he was looking for. I already knew what it was.

"I guess you think we're pretty stupid."

"Look," I told him. "When Burkett told me his story, I asked him if you guys had lifted any latents off his belt buckle. Apparently you hadn't, so Officer Fife and I did."

Alvarez threw a sharp look at Madden. "And when were you gonna share your little discovery with us?"

"As soon as you closed those four open homicides."

Alvarez rolled the mobile IAFIS fingerprint report and tapped it against his palm. He tossed it into the car.

"You're in big trouble, my friend. I've already talked to the D.A. He says you're in violation of a discovery order."

"The D.A. is wrong, as usual. I didn't know if the belt was evidence until I got the report, and I didn't have the report until after we were in court. Now I have until thirty days before trial to disclose my evidence, but then, we don't have a trial date, do we? Meanwhile, both the belt and the report are my attorney-work product."

Alvarez ran a hand over his face.

I looked back over my shoulder. "I didn't see a purse anywhere."

He didn't answer. I looked at Madden, then up at the bridge.

"And you'll want to search the neighborhood for a car."

"Get the fuck out of here, MacTaggart," Alvarez said, his neck reddening. "I see your face again and I swear to God, I'll rip it off your head."

I DIALED AS I drove. There was no answer on either of the numbers I had for Warren Burkett.

I retraced our route toward the Rose Bowl, then turned west to climb onto southbound Linda Vista. The homes on this side of the freeway were elegant, all worth a million or two apiece, but they were tarpaper shacks compared to what lay ahead of us. We crossed over the freeway, with its fleeting view of the closed-off bridge, and then we jogged onto South San Rafael Avenue, where the trees seemed taller, the streets seemed quieter, and my car seemed just a little shabbier than it had a moment before.

"What are you thinking?" Mayday asked.

None of the Arroyo-side estates was visible from the street. They all reposed atop long gated driveways curving up toward the million-dollar views at the canyon's edge. I slowed to read the numbers on the curbstones.

"I was just wondering how strong a guy would have to be to toss a hundred-and-ten-pound woman over an eight-foot fence."

"Alive and kicking?"

"Maybe."

The gates to the Burkett estate were closed. A call box was recessed into one of the stone entry pillars. I pressed the red intercom button.

"Hello?" The voice, when it came, was Hispanic, probably a maid's.

"This is Jack MacTaggart. I'm here to see Mr. Burkett."

There was silence, followed by another lengthy wait. Then, just as I was about to ring again, the gates began to part.

The driveway climbed a hundred yards through steep hillside landscaping. When it leveled out again, we found ourselves in a walled motor court. A big Dodge Ram pickup sat with its tailgate down, the truck angled in front of a five-car stone garage with iron lanterns and wooden doors made to capture a vintage 1930s look.

Two of the garage doors were open. One bay was empty, and in the other sat the gold Jaguar coupe that the mayor had described at our very first meeting.

The bed of the pickup brimmed with flowers—a lush carpet of blue and pink and yellow blooms still in nursery flats—plus stacked bags of compost or potting soil. Beside the truck was a Mexican kid in dirty jeans and a ball cap who'd set his wheelbarrow down to witness our arrival.

"*Hola*," Mayday said to the kid as we alighted. "*Está señor Burkett en casa hoy día?*"

"Hello?"

The voice came from over the wall.

"Mr. MacTaggart? Is that you?"

The portly Burkett daughter wore a blue denim dress over a black leotard top, black tights, and green rubber garden clogs. She removed matching green gloves as she approached. She was sunburned and sweating, and she ran a sleeve across her forehead.

"We weren't introduced on Wednesday night, what with all the excitement. I'm Maureen. I'm afraid you've caught us in a state of horticultural disarray, but do come, if you dare."

We followed her under a stone archway that opened onto a lawn that was wide and lush and bordered in a long ribbon of flowers. Beyond it loomed an ivy-covered palace of stone and slate that seemed, incongruously, to float in the hazy nothingness against which it stood.

"I'm afraid Daddy's not here today, but Mother is just inside."

Bobbi Burkett was in the living room. She rose from the sofa, removing her reading glasses and setting aside this morning's *Times*. The headline, I knew, read ARCHER VIDEO SHOCKER.

"Mr. MacTaggart. An unexpected pleasure, to be sure. And you'll have to forgive me, Miss...?"

"Suarez. Marta Suarez."

"Yes, of course. Please." She gestured toward the

Chippendale chairs opposite the sofa. "Or, if you prefer, we could sit outside."

She wore a long paisley skirt and a white tunic blouse. Her steel-gray hair was pulled into a tight ponytail. Other than a platinum watch and wedding band, she wore no jewelry.

"Have you been outside today, Mrs. Burkett? Out back, I mean?"

She smiled. "No, but do come and enjoy the view. Everyone likes to see it. It's the reason we moved here after Warren's retirement. His short-lived retirement."

The maid appeared through a swinging door and followed us outside, through double French sliders and onto a wide stone patio with scattered groupings of padded teak furniture. While the maid wrestled with the umbrella on an oblong table for four, I moved toward the low boxwood hedge that separated the patio from infinity.

The eagle's-nest view was everything I'd expected, and then some. Down to the left stood the bridge and the freeway overpass, while directly across the canyon rose the Vista del Arroyo hotel, six historic stories of Spanish Colonial grandeur that now served as home to the Ninth Circuit Court of Appeals.

"Isn't it lovely?" Bobbi Burkett said as she moved to stand beside me. "My parents honeymooned in that hotel, back before the war. It was kismet when this house came on the market."

She stood with one hand on her hip and the other shielding her eyes, like a ship's captain surveying a conquered land. She was a handsome woman in profile, and I tried to strip away the years and the extra pounds to see the golden young debutante I imagined her once to have been.

"The mayor's out of town, I take it?"

She nodded, still eyeing the courthouse. "In San Diego. We expect him back this evening."

"When did he leave?"

"Yesterday, after the press conference." She half-turned to face me. "For which I haven't properly thanked you. You don't know how much this all means to Warren. When a man runs for political office, it's as if the contest becomes a referendum on the man. I'm afraid it becomes quite personal."

"Was Bill Harwood with him?"

"Yes, I presume so."

A lone PPD cruiser was still parked on the bridge. Down in the depot lot, the crowd had started to thin.

"I don't know if you've noticed, but there's been some excitement on the bridge this morning. A suicide, apparently."

She adjusted her angle and splayed a hand at her throat.

"Oh, dear," she said. "Not again."

The maid returned from inside, propping the door with her hip and swinging a tray of refreshments into the sunlight. Mayday cleared some chairs in her path.

"We didn't mean to intrude on your weekend," I said. "I was hoping to have a word with the mayor, but I couldn't reach him by telephone."

Bobbi Burkett started toward the table, which the maid was now gilding with white cloth napkins and long-handled spoons. The maid was a thin, dark woman of middle years, and she eyed me warily as we approached.

"Warren often turns his phone off while on business, Mr. MacTaggart. Believe me, I should know." She nodded to the maid, who retreated to the house. "But do sit. There are things I've been wanting to ask you."

We sat in the shade of the huge umbrella. Ice sparkled in tall glasses, each garnished with an orange slice and a little sprig of mint. We laid napkins in our laps as our hostess poured tea from a glass pitcher. She added sweetener to hers, stirring daintily, the silver spoon tinkling, and then we all sipped and smiled. So polite we were, so very civilized, while just beyond our vantage point, men in white hazmat suits were scraping a woman off the blacktop with a spatula.

"Mr. MacTaggart? Is something wrong?"

"No, no. Everything's peachy. You said you had a question?"

"Yes. Now that the painting's been recovered, what will become of the charges against Warren? Surely the district attorney can't still believe he was involved?"

I glanced at Mayday. "I doubt the D.A. ever believed that. As for the painting, I'm afraid there's a small problem. You see, it hasn't been recovered."

"But I thought—"

"It wasn't at Larry Archer's cabin when the police searched it yesterday. I know, because I was there."

Her face registered surprise and disappointment in equal measure. I didn't know what bothered her more: that the painting was still missing or that she was first hearing about it from me.

"They're very chummy, aren't they? Mr. Archer and the district attorney."

"They're thick as thieves."

"You can see what Warren is up against."

"Yes, I can, and now it looks like another small complication has arisen."

"What is that?"

I nodded toward the Arroyo. "We just came from the bridge. It seems that last night's jumper was none other than our mysterious green-eyed lady."

Bobbi Burkett set her glass down carefully. "I see," she said, her gaze moving somewhere into the middle distance. "Oh, dear. How very inconvenient."

As we stepped into the backyard at Sycamore Lane, Sam bounded off in search of his tennis ball.

"I hope you eat red meat."

"Wow," Regan said, pausing to survey the flowers and the deodar cedars and the towering walls of hedge. "This is amazing."

I prided myself on maintaining Russ's property in the same general condition in which I'd received it, which had meant long weekends spent pulling weeds and hauling mulch and planting annual flowers. I hadn't spent this much time on my knees since catechism, but the effort obviously showed. My latest project, a border of new chrysanthemums rimming the patio, glowed purple in the fading light of sunset.

"Thank you," I told her, "although most of this I inherited."

Officer Fife wore baggy cotton slacks and sandals and the same linen shirt from this morning, only open now and with a white T-shirt underneath. She took the ball from Sam and flung it downslope, toward the grove of Japanese maples.

"I appreciate the dinner invitation," she said, "since the alternative was Top Ramen at home."

"The least I could do, for all your help."

I checked the barbecue coals and pronounced them worthy, then removed the cellophane wrapping from two Whole Foods filet mignons that had cost me more than my first television. They hit the grill with a mouth-watering *hiss*.

"I brought a Cab," Regan said, relinquishing the bag she'd been cradling. It was a Chateau Giroux Cabernet Sauvignon, which I knew to be wildly extravagant, especially on a cop's salary. I was going to crack wise about the last girl who'd brought a cab to my house, but I managed to restrain myself.

"Heard anything more on the suicide?"

I shook my head. "Nothing on the six o'clock news and nothing on the *Star News* Web site."

"They probably don't like to publicize the jumpers."

She made Sam sit while she wound up again and let the tennis ball fly.

"Mayday checked on art dealers in Santa Barbara," I told her. "There's a Jordan Mardian Design Studio in Montecito."

"So a Hollywood hooker named Joan Marsden jumps bail and disappears, then resurfaces twenty years later as a Santa Barbara art dealer named Jordan Mardian?"

"By appointment only."

"Montecito. It's that kind of neighborhood."

"And last I checked, they have their own bridges."

She turned to watch me battling the corkscrew. "Maybe she was down visiting friends, and had a bout of depression."

"Maybe she was down visiting enemies, who used her to make a depression."

The cork surrendered with a resonant *pop,* and I

sniffed it the way they do in the movies. Don't ask me why.

"If we're to assume the worst," Regan said, again hefting the soggy ball, "then who would have wanted her dead?"

"Let me count the ways: Burkett, for revenge. Archer to silence her, or for revenge of his own. Harwood, acting for Burkett. Tony Gags, acting for Archer or maybe himself. Angela, to protect her husband or Tony or Ricky Rio. Ricky Rio, to protect Angela or Archer, or to cover his own tracks. Any of them, for a two-million-dollar painting."

"If Detective Alvarez is right and she was still involved somehow in prostitution, then it could have been a disgruntled client."

"Or an employee. Or a rival pimp."

"But you don't think so."

"No, and neither do you."

We dined outside on the patio, by candlelight, with the house lights off and Madeleine Peyroux softly channeling Billie Holiday on the stereo inside. It was one of those balmy October evenings in which summer makes a last valiant stand against the turning of the calendar. There were gardenias, or maybe it was jasmine, blooming somewhere in the neighborhood, and the wine had the dark thrill of ambrosia. It was, to be sure, a very romantic setting.

"Will you give me an honest answer to a straightforward question?"

Her smile was enigmatic. "Fire away."

"Are you in any sort of trouble because of me?"

She reached under the table to tousle Sam's ears.

"I'm not in *trouble,* exactly. I got a lecture on chain

of command, and I had to write up a few reports. I think my sergeant was jealous more than anything else. Don't worry, Sierra Madre isn't Los Angeles."

I refilled our glasses, emptying the bottle as the stereo segued into *Weary Blues*. Sam flopped over and stretched at our feet.

"My turn?" she asked, swirling her wine.

"Do your worst."

"What is it, exactly, between you and Marta?"

"What do you mean?"

"I mean, are you some sort of couple?"

"Me and Mayday? Please. She's a nice kid, and an excellent lawyer, but our relationship is strictly business."

She watched me over the rim as she sipped.

"Really. If Mayday thinks of me at all, it's more like an older brother."

"A brother."

"Or maybe an uncle. Or a big, cross-dressing aunt."

From the breezeway came a familiar crashing sound of raccoons rummaging through the garbage. Sam was up and barking, and I excused myself and rose and followed him to the gate, clapping my hands as I approached.

"Shoo! Get out of—"

The figure was large and darkly dressed, in motorcycle leathers and a helmet. His visor was up, but his features were obscured by the darkness. He had a trash can lid in one hand and a plastic bag in the other, and he dropped them both at my approach, turning and sprinting for the street.

By the time I got through the gate, he'd already reached the sidewalk, where a Japanese bullet bike waited with revving engine, and by the time I made it out to the pavement, the bike and its two hunched passengers were receding into the distance, following their headlight, braking and leaning into the curve at the far end of the block.

NINE

We parked in the massive underground garage at the Music Center, purely out of courthouse habit, then walked the two city blocks past the Disney Concert Hall and across South Grand Avenue to the Los Angeles Museum of Contemporary Art.

To me, the museum's postmodern architecture evoked a hospital, or maybe an aquarium, with its tiled exterior and its soaring atrium glass, and today the fish were schooling at the lower-level entrance, where the word "StreetScrapes" had been sprayed across the concrete patio in huge calligraphic script.

The crowd inside the main hall was a varied admixture of older hipsters and scruffy art students, with shaved heads, tattoos, and black T-shirts, the look du jour. And that was just the women.

"If you see Alice Toklas, order me a brownie," I said to Mayday, who stood mesmerized in the center of the two-story space, studying the works on exhibit. These included a pyramid of old Brillo boxes, an all-black canvas in a silver frame, and a gigantic toy-balloon poodle.

"Warhol, Rothko, Koons," she said. "Wow."

"I'll say. Is that the bar over there, or a work of performance art?"

There was some Hollywood money in attendance, and a few genuine celebrities, including billionaire

Eli Broad and author-comedian Steve Martin, each of whom formed the center of his own small universe of admirers. More important, there were college kids in dark vests and bow ties passing hors d'oeuvres among the guests.

I left Mayday in her rapture and made my way to the bar.

The line was manageable, and while waiting I checked out the other stuff in the room. There was a hammock lying limp on the floor, and a grid of giant pegs with string, and what looked like Christmas ornaments dangling from a coatrack. There was a grand piano with the strings all cut and spilling out the top like spaghetti. There were two-tone paintings of squares within squares, and a man's suit on a hanger, and an overflowing trash bin. Then a lady wadded up her napkin and tossed it into the trash bin, so I guess that wasn't art.

Or was it?

"Bunch of goddamn crap," said the guy behind me, perhaps reading my face. "My kid could make any of it."

"Maybe your kid's a genius."

"Nah, my kid's a moron, and if he did that to my piano, I'd strangle him with one of the wires."

I was considering my beverage options when the bartender said, "Budweiser, right?" Sure enough, it was the kid from the Ricky Rio shindig, only today without his nose ring. "Just the Stella," he reminded me, jerking a thumb to the bottles arrayed behind him.

"Stella then, hold the umbrella. And a Chardonnay."

Mayday, when I found her again, was studying what appeared to be a wall-mounted bathtub before which a small group had gathered.

"Thank you," she said, accepting her drink with both hands. "Is that who I think it is? The big guy on the left? In the dark suit?"

"That's him," I said, just as Bill Harwood glanced over his shoulder. He looked north and south before ambling in our direction.

The big man had baby-blue eyes and a jaw like a steamer trunk, the effect of which, combined with his dark suit and his burr haircut, was to evoke a midsixties NFL lineman drafted from a small Methodist college in one of the *I* states. In this crowd, he blended in like a probation officer at Burning Man.

"I didn't realize you were such a discerning patron of the arts," I told him by way of greeting. "Then again, to head up the FBI's art theft unit, I guess you've had some training."

"Art Crime Team," he corrected, "and I have an MFA from Stanford."

"And I have an FYI from Pasadena. You spend an awful lot of time on the wrong sideline."

"Look who's talking. You were practically joined at the hip with Archer's wife the other night."

We held a brief staring contest, in which neither of us blinked.

"How was San Diego, by the way?"

He shrugged. "I didn't go."

"Why not?"

"I wasn't needed."

His eyes left mine to sweep the room again, and then he moved in closer, adopting a conspiratorial whisper.

"Look, I heard about the girl. I was hoping I'd see you here, so we could talk about it."

"Go ahead. Confession is good for the soul."

"I talked to some friends in the Bureau. It seems this Mardian ran an old-school escort service up in Santa Barbara. Models, college girls, would-be actresses. Thousand bucks a night, all very discreet. Arm candy for the weekend CEO crowd. Breakfast in the morning at the Biltmore, maybe spend the day on the beach. A real slick operation."

"Now tell me something I don't know."

He looked around again, as if he were about to give me the winner in the eighth race at Del Mar.

"She was also the go-to source in Santa Barbara to move artwork, antiques, jewelry. Again, all very discreet, no questions asked. Old families on hard times who don't want the neighbors to know. That was her specialty. She consigned artwork to galleries all over the country—New York, Chicago, Santa Fe. She's been on the Bureau's radar for years."

"Ricky Rio has a house in Santa Barbara," Mayday told him.

He nodded. "So does the mayor. When the Morisot went missing, the Bureau gave me a call. I've been out five years now, but they knew I was working for Burkett. I told them everything I knew, and they flagged Mardian as a person of interest from her physical description. That was on Friday. Then, lo and behold, you guys came up with the painting. That changed everything, but now the painting's gone missing again, and Jordan Mardian is dead."

"None of which explains what you were doing at Rio's party on Wednesday night."

"I could ask you the same question."

"Angela invited me, right after the debate. Fed me

some line about learning the L.A. art scene and how it might help me to represent Burkett."

He was nodding. "She invited me, too. Knew who I was, knew my background. Said it might help the mayor if I met some people she knew." He swept the room with his eyes. "Did it occur to you it was no coincidence, you and me both ending up with our faces on the wall? Like maybe she wanted to make sure each of us knew the other was there? She and this Rio character?"

I didn't answer. He lowered his voice even further.

"Did you actually see the body?"

I nodded. "It was no suicide. Nobody could climb that barrier in heels. Nobody would even try. Plus there was very little blood. Mostly around the head, which was badly crushed."

Now it was Harwood who didn't answer.

"Can you get us a copy of the coroner's report? Maybe from your friends in the Bureau?"

He nodded. "I think so."

The lights were starting to dim. At the far end of the hall, double doors opened with a bang.

I asked him, "What do you know about Tony, the brother?"

"Anthony Gagliano is a known mafioso. Born in Brooklyn, supposedly a made guy, looks out for their interests in Vegas. Definitely capable of tossing a woman off a bridge, if that's what you're thinking. I were you, I'd be more careful who I slugged."

Which was excellent advice, and I wondered if it was too late for an apology. Maybe send Tony a fruit basket. Or a box of cannoli. Meanwhile, two guys in military fatigues with aviator shades and checkered keffiyeh head scarves, like a pair of Yasser Arafat's bodyguards, had stepped through the double doors with toy machine guns. At least I hoped they were toys.

"What the hell?" Harwood muttered.

By now the hall was nearly dark. The duo raised the guns as if to fire, and the room suddenly burst into a fusillade of ricocheting laser light, like the kind they have at the Staples Center during Laker player introductions.

"Shit," Harwood said, shielding his eyes with an arm.

Behind the ersatz guerrillas, flash-bang grenades detonated, shaking the art on the walls, and as the echo from the explosions faded, rap music boomed through the loudspeakers.

"Ladies and gentlemen," a voice rumbled on the P.A., "please join us in the Eli Broad Exhibition Hall for a VIP preview of StreetScrapes, a Ricky Rio retrospective!"

The lasers quit flashing, and the room beyond the double doors brightened. The crowd began shuffling toward the light, funneling past the smoke and the soldiers, who stood now at focused attention, and into an enormous room that looked like an oversized mock-up of Ricky Rio's studio, right down to the redbrick walls and the catwalk balcony.

I hoped they'd left the porno flick at home.

There were several bars in the room, and a portable dais, and an unruly riot of graffiti artwork, from whole painted walls to smaller pieces that appeared to have been cut or ripped or chiseled from larger works off-site. There were sculptures as well: everyday street objects like light poles, parking meters, and mailboxes, but each altered in some way, either bent or twisted or welded into a fantastic new shape.

Harwood was gone now, lost in the crowd, and probably on purpose.

"What do you think?" I asked Mayday, who was turning a slow circle.

"Visually arresting, although somewhat derivative."

Once the entire crowd was inside, the doors to the main hall closed again, the ceiling lights dimmed, and a pair of spotlights up on the catwalk blinked to life, playing their beams on the blank wall opposite, like a prison-break scene from an old Cagney movie. All eyes turned to the spotlit wall just as ceiling panels opened above it and five black-clad figures dropped on nylon ropes. Each wore a climbing harness, and a full-face balaclava ski mask, and a kind of utility belt holding cans of colored spray paint.

"Now, this is interesting," Mayday said above the thumping music and the noise of the other guests.

The ninja figures hung suspended at different heights, forming a kind of pattern, and they went quickly to work, their arms moving in wide arcs and slashes, a portrait appearing by the magic of their collaborative effort.

"Isn't that…?"

Then the spotlights dimmed, and the house lights rose, and the ninjas were lowered in unison all the way to the floor. One by one they unclipped their harnesses and stepped onto the dais and removed their masks, to thunderous applause from the gallery patrons.

The first three I recognized as the guys from Ricky Rio's entourage: Benny and K-Jaw and the little guy called Mouse. The fourth figure, tall and gangly, was the girl, Legs. The last to remove his mask, stepping close to the microphone as he did, was the man of the hour himself. The applause swelled to an ovation.

Behind them, on what had been a wall of pristine white, now blazed a colorful, two-story image of *The Croquet Party*.

RIO AND HIS crew were joined on the dais by a little guy in a sport coat and tie. He blew once into the microphone.

"Good afternoon, ladies and gentlemen. My name is Jonathan Richter, and I'm the executive director of MOCA."

There was a smattering of applause.

"Street art can perform many functions. It can amuse and entertain. It can empower and inspire. And as today's demonstration illustrates, it can shine a light on social issues like hypocrisy and political ambition."

Ricky Rio, standing beside Richter, turned to admire the giant mural.

"The history of art has always been a rogues' gallery of pioneers willing to take risks and endure censure, and even ridicule, in pursuit of a new aesthetic. From the impressionists to the symbolists, from surrealism to abstract expressionism, each new movement embraced the process that Cordova called 'shouting into the void.'

"And so it is with street art. Born of the New York subways and L.A.'s Dogtown skate bowls, it is a quintessentially American art form, like jazz or rap, that has crossed both national and cultural borders to become the defining artistic genre of the twenty-first century. Egalitarian, democratic, and inclusionary, street art is the art of the people. It is the art of today. So, on behalf of all of us here at MOCA, allow me to welcome all of you to the present."

At which point Rio nudged him aside and grabbed the microphone, growling, "It's about time you got here. Now we can all have a drink."

There was sustained applause as Rio stepped away and the five ninjas linked arms and bowed, like actors at the curtain call. Then softer music whispered over the speakers as the crowd pressed forward toward the dais, engulfing Ricky Rio like a rock star.

Being contrarian by nature, I seized the opportunity to visit the empty bar and order another round. Mayday followed, and together we leaned and sipped and watched the scene play out.

"'Hypocrisy and political ambition'?"

"I know. Talk about biting the hand."

I saw her then from across the room. She was chatting with a group of high rollers that included both Broad and Martin, and when our eyes met, she excused herself and headed our way. A large man in a black turtleneck followed her.

"The hand," I told Mayday.

Angela Archer was in her campaign-wife costume: a conservative knit dress with heels and pearls. I had to admit, she wore it well. As she stepped up to the bar, her bodyguard hung back within earshot.

"Vodka tonic," she told the bartender. To me she said, "You have a lot of nerve showing up here."

"I thought I'd been invited. My name was at the door."

"An oversight, I assure you."

She swirled the drink and knocked it back in a gulp, all the while studying Mayday like a side of beef.

"Quite the little show," I said, nodding to the wall, "but not exactly the sort of publicity your husband would want."

"Ricky has a genius for two things: agitation and self-promotion. They're probably selling T-shirts in the gift shop already."

I glanced at Mayday, and then tried a different approach.

"That was a neat trick your husband pulled at the cabin. A bit late, but still neat."

"You don't know what you're talking about. My husband would never have wanted that painting, let alone stolen it, let alone displayed it in one of our homes. Art simply isn't one of Larry's interests. It never has been."

"But it's one of yours." I surveyed the room again. "Or at least I thought it was."

She set her glass on the bar.

"You're so plebeian, Mr. MacTaggart. I'm afraid I've grown disenchanted with you. Now, if you'll excuse me."

Ricky Rio, from where he stood on the dais, had been watching us the whole time. As Angela sauntered back to the high-dollar crowd, he, too, excused himself and started in our direction, with Legs following along behind him.

"My, but we're popular today."

Up close and personal, Rio was a mess. He was sweating and hadn't shaved and appeared not to have slept. He looked, in fact, like an unmade bed, while Legs, in her tight black catsuit, looked cooler than the other side of the pillow.

She ordered two Perriers from the bar.

"You were looking for a painting," Rio said, accepting one of the bottles from Legs. He drained it in a long, thirsty guzzle, then wiped his mouth with his wrist. He belched loudly. "So I made you one."

"I'm honored."

"You should be. I normally don't do commissions."

"The thing is, I found the one I was looking for."

He looked to Angela across the room.

"That's not what I heard."

We were interrupted then by a photographer, who had Rio and Legs pose side by side before an enormous blank billboard at whose center, rendered in cherry-red spray paint, was a check mark in a square.

"How long did it take to paint that one?" I asked him once the photographer had left.

Rio looked at the billboard. "Around forty years." He then turned his attention to Mayday. "I understand you appreciate art."

"I took some art history in college, and I spent a summer interning at the Timken."

"'Art history' is an oxymoron," he said, his eyes over her shoulder, scanning the room. "Art happens now, in real time. To study the history of art is to subvert its creation."

"But in order to fully understand a people or an era, you must first understand their art, don't you think?"

Rio smiled. "The cultural anthropology argument. In that case"—he made a sweeping gesture—"allow me to show you our era."

Legs set down her bottle and took hold of my arm. As she leaned her weight against me, I was reminded of a cockatoo or a macaw; some large, exotic creature impossibly lightweight for its size.

"Ricky may not show it, but he is very grateful to

you, Mr. MacTaggart," she said in her baby-girl voice as we followed Mayday and Rio.

"And why is that?"

"For exposing that horrible man for what he really is."

"You mean Larry Archer?"

She nodded solemnly.

"And what is he, really?"

Her doe eyes blinking, Legs stopped and turned to face me.

"Did you not know, Mr. MacTaggart?"

She pressed her face against mine, whispering into my ear.

"Mr. Archer is a cold-blooded killer."

TEN

In her fluttering head scarf, Regan Fife looked like a young Grace Kelly in *To Catch a Thief,* convertible top down, dreamy smile in place, motoring along the French Riviera. I'd never been to Europe, and I'm certainly no Cary Grant, but the California coastline from Ventura to Santa Barbara seemed to me as beautiful and exotic a landscape as any I'd imagined from film or literature, complete with steep, verdant bluffs and swaying palm trees and an expanse of steel-blue ocean that shimmered to a hazy infinity in the late morning sun.

"The air," Regan said, drawing a lungful. "It's so… *clean!*"

Thanks to the City of Sierra Madre's flex-staffing schedule, Officer Fife had her alternate Mondays free, and I had a lovely companion for my impromptu little road trip. I had no real agenda for the day, other than to check out a few locations and get out of Mayday's hair, but whatever fate awaited me, it was better met, or so I'd reasoned, in the company of a beautiful blond.

Better still, a blond with a gun.

In the rush of ocean air and zooming traffic, I barely heard my cell phone ringing in the console, and I made the mistake of answering it without checking the caller ID.

"MacTaggart!" I shouted.

"Hello? This is Shoshanna Gold? From Farmers Insurance?"

I held the phone outside the windshield, where it shrieked and whistled for a good ten seconds, before tapping END.

"Who was that?" Regan shouted.

"Somebody trying to sell insurance!"

We exited the freeway at San Ysidro and followed it north past East Valley Road. There, in the heart of Montecito Village, with its Mission architecture and ancient pepper trees and brilliant splashes of bougainvillea, we found a parking spot in the shade.

Regan shook her hair loose from the scarf. "What's first on our list?"

"List?" I double-checked the three addresses I'd gotten from Mayday, then slipped the phone into my pocket. "We have no list. Today we're just tourists."

It had been several years since I'd visited Montecito, and not much appeared to have changed. While most of California was still digging out from the rubble of the housing earthquake that had cut a swath of woe and foreclosure longer than the San Andreas Fault, sleepy Montecito remained as it always had been, which is to say, so stratospherically wealthy as to render irrelevant the terrestrial laws of market economics.

The first address, for the Jordan Mardian Design Studio, was on Santa Angela Lane, a quiet, mostly residential cul-de-sac lying one block west of the village proper. Regan and I window-shopped our way in that direction, stopping to ogle the thousand-dollar bottles of French Bordeaux, the ten-thousand-dollar English riding saddles, and the hundred-thousand-dollar Dutch paintings we encountered along the way. At one shop, specializing in antiquarian books and manuscripts, Regan insisted we go inside to check out an elaborately framed map of Renaissance Scotland, her ancestral birthplace.

"It's a Timothy Pont," the old proprietor called from his perch behind the counter. The map was drawn in brown quill ink, with its churches, quays, and castles depicted in exacting cartoon miniature. "It's quite rare. Most Pont maps are in the National Library of Scotland. It's over four hundred years old."

"I hope you get a discount for that."

"It's spectacular," Regan marveled.

"How much?" I called to the old man, who was standing now.

"Eight hundred"—he paused to study me over his glasses—"thousand."

Mapless, we navigated our way to Santa Angela Lane. It was a short, tree-lined street dead-ending in a traffic circle, and we actually walked past the address without noticing the discreet little sign, in gold-leaf letters on a black background, reading JORDAN MARDIAN DESIGN STUDIO, and beneath that, BY APPOINTMENT ONLY.

The building looked to have once been a house, back when people still built quaint little Victorian houses in Montecito. It had a shaded front porch and ivy-covered walls.

"What time was our appointment?"

Regan took my arm. "I hope you're not thinking what I think you're thinking."

I led the way up the walk. Wicker rockers were angled on the porch, with a mosaic-tiled table between them. Above these, where the porch ceiling met the front wall of the house, a closed-circuit security camera showed a red, unblinking eye.

The doorbell sounded a chime from somewhere deep within, and I cupped my face to the darkened window glass. The lace curtains were drawn, and there were no lights on inside.

"May I help you?"

The woman standing behind us was tall and slender and dressed like a page out of *Vogue Paris*. Stunning, in a Eurasian Russian-vodka-model sort of way. She had a hand in her leather bag, and from it, she removed a ring of keys.

"Yes, I hope you can. My wife and I have an appointment"—I checked my watch—"for eleven. With Miss Mardian. The name's Pont. Timothy Pont."

The woman breezed past us on the porch, a quiet wisp of silk and perfume, and fitted a key into the lock. With the door cracked open behind her, she turned to face us.

"I'm afraid there's been some misunderstanding, Mr. Pont. We have no appointments scheduled for today. You'll excuse me."

With that, the door closed again in our faces.

RICKY RIO'S SANTA BARBARA address was on the ocean side of the freeway, in an area called Hope Ranch, so named, I had to assume, because we all hoped one day to be wealthy enough to live there, or someplace like it. Regan navigated with my cell phone's map application in her hand, and together we found a sprawling Mediterranean villa on Mariposa Drive with a postcard view of the Channel Islands, ten misty miles offshore.

"You'd think it was a lawyer's house, or a banker's,"

Regan said, a commentary on the home's five thousand square feet of stucco-and-red-roof orthodoxy.

"'Custom will reconcile a man to any atrocity,'" I recited, "'and housing covenants to any custom.'"

Her look was quizzical.

"Shaw, more or less."

We lingered a while before returning to the car, and it was only as we swung a U-turn into the shaded lane that I noticed the dark Audi coupe, and then only because of the way the man inside raised a newspaper to his face as we passed.

OUR QUEST FOR Warren and Bobbi Burkett's Santa Barbara home led us to Veronica Springs Road, a semirural corridor of oak-studded hills running seaward from the freeway. We were stopped at the traffic signal at Las Posadas, and I was just feeding the new Brandi Carlile CD into the dashboard player, when the light changed.

A waiting mass of cars surged past us heading northbound, in the direction from which we'd come, and among them was a gold Jaguar. I rose from my seat and craned my neck for a look.

"What is it?"

"Probably nothing," I said as a horn sounded behind us, and I put the Benz in gear.

Although fully fenced and gated, Burkett's house on Cliff Drive was below the grade of the roadway and therefore visible from where we'd parked. It was a small compound, modest for the neighborhood, that included a main house, a guesthouse, and what appeared to be a barn, all in whitewashed board-and-batten and all with rusting weathervanes and curling roof shakes and tweedy, country squire charm. Eucalyptus leaves littered the driveway, with no lights or other signs of habitation inside.

I punched up both of my Burkett telephone numbers. Again I got only voice mail, and again I left no messages.

"What's next? I'm getting hungry."

"Funny you should ask."

For cuisine worthy of the company, I'd made a reservation at the Stonehouse Restaurant at San Ysidro Ranch, the überexclusive Montecito resort whose high-society notoriety included having hosted Vivien Leigh and Laurence Olivier's wedding, not to mention Jack and Jackie Kennedy's honeymoon. It was just the sort of timeless, storybook setting into which the real Grace and Cary could have stepped and felt at home.

The dining room was half full when we arrived, and we were seated, at Regan's request, by the crackling fireplace. One of the Brits from the old Monty Python troupe was sitting at a table by the window, across from a woman with a teacup poodle in her purse. The purse was on the table, and every time the woman laughed, the dog gave a little yip.

"The rich are different from you and me," I reminded Regan.

"Fitzgerald?"

"No, I think it was some writer."

We began, at Regan's suggestion, with a local Pinot Noir. She then ordered the mixed baby greens with grilled artichoke, while I went with the cheeseburger. Actually, it was an Angus burger with caramelized onions and Gorgonzola, and I think I could have bought a live steer for less at the L.A. County Fair.

After our server had retreated to the kitchen, Regan lifted her glass.

"To persistence. I'm sorry it's been a waste of time."

Our Riedel crystal *chinged*. "To persist in the presence of beauty is no waste."

"Yeats?"

"MacTaggart."

The meal proved not only outstanding, but informative. I learned, for example, that the lovely and charming Regan Fife was the only daughter of a police officer and a behavioral psychologist—her father a Catholic Scot with a high school GED, and her mother a Jewish Swede with a Ph.D. from Scripps.

It was a marriage, she said, that was doomed from the outset, and so Regan had spent her childhood shuttling between her father's tidy cop apartment in Glendale and her mother's sprawling quasi-commune in the wilds of Sierra Madre Canyon. The arrangement had lasted until age fourteen, when her father was killed in a motorcycle crash on the Angeles Crest Highway. Regan then spent what she called her "rebellious years" living with her mother, attending first the private Alverno School for Girls and then Occidental College, until her last and boldest act of rebellion, which was to follow her father's career path.

"Your mother disapproves?"

Regan shrugged over her coffee. "She got over it, eventually. My mother is nothing if not forgiving. She forgives me for everything. All you have to do is ask her—and if it's all the same with you, I'd rather not talk about it."

"Okay then, let's talk about Svetlana. What did you

think? Does she work the art side of the business or the business side of the business?"

Regan considered it.

"I would say both sides of the business, but strictly in a managerial capacity."

"Nothing too hands-on?"

"You're incorrigible."

I signaled for the waiter. "I don't know about you, but I didn't notice any untoward reaction to Jordan Mardian's name."

"Maybe she hasn't heard yet. Or maybe she's adept at hiding her feelings."

"A useful skill, in the business side of the business."

"She certainly wasn't friendly."

"I should say not."

"Are you suggesting we pay a return visit?"

"There's a thought," I said. "I'll tell her you're my niece and that you're on scholarship at UCSB, and that you need to earn some extra book money this semester."

"How about I show her my badge and tell her I have terrible news from Pasadena?"

"Then point to me?"

"Then ask to see the records of all their recent transactions."

At the table by the window, the woman laughed. The dog yipped.

WE WERE SOUTHBOUND on San Ysidro when we first heard the sirens: an atonal symphony of police cruisers and fire trucks, with an ambulance roaring past onto East Valley Road.

We saw the smoke from three blocks away, which, by the time we'd arrived, had swollen into a black and roiling column rising high above Montecito Village. A patrol car blocked the mouth of Santa Angela Lane, and so we doubled back to the village parking lot and returned on foot, elbowing our way through the gathering crowd. We slipped through the police cordon as a path was being cleared for another fire engine.

The quaint Victorian cottage that had been the Jordan Mardian Design Studio was now two scorched walls under a ten-story tower of twisting smoke and flame. The heat of it warmed our faces from across the street as the firemen fanned out, running and shouting, and the water arced and roared, and the smoke turned from black to gray to white before our eyes.

Regan wore her badge on her belt. We stood off to the side and tried to look inconspicuous as the walls collapsed inward in a swarm of orange sparks, the falling ash covering us like snow and the black water coursing in the gutter at our feet.

I draped an arm around her shoulders. We watched for nearly an hour, silent and transfixed, and by the time the fire was out and the gurney had rolled past us from the rear of the house, its slender burden zipped into a black body bag, we resembled nothing more than a pair of plaster statues.

ELEVEN

ELECTION DAY MINUS FOURTEEN.

Max Drescher scanned the documents with quiet intensity, his accountant's eye like a surgeon's scalpel probing for malignancy. He wore a white short-sleeved dress shirt and a striped necktie with an ink stain toward the bottom. There were dozens of stapled forms arrayed before him, which he'd organized into overlapping piles that blanketed every square inch of the MacTaggart and Suarez conference table.

There were Statements of Organization, and Statements of Economic Interest. There were Major Donor and Independent Expenditure Committee Campaign Statements, and Supplemental Independent Expenditure Reports. There were Supplemental Pre-Election Campaign Statements, and Recipient Committee Campaign Disclosure Forms. And there were hundreds upon hundreds of pages of Campaign Disclosure Statements, the documents collectively detailing every dollar entering and every dollar leaving the coffers of the Archer for Senate campaign committee.

And these were just the forms they'd filed with the California Fair Political Practices Commission, better known as the FPPC. Mayday had also assembled the Archer campaign's Federal Election Commission filings, the SEC filings of Archer Properties and its subsidiaries, and a grab bag of miscellaneous documents that had, over the years, been filed with the California Department of Corporations, the U.S. Department of Housing and Urban Development, and various states' attorneys general.

It was, in short, a globe-sized ball of red tape tailor-made for a man of Max's unique sensibilities—and since he never ceased pestering me about swapping professional services, thereby helping to evade the payment of state and federal income taxes, Max was the logical candidate for the job.

I lifted a document from the table and flipped through the pages. "Where's his Request-for-Permission-to-Use-the-Restroom form?"

Max peered at me over his glasses. He wasn't smiling.

"It's what this country is coming to, Mr. MacTaggart. Soon you'll need the government's permission to leave your home. You mark my words."

This was, in all likelihood, a wild goose chase, but Harwood's intel on Tony Gags, combined with Tony's role as Archer's campaign treasurer, had aroused in Mayday a certain curiosity. And who, we'd agreed, was better qualified to chase feral fowl than Max Drescher, the man who'd once told us that he couldn't be the subject of a federal indictment because he'd copyrighted his name? Who'd once told me that if the United States hadn't gone off the gold specie standard in 1861, we wouldn't have had to fake those Apollo moon landings a hundred years later?

I told him, "You can have the conference room for now, Max, but we might need it later in the week."

"I'd be happy to work from home, for another small

adjustment. That's the beauty of the barter system. With a credit for utilities, of course."

I looked at Mayday, who was trying not to smile. "Thanks, Max. We'll talk it over and let you know."

Back in my office, across the hallway, Mayday plucked the Nerf ball from the net, dribbled once, and threw up an ugly jump hook that missed the backboard entirely. I, meanwhile, paged through the Tuesday morning headlines.

The fact of *The Croquet Party*'s second disappearance had hit the street on Monday. This had triggered a fresh round of recrimination and speculation that today occupied most of the *Times*'s front page. There were also point/counterpoint Op-Eds, with each campaign accusing the other of playing dirty pool, and a political cartoon in which two figures, bears with human faces, tugged at a framed painting labeled "The Election." Rounding out the coverage was a *Times* readers' poll, in which a majority of overnight respondents stated that, if given the option, they would gladly vote for "None of the Above."

I asked Mayday, "Nothing about the suicide or the fire?"

"No, but it's only a matter of time." She dribbled the ball in a circle. "The *News-Press* up in Santa Barbara has a story on the fire, but the police aren't disclosing the victim's name until the family is notified. All it says is that the deceased wasn't Jordan Mardian, the building's owner. As soon as some enterprising reporter puts the body under the bridge in Pasadena together with the art theft in Hollywood together with the building fire in Montecito, all hell is going to break loose."

I tossed the newspaper aside. "In whose favor, I wonder?"

It was a rhetorical question. Larry Archer hadn't gotten naked with Jordan Mardian, and his house didn't look down on her death scene.

Mayday shook the hair from her face as she took aim at the hoop.

"Speaking of reporters, they were calling all day yesterday. Word is out you were at Archer's cabin."

I sifted through the phone messages. There were more than two dozen, and none was from Tom Slewzyski or Department 112. Or, for that matter, Warren Burkett.

"What's the matter?"

I was drumming my fingers on the desk.

"You told Marquez's clerk it was urgent, right?"

"He said he'd work us onto her calendar as soon as possible. Said he was a union member and a lifelong Democrat."

"We should have heard something by now. What was the clerk's name?"

"Martin something."

I opened my California Court Directory and found the direct-dial number for Judge Marquez's courtroom. A man answered on the fifth ring, sounding harried.

"Department one-twelve, clerk speaking."

"Martin? This is Jack MacTaggart, calling on the Burkett matter. We've been waiting for a preliminary hearing date, on a ten-day case?"

"Please hold," he said, and the line went silent. I covered the phone with my hand.

"Could you get me the file from Bernie?"

"Counsel?" I was on speaker now, the clerk's voice

fainter over the courtroom hubbub. "That matter has been dismissed, and all dates are vacated."

"Dismissed? When was it dismissed?"

There was a pause as he checked the docket. "Earlier this morning. State to give notice." Then the line went dead.

I dialed the D.A.'s office without setting down the handset. Mayday appeared with the file and slipped it onto my blotter.

"Case dismissed," I told her as the line rang, and she gave me a double thumbs-up.

"District Attorney's Office."

"Jack MacTaggart calling for Mr. Slewzyski in the Burkett matter."

"Yes, Mr. MacTaggart. Please hold."

"Nice of him to tell us," Mayday said, echoing my thoughts exactly.

I waited a full minute before Slew came on the line.

"Mac? Is that you?"

"Yeah, it's me. I just got off the phone with Sylvia Marquez's clerk. He told me the case has been dismissed?"

"Yep. Interests of justice."

"When were you planning to let me know?"

There was an awkward pause. "You haven't heard?"

"Heard what?"

"I got a call this morning from Tom Stark, over at Plimpton. He said they were subbing in for Burkett. Said they'd fax over the paperwork. I told him not to bother, that we'd decided to decline prosecution. This is all news to you?"

Now the pause was on my end.

"Did he say why?"

"He didn't say, and I didn't ask. As far as I'm concerned, the case is closed."

"What about the painting? And the Mardian woman?"

"The woman's dead, the painting's gone, and some of us have bigger fish to fry. In fact, I don't know why I'm even talking to you."

"And what about the fire yesterday up in Montecito?"

"What about it?"

"What *about* it? Jordan Mardian's business was torched, and a second woman was killed. That makes two murders in three days, all connected to that painting."

"Murders? MacTaggart, you've been watching too much television. Take a vacation. Better yet, go back to your fender benders and your DUIs, and leave law enforcement to the professionals. By the way, you can thank me for not charging you with obstruction. You and that surfer chick from the Sierra Madre PD. Oh, and tell your *former* client he can keep his belt. Tell him it's what married men use to keep their pants on."

The line went dead in my ear. I slammed down the handset and stalked over to the window. Outside on the boulevard, shoppers shopped and strollers strolled, and the world turned as though nothing were amiss. As though two brutal murders weren't being swept under a downtown L.A. carpet.

"There's a message slip on my desk from Terina Webb," I told Mayday. "Put her on speaker. Tell her we have a story she might like to hear."

OFFICER FIFE ARRIVED at 7:45 P.M., around an hour past sunset, and the pizza was due at eight. She'd dressed in her civvies, and together we'd retired to my study where we were surrounded by the books, photos, and assorted mementos of the late Russell H. Dinsmoor. While Russ hadn't actually died in this room, I liked to think of it as the place where his spirit still lingered, if you believe in that sort of thing. Not that I really did, but there were evenings I'd spent reading in the soft leather armchair when I'd felt a definite…*something*—call it a presence—hovering over the dusty books.

It was the writer Dan Brown, of *The Da Vinci Code* fame, who'd likened time to a river, and books to boats. I allowed myself to imagine that Russ, a yachtsman in this life, was moored somewhere nearby in the next.

"Another promo."

The Channel 9 *Action News* teaser urged viewers to stay tuned for a special report entitled "A Chair Too Big: Death and the Goldilocks Affair," for which the network's regular programming would be preempted.

"I'll bet the NCIS fans are lighting up the switchboard."

Regan fed another pretzel to Sam, who crunched it at her feet. "How did she put the story together so fast?"

"You've never met Terina Webb. You drop a hint, and she'll have it fact-checked before it hits the ground."

The broadcast finally began with a full-body shot of Terina standing on Arroyo Boulevard in twilight, the Colorado Street Bridge glowing eerily behind her. She seemed a little nervous, which was understandable given that she was about to break a story that would lead every other network's eleven o'clock newscast and every national newspaper's front page, and would, not incidentally, be her audition tape for the big leagues.

She brushed a hair strand from her face.

A stolen impressionist masterpiece. A candidate for

the U.S. Senate found naked in a stranger's bed. The painting resurfacing on a wall in his opponent's home. Even by the lights of a bruising campaign for the hearts and minds of a sharply polarized electorate, the so-called Goldilocks Affair has established a new benchmark in American political theater—some would call it a new low—that has both repulsed and captivated the nation.

A slow track, tightening on Terina.

It all began on the evening of Monday, October fourteenth, when two patrol officers here in Los Angeles responded to a residential burglary in the Hollywood Hills. What they found that night would set in motion a bizarre chain of events that would include one candidate's arrest, the apparent recovery of the priceless painting, and then its second disappearance. All of it leading to charges and countercharges of political dirty tricks.

A half turn toward the second camera, Terina now in medium close-up.

But tonight, in a Channel Nine Action News exclusive, you will learn that the scandal runs deeper than was previously reported, and that two lives have already been lost in what has all the hallmarks of a ruthless and systematic cover-up. We'll also reveal the identity of the mysterious green-eyed lady who stands at the heart of the story that America can't stop talking about. Stay tuned for this and more, after these words from our sponsors.

"Nothing subtle about that."

"Subtle is not in her playbook."

The doorbell chimed, and I hurried down the hallway, counting out bills as I went. I figured twenty bucks—or what I'd paid for the coffee at San Ysidro Ranch—should cover a large pepperoni, tax and tip included.

"Coming!"

The door exploded inward as I turned the knob, spinning me sideways, bills flying to the ceiling. And before I could find my feet again, they were on me.

Three of them, all bruisers, all in black ski masks. The first pinned my throat to the wall, while the second drove a knee into my groin. I made a noise like a barking seal, and the next thing I knew, I was on my knees with a guy on each arm and a gloved hand on my neck, forcing my face to the floor.

"Okay, sweetheart," the third guy said. He stepped forward in lug-sole boots and lifted my chin with the business end of a baseball bat. The bat was black and aluminum and cold from the outside air.

"How's about you and me play a little hardball?"

I heard Sam then, his claws clattering on the hardwood, and I felt the guy on my left arm twist around to look. I yanked away and lunged, pulling the other guy with me, and the three of us sprawled like tenpins across the foyer. Sam, not knowing what to make of it all, stopped and backed up and snarled.

"Hit him!" one guy yelled as the slugger stepped over me and moved in Sam's direction. I dove for his leg and drove my weight forward, collapsing him sideways onto the kitchen floor. I groped for the bat, but a hand grabbed my hair and jerked my head backward.

"STOP IT!"

Everyone did, and all our heads turned. Regan stood in the hallway. She had one hand behind her back.

The slugger rose to his feet, dusting at his trouser leg,

while I was lifted and shoved forward into the hallway. Now the men stood shoulder to shoulder, three black masks all facing the slender young woman beside me.

"Well, what do you know," the slugger said, tapping the bat into a gloved hand. "Boys, I think we have time for a quick pussy break."

Regan drew her gun and racked the slide in one smooth motion, pointing the muzzle between the slugger's eye holes. It was a 9 mm Walther PPS, small and black and very lethal, and she held it in a two-handed grip.

Her hands were visibly shaking.

"Police officer!" she said, the gun now tracking from mask to mask. "Put your hands on your heads!"

None of them did.

"I said hands on heads! Now!"

Sam was growling again, and I reached a hand for his collar, laying the other on Regan's shoulder.

"Okay," I announced, "here's the deal. The batting cage is down on Duarte Road, around five miles from here. It closes at ten. If you hurry, you'll each have time for a turn."

"That's not happening," Regan said through her teeth.

"Sure it is. It's exactly what's happening. Nice and slowly. Everybody cool, and nobody gets hurt."

The other two looked to the slugger. His eyes tightened, as though maybe he was smiling under his mask. Then he shouldered the bat and edged sideways toward the door. One by one, the others followed.

Regan tracked them to the foyer. My hand still on her shoulder, I felt her arm relax.

They fumbled for the doorknob as they backed onto

the porch. Then they all turned as one, nearly trampling the pimply kid in the white paper hat.

Somewhere beyond the big sycamore tree out front, doors slammed and a car started and tires squealed on pavement. The delivery boy turned a circle, all the way back to where Regan and I stood backlit in the doorway, a man and a woman joined by an orange dog, the woman still holding a gun in both hands.

"Large pepperoni, extra cheese?"

TWELVE

WITH LESS THAN two weeks to go until the election, things were starting to get crazy.

The Channel 9 *Action News* exposé had unleashed exactly the media firestorm for which Terina Webb had prayed, and on which Mayday and I had been counting. The gruesome deaths of Jordan Mardian and her "office manager," a former catalogue model named Catherine Orlov, were reported by every newspaper and television station and Internet news outlet in the country, shining just the sort of post mortem spotlight on the two women's business ventures that they'd tried so hard in life to avoid.

For two days running, the *Times* front page offered new details of the deaths, and renewed commentary on their social and political ramifications. Rumors sprouted of little black books and powerful Hollywood clients and kinky Santa Barbara orgies. There was speculation about Catherine Orlov and a certain sobriety-challenged sitcom star with whom she'd once been photographed, and there were the usual interviews with stunned Santa Barbara neighbors and public officials, all of whom vouched for the ladies' fine charitable works and sterling reputations in the community.

Down at the office of the L.A. district attorney, Tom Slewzyski had wasted no time in grabbing his baton and whistle and rushing to the head of the parade.

Jordan Mardian's death, he'd announced at a hastily
called press conference, had been under investigation
by "senior LAPD detectives" since "before her body
was cold," and he, the district attorney, was personally working "hand in glove" with the Santa Barbara
authorities. Moreover, he "declined to speculate" on
rumors that the Mardian death was other than suicide,
declaiming that "to do so would be irresponsible and
the worst kind of political grandstanding."

Larry Archer was not so reticent. The billionaire developer promptly offered, on a Fox News Radio program, a reward of fifty thousand dollars for information
leading to the arrest and conviction of "the sicko re-
sponsible for the murder of that poor woman." When
asked by his host whether he had any proof that Jordan
Mardian's death was other than a suicide, Archer had
replied, "If it walks like a duck and talks like a duck,
it ain't no spotted owl."

The election itself—at least in terms of the issues and
polling and policy speeches that are the grist of a traditional campaign—had been trampled flat in the tabloid stampede, prompting one pundit to liken it to the
spelling bee portion of a wet T-shirt contest. I caught
a news clip of Warren Burkett getting booed at a press
event for declining to discuss what he called "issues
peripheral to the election." I saw Archer interviewed
on Piers Morgan, and there wasn't a single question of
substance in the hour-long segment—making it, I believe, a typical Piers Morgan interview.

Both candidates denied any personal connection to
Mardian, or to Orlov, or to the tragic death of either.
Questions to Burkett regarding his night in the Bloom-
field mansion were dismissed as "old hat" or as "yes-

terday's news" or, in one memorable gaffe, as "water under the bridge." Questions to Archer regarding the cabin video were met with vague demurrals or with resort to the time-honored "not at liberty to discuss matters under investigation" dodge.

Even Farmers Insurance had stepped into the fray, announcing its own reward of twenty thousand dollars for the return of *The Croquet Party,* no questions asked. In making the announcement, corporate counsel Shoshanna Gold had pleaded with the thief or thieves not to allow an irreplaceable cultural artifact to be used as a political football.

Terina Webb, who'd become a regular nightly presence on her network's national news broadcast, milked the story harder than a one-armed dairyman. To her credit, though, she'd honored our agreement to keep my name out of it, citing only "informed sources" and "persons close to the investigation" as the bases for her exclusive reportage.

Unfortunately for Burkett, the scandal was breaking in Archer's favor. The mayor was, after all, the one who'd been caught with his pants down, and now the woman who'd pulled them down was dead. It was Uncle Louis's strip club prophesy made manifest, and Archer's overnight numbers spiked from a two-point deficit on Tuesday afternoon to a comfortable five-point lead by Thursday evening.

The Burkett campaign was back on life support— but not, I tried to assure myself, because of anything I had done. No confidences had been breached, and the facts, however inconvenient for my former client, would have come to light eventually. Perhaps not as soon, and probably not as noisily, but as surely as night follows day. Better that all the cards are on the table, I'd told Mayday, before the final bets are placed. As Milton said, let truth and falsehood grapple.

Such was the altered landscape to which I arrived at the office on Friday.

Max Drescher was already hunkered down with Mayday in the conference room, and no sooner had I settled at my own desk than a knock sounded and Bernie entered, waving an envelope.

"Thought you'd want to see this," she said. "It might cheer you up a little."

The envelope had a glassine window and a return address in a patriotic red-and-blue script.

"Have I been less than my merry self of late?"

I blew into the envelope and extracted the folded check. It was payable to MacTaggart and Suarez, LLP, in the sum of twenty-five thousand dollars. The memo line read "Legal Services." There was no note or cover letter.

Bernie asked, "Did he stiff us?"

"Nope." I ran the numbers in my head. "I'd say it's just about right."

She leaned in closer, jerking her head. "How long is that guy gonna be working here? He gives me the creeps."

I looked out my door. Across the hallway, Max and Mayday were huddled at their laptops, the lights from their twin LED screens reflecting off the conference room glass.

"Sometimes, Bernadette, you just have to accept a quirky personality as the price of running a business."

"Fuck that," she said, tugging at a bra strap. "I make the guy for a friggin' serial killer."

The front bell tinkled, and she hurried back to her desk. Then my intercom buzzed, but before I could answer, the door flew open and the broad shadow of Chico Alvarez darkened my day. Madden was next, with Bernadette trailing behind them. She stopped in the doorway, hands on hips.

"I told these assholes to wait."

Alvarez ignored her, looking the place over.

"Nice office, counselor."

The detectives unbuttoned their jackets as they slumped into the client chairs and made themselves comfortable. Bernie rolled her eyes and retreated, closing the door behind her.

"You let her suck your dick with that mouth?"

"Only when you're not available, Chico."

Madden covered his mouth with a fist, and even Alvarez begrudged me a smile. "Okay, asshole. So I guess we're both a couple of tough guys."

He reached into his jacket and withdrew a folded sheet. He opened it and pretended to read.

"But you do have one annoying habit, MacTaggart. Mike and me, we visit Bonhams on Sunset, and guess what? You've already been there. We run prints on a dead woman, and you've already run 'em, before she was even dead. Then we investigate a fire up in Montecito"—here he laid the folded page on my desk—"and lo and behold, you were right there when it happened."

It was a photocopy of a credit card slip from the Stonehouse Restaurant at San Ysidro Ranch. I recognized the signature.

"How was your Angus burger?"

"Medium."

"It's a sweet little alibi," Madden added, crossing

his legs. "Your reservation was at one thirty P.M., and you paid your bill at two forty-seven P.M. The maître d' says you arrived on time, never left your table, and had a cool blonde on your arm. The arson investigator says the fire started at two thirty P.M., give or take ten minutes max, which puts you right in the clear. Very sweet indeed."

Alvarez reached for the paper. As he did, he noticed the envelope and plucked it off my desk.

"What do we have here?"

He unfolded the check. He whistled. He showed it to Madden. He whistled, too.

"Legal services," Madden read aloud.

"Such a nice, round number."

Now it was my turn to laugh. "Stop it, you guys are killing me. You need an agent. You could book some club dates, maybe do *Letterman*."

"You think we're that funny?"

"Yeah, you're that funny. First of all, the cool blonde at the restaurant was Officer Fife. You remember her. We drove up to Santa Barbara to check out Jordan Mardian's studio. Just like you wanted me to, back when you fed me her name at the bridge. What I couldn't figure was why. Were you hoping I'd find something, or were you setting me up the whole time?"

"First we're funny and now we're smart, is that it?"

"I'm betting on lazy. As in, toss a bone to the bulldog and see what he digs up. That was back when you were too busy to investigate anything. Before Slew got his picture in *Time* magazine. Then again, maybe you deserve more credit than that. Maybe you're the bulldogs, but Slew had the collar too tight and the leash too short. Either way, here's the bone you wanted—the one you came all the way out here to collect. We met the Orlov woman."

"Met her where?"

I told them the story. Not the parts about Rio's and Burkett's houses, but pretty much the rest. Madden had his notebook out and was scribbling. When he'd finished, he looked at Alvarez.

"Anything else we should know?"

"Yeah. Burkett hired another lawyer. I'm off the case now, and that check makes it final. So from now on you boys will have to do your own legwork. If I were you, I'd focus on Larry Archer and his wayward wife and her crazy artist friends—one of whom, by the way, is a guy named Ricky Rio, who used to be a Hollywood pimp. Only he was Ricardo Tenorio then, and maybe he had a girl named Joan Marsden working for him."

Madden wasn't writing. He clicked his pen and put away his notebook. Alvarez tossed the check back onto my desk.

"I like you, MacTaggart. As lawyers go, you're all right. So here's some friendly advice, one tough guy to another. Tony Gags is not a man to fuck with. You go after his sister, and he might take offense. He's sensitive that way. I get the impression they're a close family. And if you do get your tit in a ringer, don't call us for help, because we probably won't answer."

"You mean, not as long as Archer's ahead in the polls."

Alvarez didn't respond. He stood and buttoned his jacket, and Madden followed suit.

"I were you, counselor, I'd work on other cases. Spring a few rapists and dope dealers. Make lots of money. Live long enough to spend it."

MAX JOINED US for lunch at our usual booth. Ordinarily he brown-bagged it, but today, he explained, his wife had left early for a weekend in Utah.

"Let me guess. Ogden?"

He nodded, studying the menu as if it were an insurance policy. "We're picketing the federal building. Then we're going to burn Orrin Hatch in effigy. Gee, this place is expensive."

"Sorry you're missing out."

He set down the menu. "Me, too, but a commitment is a commitment, and Max Drescher's word is his bond."

"That sounds like a campaign slogan."

He and Mayday shared a glance.

"What?"

Max cleared his throat.

"I was going to ask you a favor, and I guess now is as good a time as any. I've been discussing with Marta an idea I've been mulling over for the past several days. Normally I'm more decisive about these kinds of things, but for a decision of this magnitude, I've felt the need to proceed with a certain amount of caution, as I'm sure you'll appreciate in a moment."

I looked at Mayday. She looked at the menu.

"Okay."

"I've decided to announce my candidacy for the United States Senate."

He studied me for some sign of approval.

"Okay."

"I know what you're thinking, why would a fellow like me want to uproot his family and move to Washington? Why give up a successful accounting practice? But the thing is, Mr. MacTaggart, our country needs me. Things are out of control in our government, and it's in times like these that true patriots step to the fore, whatever the sacrifice. Don't you agree?"

"Absolutely, but the election's in eleven days, Max, and you're not even on the ballot. Not to be a wet blanket or anything."

He nodded gravely. "I know, and that could pose a problem, but I have a weekly newsletter with over ten thousand subscribers, and my Web site gets fifty thousand hits a month. Plus I've been in touch with Ron Paul's people. They think we can mount a credible write-in campaign, and that with all this sex and murder going on, the public will be ready to embrace a fresh new candidate on November fifth."

"Right. One with twenty-eight felony counts pending against him. One who hasn't filed a tax return in thirteen years."

He nodded excitedly. "Exactly. A candidate who'll stand up to the tyranny of a federal government run amok."

Max, I noticed, had twisted the tablecloth into a knot.

"Okay, so what was the favor you wanted to ask?"

He cleared his throat again.

"Marta says that you're a Democrat, but I was hoping you might consider letting me use your name and maybe your photograph as an endorsement. My research shows that you're very well respected in certain legal circles in Los Angeles, and it would mean a lot to me if I could list the two of you as supporters in my big rollout next week. Marta says it's up to you, and that she'll go along with whatever you decide."

I looked to Mayday, her face now fully hidden behind her menu.

"Well, Max, that's all very flattering, but here's the thing. We've already been representing one of the candidates, and we've been made privy to certain confidential information in the course of that representation. So I'm afraid there'd be ethical issues if we were to now endorse another candidate, no matter how much we'd like to do it. I'm sure you understand."

He'd been nodding as I spoke, the tablecloth twisting tighter, the silverware moving closer and closer to the edge.

"Of course, I understand completely. After all, a commitment is a commitment." He gave a little smile. "That's what Max Drescher always says."

BERNIE WAS WAITING for us when we returned, standing at her desk with folded arms and a meaningful look on her face. I furrowed my brow, and she made a small gesture with her head.

"Uh, you go on ahead, Max," I told him. "We'll join you in a minute."

We waited until Max was in the conference room, and then Mayday and I followed Bernie down the hallway where she closed my office door behind us.

"I only stepped away for a minute," she said. "I swear. It was there on my desk when I came back."

"What was? What are you talking about?"

She pointed with her chin. "That."

The package rested on the edge of my desk. It was brown and flat and almost square.

It had no return address.

THIRTEEN

"WHAT TIME?"

"I don't know. Fifteen minutes ago."

I circled the desk and stood behind it. The plain white label read, FRAGILE/DO NOT SHAKE. I opened my drawer and removed a letter opener.

"Didn't you hear the bell?"

Bernie shook her head. "I was in back, running the copier."

I sliced the brown paper tape and used tissues to lift the bright new Etch-A-Sketch from its nest of cotton batting.

I set it carefully on my blotter, where we could all read the message.

SAFE
DEPOSIT
BOX

Mayday snapped a photo with her phone, while Bernie watched over her shoulder.

"*Whose* safe-deposit box?"

"Jordan Mardian's," Mayday said, examining the image on her phone. "We should have thought of it. A duplicate set of books, or maybe some photos or videos, in case she got busted."

"Her get-out-of-jail-free card?"

"Something like that."

I sank into my chair. I told them, "There was a closed-circuit camera outside her studio in Montecito."

"Can't the D.A. get a search warrant issued for every bank in Santa Barbara County?"

I nodded. "He could, but first he'd have to think of it, and from everything we've heard about Jordan Mardian, her safe-deposit box might be anywhere. Plus if she was half as connected as Harwood says, then there are people who'd want to prevent whatever's inside it from ever seeing the light of day. Rich people. Powerful people."

"Including Larry Archer?"

"Could be. And by extension, maybe Tom Slew-zyski."

I'M NO EXPERT on estate and probate law, but common sense told me a thing or two. The first was that not many single, healthy forty-year-olds have their estate plans in order. I certainly don't, and I'm a lawyer, and all my assets are legit. I was willing to bet that our green-eyed lady—who apparently ran a prostitution ring and fenced items of questionable provenance—didn't either. Second, she almost certainly had family somewhere, and that meant heirs at law who stood to inherit whatever assets could be traced, including those found in a safe-deposit box. Third, whatever family she had may well have lost track of her long ago, and would have no reason to connect the death of a wealthy Santa Barbara art dealer named Jordan Mardian with the disappearance, over twenty years earlier, of a teenage runaway named Joan Marsden.

"So what exactly are you proposing?"

The glow from Mayday's laptop reflected in the three Chardonnay glasses that surrounded it. The Only Place was starting to fill with the early-bird dinner crowd, so we'd bypassed our usual window booth for a quiet table in back. I set down my beer.

"Find the next of kin, get ourselves hired as estate counsel, and locate the safe-deposit box before Slewzyski does. In other words, get ourselves back in the game. All before Election Day."

Regan Fife counted on her fingers. "And don't tip off the killer, and don't run afoul of the mob, and don't get yourself arrested for obstruction."

Mayday stroked her REFRESH button. "And do it all before the court appoints a public administrator, which is what will happen if nobody steps forward soon."

Regan added, "And hope that the message came from a friend, and not from someone who wants us out tilting at windmills."

"Or wants to use Jack for a friggin' piñata," Bernie added.

"Hear, hear."

Wineglasses were touched, and so was I.

"One thing I don't get," Bernie said. "If we've already been shit-canned by Burkett, then what's in it for us?"

"Well, there's the reward from Archer if we catch the killer, and the reward from the insurance company if we recover the painting. That's seventy grand right there—and if the last message is legit, we have the inside track. More important, there's the satisfaction of getting there before Slewzyski does, and seeing that justice is done, and finding out who's sending the messages."

CHUCK GREAVES · 167

Regan swirled her wine. "And payback for the other night?"

"Maybe. Speaking of which, what's the status of Operation Cannoli?"

Mayday shrugged. "Max never says, other than to mutter the occasional 'Ah hah!' or 'Nice try, buddy!'"

"I don't mind him talking to the documents," I told her, "but please let me know if they start talking back."

"He said he's taking the weekend off to campaign."

Regan frowned. "Campaign for what?"

"Don't even ask." I drained my beer and signaled the waitress for another.

"How do you propose to find her next of kin? The papers say she lived alone and that she had no known relatives."

"Jordan Mardian had no known relatives. But don't forget, Jordan Mardian is a fiction."

Mayday again stroked her REFRESH button. "Objection, not responsive."

"Which is why I've called this little meeting. I figured the three of you, working together over the weekend, could track flies at a landfill."

"There are heir-finder Web sites, you know. They specialize in this kind of thing."

I shook my head. "Too risky."

Mayday glanced up at Regan. "I can search the public records. Can you access any law enforcement databases?"

"If I knew what I was looking for."

"Okay, how about this for a division of labor? Bernie cold-calls every Marsden in the phone book, while Marta runs the public records databases, and you work your blue magic. We keep in touch by phone and then we meet back here for dinner on Sunday evening at six."

"Aren't we forgetting someone?"

"Yeah, what about you?"

"Me? I have other fish to fricassee. But I'll be working for the team. Trust me, I'm a lawyer."

Bernie cleared her throat. "What about overtime?"

"How about time and a half?"

"Double time, and an extra vacation week if I hit the jackpot."

Mayday stroked her REFRESH button. This time she sat upright.

"Okay, here it is."

She adjusted the screen, and we all moved our chairs for a better angle.

"This is the Archer campaign's Form Four-sixty," Mayday narrated as she scrolled the just-posted document on the FPPC Web site. "Today was the ten-day filing deadline, and this report covers the sixty-day period since the last filing. Okay, this is the contribution summary...and the expenditure summary...and the cash statement. Here comes Schedule A, which is the contribution detail."

The pages cascaded in a blur from top to bottom.

"Looks like lots of late money is moving to the new front-runner. Schedule B is loans received; nothing changed there. Here comes Schedule C, which is nonmonetary contributions. Campaign office...banquet hall...private jet...limousine service. Max will love these. We can skip Schedule D. Okay...here comes what we're waiting for... Schedule E, payments."

She stopped scrolling. On the screen was a grid of financial data, including payees, expense codes, dollar amounts, and descriptions for all the Archer campaign's expenditures over the last sixty days.

I frowned. "There are hundreds of entries."

"Don't worry, we can track them by code. We're looking for 'TEL,' which is TV or cable airtime and production costs."

She resumed scrolling. We all watched as the grid flickered and jumped, the moving entries reflected in Mayday's unblinking eyes.

She stopped.

"There it is," she said, leaning back in her chair as we all bent forward to look.

At the center of the grid was a single TEL entry, followed by "Environmental Regs TV Spot."

The amount paid to the videographer was $750. The name of the video company was Rio Vista Productions.

The Channel 9 *Action News* studios were located, appropriately enough, in Studio City, just off Ventura Boulevard, in the heart of the San Fernando Valley. Terina Webb had a half hour to spare between her six o'clock local broadcast and her national news segment scheduled to air at eleven. She'd agreed to meet me at Du-par's, the venerable bakery and coffee shop down on the Boulevard, where I arrived early, staked out an orange leatherette booth in the dining room, and ordered a black coffee.

I watched Terina enter, nod a few hellos, and then pause to scan the room. I raised a hand. She was waylaid twice on her way to my table, first by some news colleagues at the front counter, then by a gray-haired couple who hailed a passing waitress and produced a disposable cardboard camera to capture their Kodak moment.

"The price of celebrity," I said as she finally slid into the booth.

"I've tried obscurity. Celebrity is better."

Her face looked pink and scrubbed, and more than a little tired, and there were lines by her eyes that I'd never seen before.

"You've been a busy camper."

"Listen. In this business, you catch the wave when you can, because there's no telling when the next one will come along." She opened a little compact to check her face in the mirror. She scowled. "Did you like the special?"

"Thank you for keeping my name out of it."

"You're welcome, and I know I still owe you. This has been the biggest story of my career."

The waitress appeared, blew hair from her face, and flipped a page on her pad. Terina stashed the compact and ordered a house salad, which I trumped with the peach pie à la mode.

"How do you eat like that and still look the way you do?"

"You sound like Marta. She thinks a cheesesteak is a commodities position."

Terina produced a BlackBerry from her purse and proceeded to check her e-mail. "I don't suppose you came to tell me where D. B. Cooper gets his hair cut?"

"Actually, I was hoping to get some information from you. Starting with the arson investigation in Santa Barbara."

"Gasoline," she said, tapping at her little keyboard. "The fire started in the back office, where all the file drawers had been pulled open. They're pretty sure Catherine Orlov was alive when it burned, but probably unconscious. She was found facedown on the floor, no ropes and no gag—or handbag, for that matter. The rear door was unlocked."

"She had a handbag when she got there."

Terina's head lifted up. "How do you know that?"

"I'm just speculating. Did she have any family?"

"Excellent question. A guy turned up before the body was cold, claiming to be her husband. Calls himself a talent agent. Name of Whitaker, Alan Whitaker. He's a Brit, apparently. Lives in the South Bay. They found him inside her house."

"Doing what?"

"Counting the silver, apparently. Got all belligerent when questioned. Claims he and Orlov were married abroad, which is why there's no record of it in the States. He hasn't won many friends at the SBPD."

The waitress plunked down my coffee in passing, splashing some onto the table.

"And what about Jordan Mardian?"

Terina looked up again. "What about her?"

"What do you hear from the Coroner's Office?"

"Nothing. Slewzyski is guarding the autopsy report like it's the crown jewels"—she lowered her voice—"but I know a guy who knows a guy. He claims she was dead before impact. Something about lividity. Offered to sell me an autopsy photo." She shuddered. "Creepy business."

"So Archer's reward is still in play?"

"Tell you what. If one of us finds the killer, we'll split it."

"Unless the killer is the one offering the reward."

"Wouldn't *that* be a story?"

I lifted the mug by the handle and blew gently at the rising steam. "Did they ever find Mardian's car?"

She nodded. "It's a red Ferrari, and they found it today, parked in the long-term lot at Burbank airport. I'm breaking that little nugget at eleven."

I considered the logistics of that.

"What about her house, anything there?"

She powered off her phone and tucked it into her bag. "*That* I can answer firsthand."

"You were inside?"

"I have a source at the SBPD. He got me in on Wednesday. Very nice digs, in a low-key sort of way. Mediterranean. Classy, not flashy. Older. Partial ocean view, almost an acre. Swimming pool. What do you want to know?"

"Documents? Computers? Bank records?"

"Impressionist paintings?"

"Okay."

"I saw art on the walls that definitely wasn't dogs playing poker, but they were landscapes mostly, not what we're after. I'm told there were minimal records, just some routine household papers, like bills and magazines. No computer or iPad or smartphone, which the police regard as suspicious, since she had a Wi-Fi modem and a printer in the house, plus a DSL charge on her phone bill. Either she covered her own tracks, or someone covered them for her."

"Any evidence of that?"

She shook her head.

"What about bank statements? Or a checkbook, or a savings account passbook?"

I'd overplayed it. Terina leaned forward in her seat.

"Why the interest in bank records?"

The food arrived in the nick of time, and I asked the waitress for a refill on the coffee.

"An ocean-view acre in Santa Barbara? A Ferrari? I don't know, but it sounds to me like there's a pot of dough waiting for somebody."

"Well, they'd better claim it soon, because right now Jordan Mardian's on a slow train to Boyle Heights."

I understood the reference. The Los Angeles Office of Coroner holds unclaimed bodies for two years, after which they're cremated, bagged, and buried in a mass grave in East L.A., my old stomping ground. It's an annual ritual I'd witnessed once as a child, complete with a priest and a rabbi and a group of black-clad mourners.

There were over a thousand bags. God knows where they got the mourners.

"Sounds like the house alone is worth millions," I said, jiggling the bait. "No next of kin?"

She speared a forkful of salad and brought it to her mouth. Then she paused. "Hey. What happens to the house if there's no next of kin?"

"That depends. Each county in California has something called a public administrator. If nobody comes forward, then the public administrator takes over. He investigates, searches for assets, and looks for a will. If there are no heirs, then, in theory at least, the decedent's assets escheat to the state. But it's a rare human being who dies without heirs."

"Interesting."

"Maybe there's a story there," I said, giving it another tug. "Estate-planning lawyers have a name for it. They call it a laughing heir. Like a third cousin twice removed, who answers a knock on the door and finds out he's a millionaire."

"Could be a story," she agreed, setting down her fork and retrieving her BlackBerry. "God knows, I could use a fresh angle."

FOURTEEN

WHICH IS WORSE? I asked myself in the communal solitude of the dark and busy freeway. Being tossed from a fifteen-story bridge or being burned alive in a fire? Would your answer change if you were already unconscious? Already dead? Would it matter to you, in your last, fleeting moments, whether you'd lived a virtuous life or a life of crime and deception? Whether your last earthly acts had been greedy or selfless? Whether your killer was an acquaintance or a stranger? Whether the deed had been provoked or was simply cold-blooded murder?

It had begun to rain.

I was wired by the coffee, and distracted by my morbid meditations on life and death, and before I knew it the Mercedes had merged with the southbound traffic on the Hollywood Freeway, setting me on the fast track to the wrong side of town.

The gate was open to the Brewery parking lot, and I pulled in behind a Dumpster in a narrow side alley, as close as I could get to the old ironworks building that housed Ricky Rio's studio loft. It was a quarter past ten—late, but not too late for a Friday-night social call.

I killed the engine, turned up my collar, and ran with my head down, the splashing puddles soaking my wingtips. I caught a break when I found the stairwell door propped open by a flattened cardboard box.

I shook the rain from my jacket. Music thumped and growled above me, echoing in the stairwell and vibrating in the cold iron handrail, and I wondered how the tenants in this place ever got any sleep. Up on the second floor, a hallway side door opened, disgorging a trio of giggling teen girls in torn jeans and ratty black Cons, all borne aloft on a cloud of smoke and noise that rose and faded again as the door slammed shut behind them.

"Narc," one of them whispered, and they giggled some more, bouncing off the walls and off each other, tumbling down the staircase like a litter of newborn puppies.

The door to Ricky Rio's loft was locked, and nobody answered the bell. I felt around for a hidden key but found none, and so I retreated down the hallway, and the staircase, and back out to the Mercedes, where I inserted the key and skipped the CD changer to Van Morrison's *Saint Dominic's Preview* and made myself comfortable.

It wasn't a long wait. No sooner had the man from Belfast eased into "Gypsy" than a tricked-out Chevy lowrider swung its headlights into the parking lot behind me. Moments later, a gangling figure splashed past with a paper bag in one hand and the other hand fumbling for her keys. She was alone, and she wore an odd kind of pink plastic raincoat with an attached bubble hat, which she yanked backward as she shook her hair free and disappeared into the building.

I let the song play all the way through. Then I retraced my earlier passage up the stairs and down the hallway, where again I leaned on the doorbell. This time the eyehole darkened, and then a latch fell and the door swung wide.

Legs was stark naked.

"Mr. MacTaggart!" She stepped aside, beckoning me in. "What a groovy surprise!"

The loft seemed bigger than before. There was furniture now where the dance floor had been, a tight grouping of tattered couches and easy chairs with a low center table on which a bottle of blue liquid stood with a single glass beside it.

The floor was hardwood, paint-spattered and scuffed, and there wasn't a carpet to be seen anywhere in the room. And I mean anywhere. Believe me, I looked.

"Do you want to take off those wet clothes?"

"Just the jacket for me, thanks."

I draped it on a chair. Legs, meanwhile, had disappeared into a dark corner under the loft, from which she returned with a second glass.

"I hope you will join me for a drink. I find that it helps me to sleep."

Her skin was the color of candlewax, and as she leaned forward to pour, I could see the ribs and veins in her back, as though she were something amphibian and newly born.

"Not to be a prude or anything, but wouldn't you be more comfortable wearing some clothes? I know I would."

She giggled at that, rose to her full height, and gave me a meaningful look. Then she turned and climbed the spiral staircase.

I heard her padding around in the loft, and a drawer opening and closing, and then some soft, trancelike music seeping from the downstairs speakers.

The label on the bottle read Blue Curaçao, and the glass smelled like orange Kool-Aid.

She returned in a short satin robe, seaweed green, with a dragon embroidered across the back in heavy gold thread. She'd banded her hair into the same twin ponytails as at our first encounter, only now the highlights were neon blue, matching the color of her drink. She sat primly, tugging at her hem and batting her enormous brown eyes.

"Is this better?"

"No, but it's a lot less distracting."

She smiled at that.

"Are you expecting Ricky anytime soon?"

She slid over to make room on the sofa. When I didn't move, she patted the cushion beside her.

"Do not worry, Mr. MacTaggart. Ricky will not walk in and surprise us. He has gone away."

"Gone away where?"

"I do not know. He said that he has to be away for a while, and that I should work on my own projects until he returns."

"When was this?"

"On Sunday. After the party at the museum."

I turned a circle. With the dim glow from the floor lamps, the overall effect was of standing over a trash can fire in a shuttered train station somewhere in the Bronx. Graffiti-scarred and cavernous. All that was missing were the rats.

"Is this where you live?"

She nodded, sipping her drink.

"How long?"

"Almost a year now, I think."

"You like it?"

"Yes, very much."

I sat in the chair across from her and set my glass on the table.

"What is it you do here, exactly?"

She sat up straighter and folded her legs beneath her. They were very long legs.

"I help Ricky with his installations. I cut and copy stencils. I run errands and act as lookout. Things like that. To have the chance to work with an artist like Ricky Rio is a very big honor, Mr. MacTaggart. He is quite famous in Japan. My friends from art school cannot believe how lucky I am."

I swallowed the Kool-Aid and grimaced. She tilted forward and poured me another.

"What did you mean on Sunday when you said that Larry Archer is a killer?"

She leaned back and pouted. She studied the hands in her lap.

"You did not come here to see me, did you?"

"I've seen you plenty. Now I'd like to talk to you."

She played with one of the ponytails, swishing it back and forth.

"Who did he kill?" I pressed.

She shrugged. "I heard Ricky talking to Mrs. Archer about her husband. About what would happen if he won the election, and whether she would move with him to Washington and resign from the museum board."

"And?"

"She said that her brother, Anthony, would make her. She said that he warned her that she had better start acting like a senator's wife. She said that Anthony and Mr. Archer killed people who got in their way, and that Ricky had better be careful because Anthony did not like him anyway, and would welcome an excuse to kill him."

"Do you know why Anthony doesn't like Ricky?"

She shook her head. "I know that Anthony is a very bad man, and that Ricky is afraid of him. And Ricky is not afraid of anything."

"Now I'm a little confused. I thought that Anthony had hired Ricky to do work for the Archer campaign. To film a TV commercial."

She nodded. "That was Mrs. Archer's idea. Ricky thinks that video is the next big thing, and he told Mrs. Archer that he would film the commercial for free, for the experience, and would be reimbursed only for his costs. He is filming all his installations now. He says that he is going to make a documentary film and win an Academy Award. I bet he does, too."

"Were you with him when he filmed the commercial? Up in Lake Arrowhead?"

"No. That was just Ricky and the guys. Mouse and Benny and K-Jaw. I was helping at the museum."

"And what are the guys up to these days?"

She shrugged. "I have not heard from anybody since Sunday."

I'm not saying the puzzle pieces were falling into place just yet, but I'd definitely caught a peek at the box. If Ricky Rio had double-crossed Tony Gags, then he had every reason to be nervous at the museum on Sunday, two days after the video had gone public—and now, it appeared, Rio was in the wind.

"Do you have any way to get in touch with Ricky?"

She shook her head again. "He said that I should not attempt to contact him, and that he would call me when he could."

She slid off the couch then, untied her robe, and let it fall open. She circled to my side of the table and just stood there, like an oversized toddler with her thumb in her mouth, and then she eased herself into my lap. She smelled like orange soda, and she weighed little more than a housecat.

She batted her eyes. "Sometimes I am frightened here by myself, Mr. MacTaggart."

"There's a lot of that going around."

She ran her fingers along my face. "And yet you do not seem to be frightened of anything. Even Anthony does not frighten you. Ricky told me so."

"Don't kid yourself, kitten. Everyone's frightened of something."

I stood and hefted her in my arms and carried her as far as the sofa, where I set her down gently, stepped away, and shrugged back into my jacket.

"I have to run now. If you do hear from Ricky, tell him we need to talk."

IT WAS NOT quite midnight when I pulled to a stop before my rising garage door on Sycamore Lane. Since the new silver Porsche down at the curb was parked directly under the streetlamp, I assumed that the woman behind the wheel wasn't trying to hide. And since the raindrops dotting the hood were beaded rather than streaked, I assumed she'd been waiting there for a while.

The driver's door opened just as the garage door closed, and the slender silhouette of Angela Archer circled the car and sashayed in my direction, putting a lot of English into the effort. This was the candidate's wife edition, complete with black cocktail dress and heels, swinging a black quilted handbag over her shoulder.

I looked at my watch and frowned.

She paused long enough to pose with a hand on her hip. She wore crimson lipstick and above-the-elbow opera gloves. She seemed a little unsteady, and her eyes shone like obsidian in the light above the garage.

"Don't just stand there. Be a gentleman, and offer me a drink."

I led the way, across to the house and onto the stoop, where Sam gave Mrs. Larry Archer the Big Sniff as he tumbled out to greet us. She ignored us both, brushing past me in the doorway. She paused in the foyer when the lights came on, removing her gloves as she turned a circle, giving the house the once-over. She looked like the Dutchess of Kent visiting a refugee camp.

"You live all right for a small-time lawyer," she said, slapping the gloves to my chest, where they slid to the floor. I followed her into the living room.

"How's about that drink?"

"Vodka?"

"Grey Goose if you've got it." She set her bag on the coffee table.

I knocked around in the kitchen, and when I returned with her gloves, the vodka bottle, and two glasses of ice, the room was empty. Then the toilet flushed in the hallway bathroom, and the water ran, and she teetered back into the living room. She fell into the sofa and crossed her legs with what I would have to call deliberate effect.

They were very nice legs.

The label on the bottle read Smirnoff's, and she wrinkled her nose as I poured both glasses full.

"I heard you got the ax," she said, leaning back and tasting her drink.

"'Substituted,' we like to say."

"Like in football. Sent to the bench, to bleed and lick your wounds."

"An interesting metaphor."

She rattled her ice. "I'm an interesting woman. I know all kinds of things."

"I'll bet you do. Did you know that your brother sent some goons out here the other night to use my head for batting practice?"

She leaned to the side and looked me over.

"You're still in one piece."

"I had help, and not from my dog."

Sam, who'd sat on the floor beside me, lowered his ears.

"I'm glad to hear it. I'd hate to see that face of yours all lumpy and blue."

I sat in the chair across from her.

"I tried visiting your protégé this evening, but he seems to have taken a trip."

"If you mean Ricky, he does that. In his business, you don't advertise your next project."

"I had the impression he was hiding. From your brother, as a matter of fact."

She downed the rest of her drink, the ice clattering against her teeth.

"Lots of people hide from Tony. It's a healthy thing to do." She dabbed at her lips with her thumb. "Kind of like jogging. Or vitamins. How's that for a metaphor?"

"Turns out it was Ricky who shot that campaign video at your cabin in Arrowhead. Seems to me that's as good a reason as any to be hiding out from Tony—and your husband, who I'm told doesn't care much about art."

"You think you have all the answers, don't you?"

"No, but I've got a few. Want to hear them?"

She leaned forward and refilled her glass. "Sure, why not."

"First the questions. Like, why did you and Ricky try to set me up at your little postdebate shindig? Maybe you thought I'd be slow on the uptake, and that I wouldn't notice. Then, if I did, maybe I'd think you wanted me to suspect Harwood, and vice versa, and then we'd both think you were trying to take the heat off your husband for the Bloomfield job. It worked with Harwood, by the way. Am I going too fast for you?"

She took another gulp, her eyes smoldering, her lipstick smeared on the glass.

"Then I found out that you and Ricky both knew something we didn't. You knew the video was out there, and you knew what was in it. So what were Harwood and I really doing at that party? I'm thinking we were there for Tony. Once the video went public, Ricky would be a dead man walking. He needed something to put Tony off the scent, and that's where Harwood and I came in. It was a weak play, but at least it was something. What lawyers call reasonable doubt. Only it didn't work, and now Tony's on the warpath, and Ricky's off the reservation, and you're the one left guarding the teepee and hoping your brother's too dim to figure out your role in the whole sordid mess. How'm I doing so far?"

She lifted her glass again. This time her hand was a little less steady.

"Keep going, this is ever so fascinating."

"Okay, but here's where it gets murky. Ricky took an awfully big chance, given your brother's reputation, and he doesn't strike me as the type to lose sleep over elective politics. I'd say he's more of an enlightened self-interest kind of guy. And that brings us back to you. With you out of the L.A. picture, Ricky Rio loses money, clout, and contacts. He loses his patron, and that's worth taking a risk for. Maybe it's even worth killing for."

"Ricky wouldn't hurt a fly."

"That's where you're wrong, angel. Ricardo Tenorio has hurt lots of women. One of whom may have gone on to be big in Santa Barbara hospitality."

No comeback this time. No haughty sneer or dismissive gesture. She just stared into her drink, as if I were telling her things she hadn't considered. Or things that she had, and now she was considering them all over again.

"Only, here's the thing. Killing Jordan Mardian doesn't hurt your husband; it helps him. So, despite all the evidence, I don't like Ricky for the bridge job."

She looked up. "Then who?"

"Your brother would be high on anyone's list."

She shook her head. "Tony has his faults, but killing women isn't one of them."

"All right, have it your way. But you didn't drive clear across town just to drink my cheap vodka. What is it you wanted from me?"

"I'm not sure." She stared again into the glass. "No, that isn't true. I know what I wanted, and I think you've given it to me."

She stood then, and so did I. She circled the table and grabbed my jacket and pulled me close enough that I could smell her lipstick.

"My husband is a powerful man, and like all powerful men, he has ways of making things turn out the way he wants them to. Between Tony and the police and the district attorney, my husband has the power to make Ricky appear guilty for that poor woman's death, and he's angry enough and rotten enough to do it."

"What do you want me to do about it?"

"Want?" Her fists tightened. "I want you to stop him, that's what. The police certainly won't, or the district attorney. You're the only one who can. And you care; I know you do."

"You love Ricky, don't you?"

Her grip softened. She nodded. "Yes. Yes, I love Ricky."

"Okay, then here's my advice: If you have evidence against your husband or your brother, take it to the police."

"And wind up under some bridge?" She pulled me closer. "Is that what you want? Is it?"

She kissed me then, long and deep, and I kissed her just as hard. Don't ask me why. Maybe it was the booze, or the hour, or the weepy yarn she'd just spun for my benefit. Maybe it was the novelty—the cheap thrill of seducing the wife of our next U.S. senator—or a thumb in the eye to her asshole husband and her Neanderthal brother.

Or maybe it was just that she was beautiful and frightened and asking for my help. That was generally all it took.

She'd have figured that out by now.

FIFTEEN

THERE WERE NO phone calls on Saturday. No visits from the goon squad, or come-ons from amorous femmes fatales or naked cartoon schoolgirls, even in my dreams. I slept late, and I woke up with a hangover, and then I spent the day working in the garden before taking Sam on a late-afternoon stroll through the neighborhood. We met a few new dogs and saw a few new people, one of whom chewed me out in Mandarin for letting Sam take a leak on his gingko tree. In the evening I caught up on the news and had a cold beer and watched USC beat Notre Dame in South Bend in the shadow of Touchdown Jesus.

On the whole, it was an excellent day.

There was some late-night campaign coverage, but it focused mainly on the new polling and fund-raising numbers. Larry Archer had spent his Saturday addressing an audience of Silicon Valley executives in Palo Alto, calling for new trade sanctions against China, while Warren Burkett had attended an outdoor rally in San Jose, appearing in shirtsleeves before hundreds of broom-wielding *unionistas* chanting *"Sì, se puede."*

None of the networks even mentioned the Goldilocks Affair, which seemed to be losing a little momentum in the flashing tilt-a-whirl of the twenty-four-hour news cycle. Even Terina Webb was AWOL from her post— out beating the bushes, I hoped, in search of laughing heirs. The consensus among the pundits was that Archer had survived the scandal in Lake Arrowhead and was on his way to a hard-fought victory.

I had another beer.

I expected an empty office on Sunday morning, but found, to my surprise, the hunched figure of Max Drescher at the conference room table. I knocked before entering, and he practically jumped from his chair.

"You startled me, Mr. MacTaggart. My goodness." He touched a hand to his chest. "This project is giving me the willies."

"I thought you were on the campaign trail this weekend."

"I was, but I had a couple of hours free, so Marta let me in. I hope you don't mind."

"Where did she go?"

"To church, I think. She said I should close the door when I leave."

I walked around to examine his laptop. I recognized his Web site, Tax Myths and Methods, but with a new yellow banner screaming, SEND A *real* TAX REFORMER TO WASHINGTON.

"Catchy."

"You think so? We've had over ten thousand signatures. I'm quite encouraged." He moved the computer aside. "Since we're both here, do you mind if we go over what I've found so far? I think you'll find it all very interesting."

The documents on the table had been rearranged, from dozens of smaller piles to a trio of tall stacks. He pulled one closer with both hands.

"What do you know about money laundering?"

"Generically? It's the process of running illicit cash through a legitimate business."

Max nodded. "The Federal Election Commission oversees a complicated system of campaign contribution rules and limits—all of it unconstitutional, of course, but for now, lawyers and accountants make careers out of helping candidates navigate their way through the maze. Some candidates play it pretty safe, while others operate closer to the edge. That's where things like intercandidate transfers and 501(c)(4) spooky PACs come into play."

"Okay."

"But even in this highly regulated environment, there's still room for some old-fashioned money laundering. Let me show you some examples."

He paged through the pile of documents and extracted three that he'd tabbed with Post-it notes. These he arranged in a row before him.

"You're familiar with *Citizens United*?"

"Sure, that was the Supreme Court decision allowing unlimited campaign contributions by corporations. Now corporations are treated like people. More like Nevada prostitutes. You can't marry them, but now you can legally get fucked by them."

"Actually, *Citizens United* allowed for unlimited *independent* spending by corporations and labor unions. This has led to the proliferation of so-called independent-expenditure political action committees."

"Super PACs."

He nodded again. "Under current law, corporations and labor unions are still prohibited from making direct contributions to candidates. So I ran a little stress test on the sources of Mr. Archer's campaign contributions, and I found that an unusually high percentage came from individuals. These are the so-called hard-money contributions that are still subject to a strict per-person limit."

"Okay."

"What's more, I found that an unusually large percentage of Mr. Archer's hard money is coming from donors employed by companies based in Nevada."

"That makes sense. Archer Properties is headquartered there."

"Yes, but these contributors include thousands of lower-level employees—administrative assistants, Realtors, construction workers. There are any number of hotel maintenance personnel, for example, who made the maximum contribution. I'm talking about maids and janitors. Plus cocktail waitresses, bartenders, and card dealers—all contributing to the maximum limit. Here, let me show you some examples."

He'd highlighted several entries on two different copies of Schedule A to the FPPC's Form 460—the same form I'd seen Friday afternoon on Mayday's laptop. These were the schedules detailing campaign contributions made during each relevant filing period.

"Take a look at these contributors. All work for different companies. Sterling Hospitality Group, Bacchus Entertainment, A-1 Custodial Services, Union Street Management—all either operate or contract with casinos in the state of Nevada, but all are subsidiaries, either directly or indirectly, of a company called Global Gaming, LLC. Global Gaming owns the Hemisphere Hotel and Casino in Vegas."

The third document he'd highlighted was a page from the SEC's Form 10K for Global Gaming, listing its board of directors. One of whom was Anthony Gagliano.

"Are you saying Tony Gags puts the arm on these employees to contribute to Archer's campaign in California?"

"More likely they're instructed to make a contribution, and they then receive a corresponding bonus in their next paycheck. Or else they're bypassed altogether, and the contribution is made in their name, using information already in the employer's possession. It's an old scheme, but it's tried and true. I've just never seen it used on this large a scale. We're talking millions of dollars here."

I slid into the chair beside him. "So Global Gaming is making direct hard-money contributions to the Archer campaign, laundered through the employees of these subsidiary companies?"

"So it appears."

"But if you could uncover all this in just a few days of research, working by yourself from public records, then surely the authorities—"

"If they wanted to, Mr. MacTaggart, and if they had the resources. Schemes like this are very difficult to prosecute, and even if pursued, it's always after the election. And it happens on both sides, Republican and Democrat, corporations and unions. That's democracy in America, Mr. MacTaggart—and that's not all."

He pinched another tier of documents from the pile and fanned them out before us.

"There are other suspicious transactions, like unsecured loans long outstanding and charitable deductions that correspond to third-party campaign contributions.

The list goes on, but I haven't had time to pursue it all. Let's just say that Larry Archer's entire campaign stinks, and that the odor seems to originate from the general vicinity of Las Vegas."

Until now I'd been operating under the assumption that Larry Archer used Tony Gags the way he used his other levers of power: to get the things he wanted. Now I wondered if I didn't have it all backward.

"Any chance you could type this up into some kind of report? Maybe just an executive summary, with a few key exhibits as backup? Enough to interest the press and give them a place to start?"

He squirmed in his chair. "I don't want to get in trouble with these kinds of people, Mr. MacTaggart—and neither do you."

"Come on, Max. Where's that revolutionary zeal I saw in court?"

"That was for a good cause. What's in this for me?"

"Archer's the front-runner, Max. If he throws a shoe, it's anybody's race."

"As long as the shoe doesn't hit me in the head."

"We'll keep it on the down-low. Our discussions are protected by attorney-client privilege. Nobody will ever trace it back to you."

"You're sure about that?"

"Trust me, Max. I'm a lawyer."

IT WAS 6:05 when I arrived at the Only Place, where Regan and Mayday were already ensconced at the same little table in back. Both had ordered iced teas, and they were passing documents back and forth between them.

"Well, if it isn't Long John Silver," Mayday said, moving her laptop and clearing a space on the table. The documents, I could see, were screen grabs printed from sites like Facebook and LinkedIn and Ancestry.com. They were dog-eared and highlighted and heavily annotated in the margins.

I looked from one woman to the other.

"Shall we order champagne?"

"Try the hemlock," Mayday said, squaring the pages and pushing them my way. "I've spent two whole days chasing shadows. There are dozens of Marsdens in L.A. County, but none of them connects to a Joan Marsden born between 1970 and 1975. At least none that I could find."

I turned to Regan, who looked positively angelic in a snug black T-shirt and matching silk blouse, her hair down loose on her shoulders. She was even wearing a little makeup.

"Nothing on my end. The bench warrant from 1990 is still outstanding. There was a skip trace that went nowhere. There are no missing persons, no parking tickets, and no other wants or warrants."

"What about the bail bond?"

"I checked. It was a five-grand signature bond, with Marsden herself as the indemnitor. What's worse, the company's out of business."

"I can see why."

"But I did find something you should know about," Mayday said, lifting the lid on her computer, her expression suddenly sober. "Have you seen today's *Times*?"

She turned the screen to face me. It was a small item on the Crime page of the newspaper's Web site, under the headline BEATING VICTIM IDENTIFIED. The first paragraph read:

The body discovered early Saturday on a bridle
path in Griffith Park has been identified as that
of Kevin Jaworsky, age 27. A 2009 graduate of
CalArts in his hometown of Valencia, Jaworsky
was a noted L.A. street artist. Police are investi-
gating a possible connection between Jaworsky's
beating death and the sometimes-violent rivalries
between competing "crews" of urban graffiti artists. (more)

"K-Jaw?"

Mayday nodded. "Murder number three."

"Shit. Do they have any leads?"

"Apparently not"—Mayday turned the laptop, keeping her eyes on me—"but they think the murder weapon
was a baseball bat."

I sat. Regan touched a hand to my arm.

"Now you *have* to report what happened at your
house."

I looked at my watch. "Has anyone heard from Bernie?"

"Not yet."

"Me neither."

We waited another half hour, then went ahead and
ordered. I recounted the fruits of my busy weekend,
leaving out certain sartorial and osculatory details. The
food arrived at our table just as I'd arrived at Max's
conclusions.

"Hold on," Mayday said. "If Ricky planted the painting during the video shoot, then he had to have been in
cahoots with Mardian. Or Marsden. Which confirms
what we've always thought. Still, it doesn't square with
his wanting Archer to lose the election. Like you said,

Archer was already losing. Why would they set Burkett up in the first place?"

"Maybe Rio didn't," Regan said. "Maybe Tony Gags did it, and Rio found out."

"Then somehow got hold of the painting?"

"Sure. Maybe Rio was supposed to fence it, but then he double-crossed Tony and Archer."

"Or maybe Rio's been playing both sides all along," Mayday said, excitement in her voice. "Wooing Angela, pretending to help Archer, then pulling a U-turn. That way Archer loses the election, and Ricky keeps both Angela and the painting. And while Tony was out hunting for Rio, he found K-Jaw instead."

I said, "At least we know who's been sending the messages."

Regan frowned. "We do?"

Mayday fielded that one.

"It had to have been someone at the video shoot. Someone who wanted to take Archer down, and now someone in a position to know what might be inside Joan Marsden's safe-deposit box."

"Ricky Rio."

"Which means that Rio and Marsden *are* connected."

Regan frowned. "But why kill Marsden and Orlov? To flip the polls? That's an awfully big risk for a doubtful reward."

"Whoever killed Orlov was covering tracks. They were after Marsden's records."

"So if you find who hired Marsden, you find who killed her."

"And if Rio wants us to find Marsden's records, then he's not the one who hired her."

"Which puts us right back where we started." Regan

slouched in her chair. "It's like one of those M. C. Escher staircase drawings."

My phone vibrated, and I dug it out from my pocket. These two didn't need me anyway.

"MacTaggart."

"Sorry I missed the dinner, boss," Bernie shouted, "but I got hung up in Riverside."

I could hear honky-tonk music and laughter in the background.

"Riverside? Are you all right?"

"I'm right as rain, but you're gonna have one hell of a bar tab come Monday."

"Oh, yeah? Why is that, exactly?"

"Because," she said, lowering her voice a notch, "these Marsden girls drink like fuckin' catfish."

SIXTEEN

NEITHER WOMAN, OF COURSE, was named Marsden.

The elder, Michelle, had divorced an auto mechanic named Johnson, whose name she'd kept "'cause of them lines down at the DMV." Rawboned and haggard, with small eyes and birdlike features, Shelly Johnson currently lived with her son's pregnant wife in an apartment complex in Victorville, her son being "off in Afghanistan, fightin' for our freedom."

Younger sister Pamela was still married, in her case to a man named Lester Sylbert, a fact that in no way seemed to dampen her enthusiasm for tight jeans, big hair, and exceedingly small T-shirts. It was this combustible combination that accounted for the three Barstow cowboys who crowded our little conclave like crows on a roadside carcass.

"Lester don't like bars," Pam shouted over the jukebox strains of Waylon Jennings's "Lukenbach, Texas."

"He says he'd rather fight and fuck and puke in the comfort of his own home."

We were in a roadhouse honky-tonk called the Spoke, just off the 215 Freeway on the outskirts of Moreno Valley. Regan was beside me, while Bernie smiled at both of us from farther down the bar. She raised her glass, knocked back the shot, and bit into a lime wedge.

"So where exactly does Joan hang in the family tree?" I asked Shelly, who seemed the soberer of the two.

"Joanie come after me and before Pamela."

"I'd never come before Pamela," one of the cowboys offered, poking his hat into the conversation, "and that right there is a promise."

Pam whooped and lassoed him with her arms, and together they toppled sideways into the bar, like a tree collapsing onto a house. Regan rescued her Diet Coke just in time.

"When was the last time either of you heard from Joan?"

Shelly's face pinched. "You ask a lot of questions, do you know that? How do we know you ain't a cop or some kind of a spy or somethin'?"

"Hey," Pamela addressed herself to Regan, reaching a hand over the cowboy's shoulder, "is that really your hair? 'Cause that's about the prettiest damn hair I ever seen."

"Why, look! An open booth," I said, extending an arm toward some departing patrons. "If you boys will excuse us, we have an important matter to discuss with these ladies in private."

With Regan's help, I was herding the sisters Marsden toward the still-cluttered table when I felt a hand clap onto my shoulder.

"Hey. Who the fuck do you think you are, buddy?"

I pried the hand loose and spun the cowboy around, shoving him facedown on the bar with his hat cocked and his arm behind his back. His friends each took a giant step backward.

"I'm the guy who's gonna let you keep all your teeth tonight, Rango, provided you mind your manners. How does that sound to you?"

"Sounds good, hoss," he said, his breath fogging the bartop.

I left them in Bernie's dubious care and joined the women in the booth, where a waitress was collecting empties and wiping the table with a rag.

"Pardon the interruption," I told the sisters, who, side by side in the roseate glow of neon, could have passed for mother and daughter. Pamela, the youngest, had her late sister's coloring—brick-red hair and eyes the color of jade—to go along with her Barbie doll physique. I'm sure she was a big hit down at the Grange hall, crushing beer cans on her forehead.

"My sister asked you a question," Pamela said, rooting through the purse in her lap.

It wasn't clear to me how much Bernie had told them, other than the fact that I was a lawyer who wanted to talk to them about their long-lost sibling.

"I'm afraid I have news," I said.

Pamela stopped fumbling. "She's dead, ain't she?"

I nodded.

"Shit fuck." Pamela produced a cigarette and a green plastic lighter. In California, it had been illegal to smoke in bars since 1998.

"When?" Shelly asked.

"Last weekend, in Pasadena. She fell off a bridge. Or maybe she was pushed. That's what we're trying to find out. We were hoping you could help us."

"Help you how? And how come we're talkin to you and not the police?"

I looked at Regan, and she at me. She shifted on her hip and produced a black leather case and discreetly showed her badge.

"I should've known." Pam drew on her cigarette,

flipped her wrist, and sent a blue cloud across the table. I addressed myself to Shelly.

"What can you tell us about Joan? Starting with when you last saw or heard from her."

"Mister, Joanie run off when she was sixteen. 'Goin' to Hollywood,' she said. 'Gonna be a movie star.' We got one postcard from her, maybe six months after that. Said she was makin' good money and livin' the high life. Then nothin'."

"Did you ever try to track her down?"

The jukebox segued to Lynyrd Skynyrd's "Free Bird." Shelly shook her head.

"I figured wherever she was at, it was better'n where she'd been."

"Where was that?" Regan asked her.

Pamela ground her half-smoked cigarette into the tabletop. "You wouldn't know shit about it, blondie."

"Why don't you try me?"

Pam turned her attention to the wall.

"Our mama died right after Pammy was born," Shelly said, patting her sister's hand. "Daddy done what he could. Then the county come and took us girls and placed us in foster care. 'Placed'—that's what they always say. Like it's all gentle and careful-like. Me and Joanie, we was kept together, but Pam got separated. Joanie was five or thereabouts. Pam was just a little baby."

"Is your father still alive?"

Shelly shook her head. "The cancer took him, maybe fifteen years ago."

"No other brothers or sisters?"

"Just us girls. Joanie and me, we moved around some. Then, when I was fifteen and she was thirteen and Pam here was eight or thereabouts, we was reunited, you might say."

"I was nine."

"Pam was nine. We got placed with a man in Barstow had a half-wit for a wife. He wasn't a minister, exactly, but more like what you'd call a deacon. He was a drunk and a pervert, and he took a special interest in Joanie, if you get my meanin'. She run away once, and he caught her and whaled the tar out of her. Next time she run, she never did come back."

I felt Regan's grip on my arm.

"Were any of you ever adopted?"

Shelly shook her head. "When I turned seventeen, I went to the judge and got me a order to move out and take Pamela with me. She finished her school while I worked at the base out there at Fort Irwin. After that, I guess we just growed up."

As a juvenile court proceeding, that case file would've been sealed. I glanced over at Bernie, laughing with the cowboys.

"And other than the one postcard, you've had no contact with Joanie for, what, twenty-four years?"

The sisters shared a look, and Shelly withdrew my business card from her pocket. She examined it front and back.

"Why do you care about all this?"

"As far as we know, your sister never married. When she died, she left a house up in Santa Barbara, plus a car and some artwork. Possibly some bank accounts. We won't know the extent of her estate until an executor is appointed, and we can gain access to her records."

"What car?" Pamela asked, showing renewed interest in the conversation.

"Hey, you two," the cowboy interrupted, newly fortified, "we're gettin mighty lonesome over here."

"Fuck off, pencil-dick," Pam told him, and he showed his hands in retreat.

Shelly leaned across the table. "I asked it before, and I'll ask it again. What's your interest in all this?"

"He's trying to help you," Regan told her.

"Honey, the last man offered to help me stole my satellite dish."

"Look," I said. "I was there when they found your sister's body, okay? Three days later a woman who worked for her was killed in a fire. I think both women were murdered, and I intend to find out who did it, whether you help me out or not."

The sisters shared another look.

"Joanie's body is at the Medical Examiner's Office in Los Angeles," Regan told them. "It needs to be claimed and given a proper burial."

"I need to pee," Pam announced, shoving at her sister's shoulder. "Come and powder your nose."

They slid from the booth and worked their way toward the back, with Pam stiff-arming the cowboy in passing.

Bernie slid from her barstool and joined us.

"How's it going?"

"How did you ever find these two?"

She scooted into the cracked Naugahyde, grinning from ear to ear. She was pretty clearly drunk.

"I wasted the whole day Saturday calling Marsdens from the phone book, and I didn't find shit. Then I stopped for a minute to think about it. I figured that a teenage girl who runs away must have problems at home, right? So then I got to thinking about family problems that might leave some kind of record. I went to the library on Saturday night and started looking at obituary notices. They have them all on microfiche."

She dug into her pocket and laid some folded pages on the table.

"I found a Helen Marsden who died in Fontana. It said she was survived by her husband, Thomas, and her daughters Michelle, Joan, and Pamela."

I unfolded the papers. The first sheet bore the scanned image of a newspaper obituary page with one entry circled. The date was June 12, 1979.

"Three girls, all now adults. So the next thing I did was search for wedding announcements in San Bernardino and Riverside Counties." She gestured with her chin. "That's what I found."

The second sheet was from something called the *Redlands Daily Facts.* Under the heading "Wedding Bans" was a small mention of the Marsden-Sylbert nuptials.

"There were only a few Sylberts, and they're all fuckin' related. I told 'em I was an old girlfriend of Lester's."

I handed back the sheets. "I'm speechless, Bernadette."

"Yep." She sighed, arching her back and folding the papers back into her pocket. "I'll remember it fondly as I sip my margarita on Rosarito Beach."

"What do you think?" I asked Regan.

She shook her head. "They haven't told us everything."

"I agree. I think there was more contact than the one postcard. With Shelly, would be my guess."

"Here they come."

Bernie returned to the bar as the sisters Marsden resumed their places in the booth.

"So let me get this straight," Shelly said, leaning on her elbows. "You want us to hire you so's you can represent us in handling Joanie's estate?"

"That's right."

"And that will help you to find out who killed her?"

"We think so. We think your sister might have kept records in a safe-deposit box and that those records will lead us to the killer"—I glanced at Regan—"and maybe stop him from killing again."

"What do you need us to do?"

"Right now we don't know whether Joan left a will. If she did, it will probably be in the box. Either way, we need to have one or both of you appointed as the administrator of her estate. That involves a bunch of paperwork and a court order, but first it involves you hiring me as your lawyer."

"What will that cost us?"

"Nothing. We'll do all the work for free, but we need to find that box in the next nine days."

"Why nine days?"

"Election Day. It's a long story. Let's just say that if we don't find her killer by then, he might get away with murder."

Shelly reexamined my card. She flicked it with a fingernail and looked at her sister. "Excuse us," she said, and again they slid from the booth, this time crossing only as far as the bar.

The cowboys, it seemed, had moved on to the next roundup. Bernie slipped back into our booth.

"What's taking so friggin' long?"

"Shhh."

"Shush yourself. I've been drinking tequila since six o'clock."

"Also known as Sunday."

"Just don't expect much work from me tomorrow."

"Also known as Monday."

Regan nudged my leg.

The women returned with the waitress in tow. "Slide over, honey," Shelly told Bernie, and the sisters shouldered in beside her. The waitress swung her tray and set down five shot glasses brimming with a clear golden liquid. Shelly lifted hers.

"I ain't never had me a lawyer before," she said, "but I guess there's a first time for everything in this world. Here's to Joanie."

We raised and touched our glasses.

"Now let's get the sonofabitch what killed her."

SEVENTEEN

"EIGHT DAYS IS IMPOSSIBLE," Mayday said. She removed a book from the credenza behind her. It was a desktop edition of the *California Probate Code*.

"A hearing on a petition for the appointment of an executor requires at least fifteen days' notice. The code requires personal service on all known heirs, plus publication in a newspaper of general circulation." She flipped pages until she found the applicable statute. "I quote: 'The court may not shorten the time for giving notice of hearing under this section.'"

"All true," I told her, "but you're swimming in the wrong stream."

"What do you mean?"

"I mean there's a whole chapter in there on the appointment of a special administrator, with or without notice, where circumstances require. All we need to do is convince a judge in Santa Barbara that there's an emergency that makes the appointment necessary."

"An emergency. Like electing a murderer to the U.S. Senate?"

"I'd start with the fact that the decedent was implicated in a public scandal, that she then died under suspicious circumstances, that her business records were destroyed in an arson fire, and that we have good cause to believe that a clue to the killer's identity might be found in her safe-deposit box."

Mayday looked up from the book. "Filed under seal, I presume?"

"Definitely not."

"Hold on. You're going to put all that in a public document?"

"I am, and then we might even leak a copy to Terina Webb."

She pushed back from her desk. "If you do that, you'll turn this into a bigger circus than it is now, if that's even possible. Not to mention put a bull's-eye on your back."

"Think, Marta. We have no admissible evidence that Joan Marsden's death was anything other than suicide, and we have no admissible evidence that a safe-deposit box even exists, let alone what might be inside it. So just getting the order would be a minor miracle—and even if we were to get it, we don't know where to find the box, nor do we have a key for it even if we did. There are only six business days left until the election. It's late in the fourth quarter, we've used our last time-out, and the clock is ticking. The best we can hope is that by filing the petition and making it public, we'll somehow flush out the killer."

"So we're not even trying to find the box?"

"Oh, we'll try, but it's a ten-to-one shot at best. If we fly under the radar, the odds are that we crash and burn. But if we make a sonic boom, then at least we'll rattle some windows on the way down."

I LEFT MAYDAY to handle the paperwork, and Bernie to nurse what looked like an ear-bleeding hangover. I'd probably overstated the odds against us, but they were still longer than a Russian novel. My job now was to whittle them down to size.

I knew in my heart that Joan Marsden's death hadn't been a suicide, but knowing is one thing, and proving is something else altogether. Proof, in the courtroom sense, meant getting our hands on the official coroner's report.

There were lawful ways to go about that, like filing a Public Records Act request. The newspapers, I'm sure, had already done so, but the law gave Slew ten days to respond, plus a bagful of loopholes he could use to run out the clock—and with Archer ahead in the polls, Slew wasn't about to do anything that might rock the electoral boat.

We didn't have weeks, or even days, but I did have one thing: a promise from Bill Harwood that he'd get me a copy through his FBI contacts. The problem was, he'd made that promise when we were both still playing ball for Team Burkett. It was time to see if his word had survived my demotion to the minors.

I had no phone number for Harwood, but according to the Burkett campaign Web site, the candidate was slated to speak at a literacy event in Pasadena at noon, at the old Central Library on Walnut Street, and the book-loving public was invited to attend.

It was already 12:05 when I reached the little parking lot in back of the building, but the lot was already full, and the attendants were waving late arrivals northbound onto Garfield Avenue. I finally found a spot two blocks away, and returned to the library at a trot.

Built in 1927 in the Moorish architectural style, the Pasadena Central Library building was designed by Myron Hunt, whose other claims to fame included designing the State Capitol building in Sacramento. Walking into the main hall, with its soft cork floor and dark oak wainscoting, passing under its pendant lights and forty-five-foot corbelled ceiling, was like stepping into the sepia-toned Los Angeles of Nathanael West and Raymond Chandler.

I paused for a moment to scan the inscriptions carved in stone under the high southern windows. One was from Marlowe, and I don't think it was Philip. It read: *infinite riches in a little room.*

There were signs directing the voting public toward the west end of the building, to the Ernestine Avery Children's Wing, where a small crowd was gathered in the innermost reading room. It was strictly a photo-op, with more reporters than civilians, and thus perhaps an indicator of the mayor's fading electoral prospects.

Burkett sat in a straight-backed chair with a book in one hand and a squirming four-year-old in his lap. Standing beside him was the kid's mother, a real looker in the Jennifer Lopez mold. Arrayed around them on a small amphitheater of carpeted risers were a dozen more kids, scrubbed and fidgeting and paying more attention to the photographers than to the silver-haired man in the chair. Burkett, for his part, looked like he'd rather the kid and the mother switched positions.

Harwood, of course, saw me enter. He'd been leaning on a bookshelf by the fireplace, and now he moved quietly around the perimeter of onlookers. I stepped back through the opening to the outer room.

"I wondered when you'd show up."

He wore his standard uniform of dark suit and white shirt and solid tie, carefully chosen to blend into a crowd as best as a six feet two inch, two-hundred-forty-pounder can blend. Apropos of our surroundings, I replied with a snippet from Brontë.

"'As children hope, with trustful breast.'"

The Stanford man didn't miss a beat. "'I waited bliss and cherished rest.'"

We shared another stare.

"When last we spoke," I reminded him, "you offered to get me a copy of the coroner's report."

At first he didn't answer, and together we stood shoulder to shoulder, watching the mayor perform. He was reading from Dr. Seuss, *Green Eggs and Ham,* and he sounded a little rusty.

"As I recall the conversation," Harwood finally said, "you asked if I could get you a copy, and I said maybe."

"Let's not quibble, darling."

"Why do you want it?"

"I have my reasons."

"You after the reward money?"

"Could be. I lost a client, and the rent is coming due."

"I don't see how the coroner's report will help you find the painting."

"Let's quit fencing, shall we? I don't give a shit about the painting or about any reward. I don't give a shit about the election or Warren Burkett or Larry Archer. All I care about is the fact that two women are dead, and the D.A. doesn't seem to care, and the cops are—"

"Shhhh."

A woman had turned, a finger to her lips. We moved deeper into the adjoining room.

"I'd think that with Burkett running second, you'd welcome all the help you could get."

"We would. The problem is, every time there's a story about that woman's death, we lose more ground."

"Marsden."

"What?"

"Her name was Marsden, Joan Marsden—and if that were the case, then the D.A. would have released the report on his own by now. Like maybe on a billboard."

"You know the drill. Archer's on top, so the D.A. doesn't want to make waves." He turned to face me. "Let's say that the report points to murder. Hypothetically speaking. How could that possibly help the mayor?"

"I'll make you a deal. You get me the coroner's report, plus all the LAPD's forensics, and I'll give you something guaranteed to put a stick in Archer's spokes."

"What something?"

"A little surprise I've been working on. You'll like it. Trust me, I'm a lawyer."

Applause broke out in the other room, where Burkett stood posing for a photo with the little kid's mother. He had his arm around her waist.

"I'll need the mayor's permission," Harwood said.

"That's fine. Tell him he's got nothing to lose and all of Carthage to gain."

We watched as the crowd fragmented into clusters. The kids were being herded by the shushing librarian, and the cameramen were packing up their equipment. Burkett, meanwhile, had steered the kid's mother into a corner.

"Got to go," Harwood said. "I've got your number."

"Yeah, I'm sure you do."

I stood for a while and watched. After another round of glad-handing, Burkett and Harwood moved in my direction, the mayor pulling up short as I came into his headlights.

"Well, there," he said, offering a hand. I shook it.

"Nice to see you again."

"You, too." He tapped me on the shoulder. "Got to run, but we'll talk soon."

I waited around for a while after they'd left. The kids were all at tables now, dutifully paging through picture books while the press filtered out in ones and twos.

I was watching the mother.

She was standing by the fireplace, looking a little lost. She rummaged through her handbag. She looked at her son, who was seated at one of the tables. She checked her watch, and I did the same.

"Pardon me," I said as I approached her, patting at my pockets. "This is really embarrassing, but I seem to have left my cell phone out in the car, and I need to call my daughter's school. Would you mind terribly if..."

"Oh, sure," she said, digging back into the bag. "Not a problem."

I backed a step while dialing. I smiled at her, and she smiled back. Burkett answered on the first ring.

"That was fast," he said in a low voice.

"And so are you. You really need to watch that. Meanwhile, I made a proposal to your man Harwood, and I need an answer by today. You're running low on options, senator, and I can help. Harwood knows how to reach me."

I hung up without waiting for his reply. The mother smiled again. She had a great smile.

"That was fast," she said.

"Aren't we all."

THE ADDRESS I'D gotten from Terina Webb was on the Strand, between Fifteenth and Sixteenth streets in

Hermosa Beach, the middle jewel of the Manhattan-
Hermosa-Redondo triple crown of small beachfront
cities that constitute L.A.'s fabled South Bay. I parked
on Hermosa Avenue and put up the convertible top and
stripped off my jacket and tie. I rolled up my sleeves
and fed four quarters into the meter. Then I stopped and
returned and pumped in another buck.

I was immediately assaulted by a cool sea breeze and
a sidewalk crowded with scruffy boys on skateboards
and sunburned girls in baggy sweatshirts over bare legs
and flip-flops. One of the girls sported a red Mohawk.
One of the boys had a live parrot on his shoulder.

The kids weren't alone. There were also joggers, and
Rollerbladers, and grown-up dudes on beach cruisers.
There were seagulls and palm trees, and little banga-
low homes with little bungalow lawns framed in banana
fronds and pink bougainvillea.

I walked to Sixteenth Street past Beach Drive and
continued out to the Strand. Beyond the low seawall was
a wide sand beach with a lifeguard tower and some volleyball courts and scattered groupings of sunbathers. I
turned south and read the numbers on the tidy beachfront homes wedged cheek by jowl with their neighbors,
and it occurred to me that for what these places must
cost, I'd want a tad more privacy for my housing dollar.

The address I was after belonged to a two-story faux
Mediterranean shoehorned between its more contemporary glass-and-cedar neighbors. All the homes had
picture windows behind seaside balconies, but this
one featured wrought-iron railings and a Saltillo patio
with a small, gurgling fountain. The little iron gate was
propped open, and I heard both music and a television
set blaring from inside.

I knocked loudly. The blonde who answered wore a yellow bikini top and cut-off denim shorts with the combined surface area of a greeting card.

"You're late," she said, giving me the once-over, "but come on in."

There were a half dozen guys in the downstairs living room, all of them young and fit and all of them wearing nothing but white Jockey underpants. Some were reading, and some were watching a soap opera on the tube. A few nodded hellos. The house smelled faintly of coconut butter and body odor and marijuana.

The girl from the front door disappeared into a back bedroom and returned with a tighty whitie that she balled up and tossed in my direction.

"Thirty-four okay?"

"Sure," I said. "Thanks."

"You can change in back." She sidestepped into the kitchen. "You want a drink first?"

I followed her to the blender on the kitchen counter. There she measured tequila and triple sec and sour mix and ice scooped with her hands from a ripped plastic bag in the sink. She threw the switch.

"You're a little old for this gig," she shouted over the blender, "but I like your face."

When the whirring had stopped she took down a glass from the cupboard. She looked at me and smiled and wet the rim with her tongue. Then she crunched the rim into a salt dish shaped like a sombrero and filled the glass. She garnished her creation with a lime wedge from the cutting board.

"Thanks," I told her, lifting the drink, "but there seems to be a misunderstanding. My name's MacTaggart. I'm a lawyer, and I'm here to see Alan Whitaker."

I set down the underpants and handed her a card. She put a hand to her mouth and giggled.

"Alan's upstairs," she said. "They're almost done. You can hang out here, or you can wait outside." She picked the underpants up off the counter and flapped them once, then held them against my crotch. "Sure you won't try these on for me?"

I waited outside. The sun was high, and the swell was small, and the only sound from the ocean was the flat and intermittent slapping of shorebreak against sand. Gleaming people walked and jogged and Rollerbladed on the pavement, their iPod cables swaying in the ocean breeze. On the beach, the volleyballers scrambled and leaped and stood doubled over, sweating and breathing hard.

My phone vibrated, and I checked the caller ID.

"MacTaggart."

"Burkett's house at five," Harwood said. "Don't be late; we need to catch a plane."

"You've got the reports?"

"I called, didn't I?"

"Okay," I told him. "Five o'clock sharp."

I tapped END and punched up the office. Bernie sounded as if she'd been asleep.

"MacTaggart and Suarez."

"It's me. Is Marta there?"

She groaned. I was placed on hold until Mayday came on the line.

"Jack?"

"Do me a favor, would you? Call Max and tell him I need his report on my desk by four o'clock today. No names, and no way to trace it back to us. Don't take no for an answer, no matter what he says, okay?"

"What's going on?"

"I'll tell you later. How's the application coming?"

"Okay, I guess. I'll have it on your desk by five."

"Keep it in draft," I told her. "I may have something important to add."

EIGHTEEN

I WAITED ALMOST an hour, watching the volleyball and the bikinis and the action on the esplanade, before the door to the house opened and a man stepped squinting into the sunlight. Average build, roughly my age. Light complexion, slightly sunburned. He wore a two-tone Tommy Bahama bowling shirt over baggy linen slacks and black-and-white striped espadrille slippers. His ginger hair was slicked, and he sported sharp sideburns and a three-day beard. He removed a pair of Ray-Bans from his shirt pocket and slipped them onto his face. It was a handsome face, and he seemed a little reluctant to hide it.

"You Jackie? I'm Alan Whitaker. You've got two minutes."

He didn't offer a hand. He stood beside me facing the ocean. He waved to somebody on the beach.

"I represent the family of Jordan Mardian. She owned the building in Montecito where Catherine Orlov was killed. We—"

"Whitaker. Catherine Whitaker."

"Right. We—"

"Wait a sec. Are you with the insurance?"

"What?"

"Is that your game? Cage the grieving husband and get him to settle on the cheap? Well, you can piss off.

I've hired the best lawyer in Beverly Hills. You'll be hearing from him soon enough."

I turned and stood before him, invading his personal space.

"Catherine Orlov was murdered, Mr. Whitaker. The building was torched, either to destroy records in the office or to hide what records were stolen. Jordan Mardian, Catherine's employer, was—"

"Yeah, yeah, I know all about it. Took a swan dive off a bridge. I don't live in a bloody cave. What's it got to do with me?"

The door opened behind us, and two of the models emerged, both fully dressed. Whitaker broke away to shake their hands and tell them he'd be in touch. He checked his stainless Rolex as he returned.

"I'm afraid your meter's about to expire, Jackie boy."

He flinched when I snatched the sunglasses from his nose.

"All right, let me put this in terms you might understand. Somebody killed Catherine Orlov. If she was really your wife, then you have a slam-dunk wrongful-death case against the killer. If the killer has any money, then you've just hit the jackpot."

"Go on."

"But first we have a little problem. First we need to identify the killer, and to do that, I need to know a few things."

"Such as?"

"There was a ring of keys in Catherine's purse on the day she was killed. The purse was never found. I need to know if the keys ever turned up. If so, I'd like to have a look at them."

He shielded his eyes with a hand. "Don't know about

keys. Had to call a locksmith just to get inside the house. Now they want to nick me for burglary, if you can believe that."

"All right, second question: Did Catherine do any banking for the Mardian business? Were there any bank statements or checkbooks in her house?"

He lowered his hands to his hips.

"Banking papers and keys? What's your game, Jackie? You're after something, and it damn well isn't any killer."

I looked back at the house. The blonde was on the balcony now. She waved.

I drew my phone from my pocket.

"You're too sharp for me, Alan." I handed him back his shades. "I'm gonna give you a number, and you'll want to write it down."

I showed him my call history. He removed his own phone and tapped on the keypad.

"Who's this?"

"A woman you'll want to talk to. She's from Farmers Insurance. Her name's Shoshanna Gold. Just tell her I asked you to call."

I BATTLED FREEWAY traffic all the way to Sierra Madre, but I still made it by 4:30. Bernie sat at the reception desk in a pair of oversized sunglasses. I waved a hand in front of her face.

I found Mayday in her office.

"There it is," she said, nodding to a folder on the edge of her desk. "He wasn't happy."

I opened the folder and flipped through Max's report.

"Are you giving that to Terina, too?"

"Uh-uh. This I'm trading to Harwood for the coroner's report and the LAPD's forensics on Marsden."

She reclined in her chair, lacing her hands behind her head.

"So let me see if I follow: We're now working for free, essentially, on Max's case, so that we can work for free on the Marsden case?"

"Something like that."

"And for this I gave up a job downtown?"

"And two thousand billable hours a year."

"And a six-figure salary."

"You're forgetting the reward money."

"Ah, the reward money. Thank you for reminding me." She shuffled some papers on her desk. "Regan called. She wants to know what's going on, and I didn't know how much I should tell her."

"Tell her we'll fill her in later."

"Also, I asked Shelly and Pam to come in tomorrow afternoon. Once they sign their declarations, we'll be ready for court on Wednesday."

"New timetable. Have them come in the morning dressed for court. We'll drive up in the afternoon."

"Tomorrow? Are you sure?"

"Sure? Hell no, I'm not sure. I'm making this up as I go."

I DIALED TERINA WEBB on the drive over to Burkett's house. I left a message that the porridge was getting hotter and that if she said pretty please, she could have the first taste.

As I crossed the freeway overpass and turned onto South San Rafael, I saw the black Town Car in the street, pointed in my direction. I pulled to a stop at the curb opposite. A rear door opened as I killed my engine, and Harwood stepped out with a large envelope in his hand.

He looked in both directions before crossing the street toward my car. He was careful that way.

"That looks a little thin," I told him, reaching for the envelope.

He snatched it away. "You first."

I handed him Max's report. He opened the file and skimmed the first page. Then he flipped to the exhibits. He whistled.

"This is good stuff."

"It won't hold up in court, but it'll sell newspapers."

"Wait here a second."

He walked the file back to the limo, where a rear window slid open. He passed the file through and waited. Words were exchanged, and then he returned.

He handed me the envelope. I opened the flap and extracted a photocopy of the coroner's case file.

"That's all I have right now." He leaned a forearm on my window frame. "I'm working on the rest, but it may take a day or two."

I tapped the envelope on the steering wheel.

"Don't worry," he said, "you'll get it."

"That's what I'm afraid of."

Again his eyes scanned the empty street, up the block then down.

"You read the *Times* lately?"

"You mean about the kid? In Griffith Park?"

"Yeah." He glanced over his shoulder as he bumped the window frame with his fist. He sighed. "Believe me, MacTaggart. I don't like this any more than you do."

THE WORD "autopsy" is from the Greek, meaning "see for yourself." I'd witnessed an autopsy once, and it had left an impression. Kind of like the claw end of a hammer leaves an impression. Deep enough, in my case, that I hoped never to witness another.

In the matter of the autopsy of Joan Marsden, a.k.a. Jordan Mardian, the coroner's case file was twelve pages in length. It consisted of a one-page case report, followed by an investigator's narrative, the autopsy report itself, and then a medical report. Various forensic consultants' reports were referenced, but were not attached to what Harwood had given me.

At the top of the case report, under the heading "Apparent Mode," appeared the word "Homicide." I should have quit right there and left the rest to Mayday, the doctor's daughter, but I couldn't stop myself.

I pictured the procedures that the medical examiner would have followed. The body being wheeled from the cooler and placed on a stainless-steel autopsy table. The M.E. and his assistant, each in scrubs and visors and two pairs of rubber gloves, weighing and measuring the body and conducting an external examination. Then placing a body block under the torso and making the big Y-shaped incision from shoulders to sternum to pelvic bone. Then peeling the chest flap upward until it covered the face, and opening the rib cage to expose the internal organs.

According to the case report's synopsis, the proximate cause of death was acute trauma to the posterior skull, probably from a heavy instrument, with a crushing blunt-force impact to the head and body occurring only post mortem. According to the autopsy report, there were no other conditions, toxicological or otherwise, contributing to the cause of death.

Once the body is opened, organ removal is conducted using what they call the Rokitansky method, in which the viscera are removed en masse, as a hunter might field-dress a deer, and are placed on a separate table for dissection. The assistant then uses brightly colored string to tie off the carotid and subclavian arteries in the neck and upper chest before severing them. This enables the mortician to find them later, in order to inject the embalming fluid.

The investigator's narrative included statements from the jogger who'd found the body, from the Pasadena PD sergeant in charge of the crime scene, and from LAPD Robbery-Homicide detectives Carlos Alvarez and Michael J. Madden. Alvarez, it read, had stayed to witness the autopsy.

Once the viscera are removed, the body block is then shifted upward and placed under the head like a pillow. The scalp is peeled backward and forward, again covering the face, and a Stryker saw is used to open the cranium. It opens, as I recalled, with a distinctive sucking sound. Since the human brain is roughly the consistency of toothpaste, it is removed with great care and suspended by means of mesh netting inside a jar of formalin solution, where it will remain for a period of weeks. This fixes the brain tissue, preserving it from decay and firming it up for easier handling.

According to the investigator's narrative, the deceased's personal effects were tagged as evidence and remanded to the custody of the LAPD. No inventory was attached. No next of kin were available to approve tissue donation. Both Detective Alvarez and District

Attorney Slewzyski requested to be copied on the final autopsy report.

I left the envelope on Mayday's desk. Then I walked two blocks to the Buccaneer Bar and ordered a double Scotch.

NINETEEN

ELECTION DAY MINUS SEVEN.

We drove in Mayday's Lexus, with Shelly up front and Pam and me folded into the little backseat. I'd figured on an hour to Santa Barbara if the traffic was light, so we'd eaten takeout sandwiches at the office and hit the road at 11:30, leaving plenty of time to make the 1:30 calendar call.

In the trunk was Mayday's briefcase, and inside Mayday's briefcase was our formal application to appoint Shelly and Pam jointly as special administrators of the estate of their late sister, Joan Marsden. Supporting the application were declarations from the sisters attesting to their status as Joan's sole surviving heirs, and a declaration from yours truly both authenticating the coroner's autopsy report and making, as best we could, our case for the emergency nature of their appointment.

We'd sent a copy of the application as an e-mail attachment to Terina Webb just before leaving, with instructions that while she may refer to and report on its contents, she may not publish the actual document until we sent her a new face page after the hearing. That face page would bear a court clerk's stamp that would read either RECEIVED or FILED, depending on the outcome of our ex parte application. Were she to publish the application beforehand, without the official court stamp, it would betray the fact that she'd received it from a source other than the clerk's window at the courthouse.

The holes in our presentation to the court were, first, our grounds for believing that a safe-deposit box existed, and second, our reasons for believing that the box, if it existed, might actually contain time-sensitive evidence. These Mayday had tried to paper over with some vague language about "good cause to expect" and "reasonable grounds on which to believe." The result was like a do-it-yourself home repair, in which the walls looked pretty good unless you gave them a close inspection.

Between the coroner's report and Mayday's deft obfuscation, I figured the odds for winning the court's approval had narrowed, to maybe five to one against. We were still underdogs, but at least we now had a puncher's chance.

"Can we drive by afterward and look at the house Joanie lived in?" Pam wanted to know.

"Sure. I'd like to see it myself."

Joan Marsden's kid sister wore a short black skirt with a cream-white blouse and a Kelly-green sweater. Big sister Shelly wore a black wool suit that smelled faintly of mothballs. Pam had her hair clipped back and wore a string of imitation pearls, the effect of which was to further accentuate her resemblance to their late middle sister.

"What happens if the judge turns us down?" Shelly asked into the rearview mirror.

"Then we'll reapply with regular notice, but in the meantime, we'll have tipped our hand to the world."

"And you think that'll bring the rats out of the basement?"

"That's what I'm hoping."

In Santa Barbara County, estate and probate matters are heard at the Anacapa Division courthouse, in beautiful downtown Santa Barbara. We parked in the public library garage and crossed the street to the main courthouse entrance. From there we were directed to the office of the probate examiner, who prescreens all trust, estate, and probate matters for proper form and format before they're allowed into court. The examiner acts as a kind of filter, either rejecting matters outright, recommending them to the court for approval, or leaving them for the court to decide.

There were three cases ahead of ours when we arrived at the examiner's office, and so we found empty benches in the narrow hallway outside. The time was 1:15.

I checked my phone and found three new voice messages. The first was from Terina Webb, confirming that she'd received our e-mail and offering to have my love child. The second was from Max Drescher, alerting me to a so-called virtual campaign rally to be held that evening on his Tax Myths and Methods Web site. The third was from Shoshanna Gold of Farmers Insurance, asking, with a palpable note of irritation, that I ring her back at my earliest convenience.

When our matter was finally called, I sent Mayday, who had drafted all the paperwork, in to see the examiner. She emerged ten minutes later, and without speaking, she handed me the application, on whose cover page the examiner had scribbled, "JTD."

Judge to Determine.

"A chip and a chair," I said aloud, quoting Uncle Louis. We headed for the elevators.

The courtroom of Judge Sheila Lawton-Coen was on the second floor, in Department 5. There we encountered the same gaggle of lawyers we'd seen outside the examiner's office, minus those whose paperwork had been rejected.

The judge's bench was empty, and the clerk and bailiff were huddled at the bailiff's desk, so we placed our papers and business cards neatly on the clerk's desk and took seats in the back of the courtroom. There was no court reporter.

"What's going on?" Shelly whispered.

"It looks like she's hearing matters in chambers. In her office, in back."

After a few minutes, two lawyers, one smiling and one not, strode forth from the open door behind the bench. The clerk looked up and called the next case.

"Estate of Turner," she said. "The judge will see you in chambers."

An elderly lawyer rose and straightened his tie and stooped for his battered briefcase. He shuffled through the gate and past the clerk's desk and around the witness box to the open doorway. He paused and took a breath before stepping inside.

"It ain't nothin' like on the TV," Pam observed.

Twenty minutes later, our case was finally called. By then the clerk had skimmed our paperwork, made a few clucking sounds, and carried it back to the judge.

"Estate of Marsden," she intoned, and we all stood.

The chambers of the Honorable Sheila Lawton-Coen came straight from the municipal prop department, with their wood-paneled walls, bookcases filled with tan leather volumes, hanging plaques and framed citations, a black robe on a coatrack, half a dozen chairs in brown leather and rivets, and a desk big enough on which to shoot billiards. To these she'd added a few feminine touches, like cut flowers in a vase and, this being Santa Barbara, some white orchids in little twig-and-moss baskets.

There was nothing feminine, however, about the woman behind the desk. She was a hard case who wore like battle scars on her weathered face every sob story and wild alibi she'd ever been fed and every harsh judgment she'd ever handed down over the course of her many years on the bench. It was a face that had seen it all and heard even more, and was in no mood to hear it again.

"Sit down," she said without looking up from our papers. "We'd better put this on the record."

She pressed a buzzer, and a side door opened to a young man with a stenographer's *ticky-tak* machine on a portable stand. He entered quietly and sat down and threaded his roll of folded paper. He nodded.

"Estate of Joan Marsden, Deceased, case number P-three-eight-six-three-nine-eight. Counsel will state your appearances."

"Jack MacTaggart and Marta Suarez for petitioners Michelle Johnson and Pamela Sylbert, both of whom are present."

She lifted a gimlet eye.

"Jack?"

"Yes, Your Honor."

"Not John or Jackson?"

"No, Your Honor. Just Jack."

She grunted. "All right then. The petitioners are before this court on an application for their appointment as special administrators of the estate of their late sister, who appears to have died in Los Angeles County under circumstances suggestive of foul play. The court will note here that this is a matter of no small public interest, involving, as it does, a rather high-profile series of events that pertain, either directly or indirectly, to the pending senatorial election. Not to mention, as the petitioners' papers do not, a second case of apparent homicide occurring here in our jurisdiction."

She pursed her lips, looking past our heads toward the open doorway to the courtroom.

"The court finds that petitioners have made a prima facie case that they are the sole heirs of the decedent, and are otherwise qualified to act as special administrators of the estate. The court is troubled, however, with petitioners' showing that the circumstances of the estate require the immediate appointment of a personal representative to act as special administrator. The court therefore invites further argument of counsel."

Her eyes, cold and unblinking, shifted to me. I cleared my throat.

"As we've noted in our petition, we have reason to believe that a safe-deposit box exists and that—"

"Cut to the chase, counsel. What reason?"

I looked at Mayday, and back at the judge. I shifted in my seat.

"Has Your Honor ever played with an Etch-A-Sketch?"

She raised an eyebrow, reclining into her seat.

"Not for some time."

"Neither had I—and then I had one delivered to my office by messenger a couple of weeks ago. It was on the day after Warren Burkett had been arrested for breaking into a stranger's home from which a painting was found to be missing. That was three days before a video turned up on the Internet showing the missing painting hanging in Larry Archer's dining room. That video, the court might recall, showed the lower-left corner of the painting, in which only a croquet ball was visible."

"And the Etch-A-Sketch?"

"It came with a message that read, 'Keep your eye on the ball.'"

Her eyebrows moved.

"Now we fast-forward around ten days or so. The painting's gone missing again, and several people are dead."

"Let me guess. Another Etch-A-sketch."

I looked to Mayday, who powered up her cell phone. When the image came up, she passed it across the desk.

"'Safe-deposit box,'" the judge read.

"I know it's not admissible, but I trust the sender."

"Because of the croquet ball."

I nodded.

"The sender being?"

"That I don't know. I have a suspicion, but only that."

She returned the phone to Mayday and reclined again into her chair.

"An anonymous but reliable source," she mused aloud. "Evidence better suited for journalism than a court of law."

"Yes, Your Honor."

She raised a hand to her mouth. She rocked in her chair.

"The standard is pretty flexible," I reminded her, quoting from the statute. "Letters will issue 'if the circumstances of the estate require.'"

She looked at me again, and then at the two women

sitting stiffly beside me. She sat upright and turned to face the court reporter.

"Upon consideration of the petition and the arguments of counsel, the court finds that good cause exists for petitioners' appointment as special administrators of the estate of Joan Marsden, a.k.a. Jordan Mardian. The appointment shall be for a term of ten days only, however, and shall be for the limited purpose of locating any safe-deposit boxes that might exist in the name of the deceased, or in the name of her alias, or in the name of her business, and for the limited purpose of taking possession of and holding for safekeeping as officers of the court the contents of any such safe-deposit box or boxes. Petitioners are to serve without bond, and letters shall issue forthwith reflecting the foregoing order of this court."

She rose from behind her desk, and we all followed suit. Again she half-turned to the court reporter.

"Off the record."

He typed a few more keystrokes, then stood and gathered up his machine and disappeared through the door from which he'd come. The judge turned her gaze back to me.

"Happy hunting, Mr. MacTaggart." She extended her hand. "Whoever's behind all of this, I want you to nail his hide to the wall."

WE REPAIRED TO the public library across the street, where Mayday, using a combination of her laptop, the court's online probate forms, and the library's printer and photocopier, cobbled together the necessary paperwork for the judge's signature. By the time we'd returned to the courthouse and walked the documents back through the system—including another session with the probate examiner—it was already 4:30, too late to visit any of the local banks.

"Can we look at Joanie's house now?" Pam implored.

The house was in Montecito, but in one of the older neighborhoods, where the homes had been built on a human scale more than fifty years earlier. Pam pressed her nose to the rear-seat window as the olive trees and eucalyptus trees and royal palms scrolled past. She craned to see the houses, glimpsed only through open gates or through gaps in stone walls. When we rolled to a stop before a landscaped entry gate, she jumped from the car like a kid in the Disneyland parking lot.

"Oh my God!" she said, leaning over the gate for a better angle. We all got out and joined her.

There was an SBPD DO NOT ENTER seal on the gate, with yellow crime scene tape visible in the home's entrance alcove, which we glimpsed across a wide expanse of lawn.

"We can't go in," I told her.

"Why not? It's ours now, ain't it? We got a court order."

"We have an order that allows us to access safe-deposit boxes in your sister's name. The house belongs to the estate, for which no permanent executor has yet been appointed—and remember, you're an heir only if there's no will leaving it all to somebody else."

"Shit."

Shelly rested a hand on her sister's shoulder. "When will we know about the safe-deposit box?"

"We'll walk the order around Santa Barbara tomorrow, hitting as many different banks as it takes. Finding the right bank, however, is only half the battle. We still don't have a key, which means we'll have to get the box drilled. That will involve internal red tape at the bank, assuming we can find the right bank."

"There are only five banking days left until the election," Mayday reminded us. "And that's if you count Saturday."

Pam's eyes were still on the house. "What can we all do to help?"

"Someone needs to claim Joan's body from the coroner's office and make the funeral arrangements."

"I'd like to do that," Shelly said.

"What if you and Marta deal with the coroner, while Pam and I drive back up here tomorrow?"

"You should book a hotel," Mayday said. "It could take several days."

"Can you babysit Sam? You and Shelly could stay at my place."

Mayday nodded.

"Okay, then," I said, pushing away from the gate. "I'd call that a plan."

TWENTY

ELECTION DAY MINUS SIX.

I found nothing in the *Times* about the autopsy report or the safe-deposit box, and so I carried my second cup of coffee down to the den to check the morning news shows, with Sam hopping up and settling onto the couch beside me.

GOLDILOCKS DEATH A HOMICIDE—L.A. CORONER read the crawl on CNN as the anchors dealt with lesser tales of war and famine and natural disaster. Then, at the top of the seven o'clock news hour, I got the whole enchilada:

In our top story, the Los Angeles County Coroner's office has ruled that the death of Jordan Mardian, originally thought to have been suicide, was in fact murder. Mardian was the woman at the center of the so-called Goldilocks Affair that has rocked the California Senate race ever since Democratic candidate Warren Burkett was found by Los Angeles Police in the bed of a stranger's home from which a priceless painting was missing. The coroner's report came to light yesterday in a court filing in Santa Barbara County, where heirs of the late art dealer sought permission to search for a safe-deposit box that they believe might contain clues to her killer's identity. We turn now to CBS News special correspondent Terina Webb for the latest.

Terina was back at the bridge. It was a live shot, with

freeway traffic droning overhead. She wore a belted trench coat, Brian Williams style.

The latest bombshell to alter the California political landscape landed yesterday afternoon, exactly one week before the election, when lawyers for the family of the late Jordan Mardian filed with the court in Santa Barbara County a copy of the coroner's autopsy report from Los Angeles, which concludes that the forty-year-old art dealer's death was in fact homicide, the result of a blow to the back of her skull with a heavy object. The coroner's findings suggest that Mardian's body was then thrown from the Colorado Street Bridge here in Pasadena in an effort to conceal the true cause of death. What's more, the Santa Barbara Superior Court filing alleges that the deceased, whose real name was Joan Marsden, left clues to her killer's identity in a safe-deposit box. Los Angeles attorney Jack MacTaggart, who represents the Marsden family, yesterday won a court order allowing him to search the box for this potentially explosive new evidence. MacTaggart, you may recall, also represented Democratic candidate Warren Burkett when the painting that had gone missing from the Bloomfield residence on October fourteenth turned up in a campaign video shot at the home of Republican candidate Larry Archer. Neither the Burkett nor Archer campaign has yet weighed in on these new revelations, while MacTaggart has been unavailable for comment. For CBS News, this is Terina Webb, reporting from Pasadena.

I switched off the TV and powered on my phone. There were eighteen new e-mail messages, all from media outlets, all within the past hour.

The big dogs were running again. Only this time, I was the rabbit.

The phone vibrated in my hand, and I read the caller ID.

"Hey."

"Are you watching? We're the lead story on every network, and they all mention you by name." Mayday sounded more concerned than excited.

"I know. Mission accomplished."

"I hope you know what you're doing, Jack."

"What's the matter?"

"I don't know. It's just that, now that we have the order, I wish we'd been more circumspect. You're going to have reporters following you everywhere."

I moved to the front window and peeked through the blinds. The street outside was empty.

"Nobody here yet."

"Just the same, maybe we should meet at my place."

The phone vibrated, and again I checked the ID.

"I need to take this. I'll be at your place at nine."

I dropped Mayday and took the call from Terina Webb.

"MacTaggart."

"Are you watching any of this? I'm on every fucking network in the country!"

"I just saw you on CNN. The trench coat was a nice touch."

"You need to come on camera, Jack. I can get us a deal with Fox. Ten grand apiece for an hour's work downtown. You'll be finished before lunch. Wait a minute."

She lowered the phone and spoke to somebody there. The freeway traffic sounded heavier.

"I need to run. What do you say?"

"Pass. I'd like to, but I have other plans."

"Never say never, Jack. I'll talk to you later—and when you find that box, you'd better call me first!"

The phone vibrated again as I was rinsing the breakfast dishes.

"Hi."

"Hey, you." Regan Fife sounded sleepy. "I just spoke with Marta. When do we leave for Santa Barbara?"

"We?"

"Heck, yes. I feel a cold coming on, and I have two weeks of sick leave in the bank."

"If you mean that, I could really use your help. We can take Bernie along and split into two teams and cover more ground."

"Where do I sign up?"

"Marta's condo, nine o'clock. Ask her to call Bernadette. Do you have the address?"

"I'll see you there."

The phone rang twice more while I shaved. It rang a third time while I dressed, and again as I loaded my briefcase. I checked my watch. It was 8:10.

I dialed 411 and made my request to the robotic operator, then waited through three rings before a woman answered.

"Santa Barbara Police Department, how may I direct your call?"

"I'd like to speak with whoever's in charge of the Catherine Orlov arson investigation. My name is Mac-Taggart. I'm a lawyer here in Los Angeles."

"Hold please."

I sat on the bed and waited. Sam brought a toy and placed it beside me.

A man came on the line. "This is Detective Sergeant Lillevick."

"This is Jack MacTaggart. I'm a lawyer in L.A. who—"

"I know who you are."

"Then maybe you know I have a court order allowing me entry into any safe-deposit box rented in the name of Joan Marsden. That's Jordan Mardian to you, Catherine Orlov's employer. Or should I say Catherine Whitaker?"

"It's Orlov, and I'm listening."

"I went by the Mardian home yesterday, and the place is under seal. I'd like to get inside."

There was a brief silence as he weighed the pros and cons. Which was worse, he had to be thinking, an out-of-town lawyer nosing into his investigation, or said lawyer calling him uncooperative on national television?

"That might be arranged," he finally said. "When?"

"How about 10:30 today?"

"All right. I'll meet you at the front gate."

FIVE OVERNIGHT BAGS lined the wall of Mayday's living room when I arrived. Bernie looked like Garbo, in big shades and a head scarf, while Mayday, in a blue business suit, poured coffee for Regan, whose hair was still wet from the shower. Mayday nodded to a printout on the table.

The screen grab from Google showed fourteen different banks in and around Santa Barbara, and most had multiple branches.

"That should keep you busy," she said.

I studied the list. "We have a ten-thirty appointment

at Joan's house with the SBPD. That might help narrow the field."

"Hot damn," Pam said as she emerged from the bedroom, her sister trailing behind her. Both women were dressed in jeans and cowboy boots.

Regan tasted her coffee. "What's our deployment?"

"Marta and Shelly stay here to handle the coroner's office, while the rest of us head up to Santa Barbara. We'll take two cars—Bernie rides with me, Pam with you. You can follow me to Joan's house in Montecito. If we get separated on the way up, we'll meet where we parked before, at the lot in the village. How's your gas?"

"Full."

I turned to Shelly. "I'm sorry I won't be there to deal with the coroner, but I can assure you that you're in good hands with Marta."

I looked at Mayday.

"Don't forget Joan's personal effects at the Police Administration Building. You might want to call ahead and talk to Alvarez. Some of it may be evidence, like maybe the car and the clothes, but probably not the jewelry. Just try to get what you can."

I kept the top up and the pedal down, and we made it to Montecito Village in just over an hour. Bernie kept her earbuds in the whole way, alternately dozing and nodding along with her music. I listened to KNX News Radio, which reported newly issued press releases from both the Archer and Burkett campaigns. Both were shocked to learn of the coroner's findings. Both offered their condolences to the family of the deceased. Both pledged their full cooperation to the authorities.

I saw no tail, either leaving Pasadena or waiting for us in Montecito, and I felt silly even to be looking.

I swung into the village parking lot and lowered my window as Regan rolled her Toyota up beside me. I checked my watch.

"We're right on schedule. There's a restroom in the drugstore if anyone needs to stop."

She looked to Pam. "We're good here," she said.

"Okay then."

A blue Chevy Caprice idled outside the gate leading to Joan Marsden's driveway. A man in a sport coat alighted as we pulled in beside it. He was tall and blond, with a rugged face and piercing blue eyes.

"Look," Bernie said, finally removing her earbuds, "a friggin' surf Nazi."

I lowered my window at the man's approach. He appeared annoyed.

"I wasn't expecting a parade."

"I'm Jack MacTaggart. We spoke on the phone. This is my assistant, Ms. Catalano. In the other car are Officer Regan Fife and Pamela Sylbert, who is the cospecial administrator of her late sister's estate."

I gave him my card, and he frowned as he read it. He leaned in and looked at Bernie.

"Okay, MacTaggart, here are the ground rules. We stay together at all times. Nothing is touched without my permission, and nothing is removed without a court order. You've got a half hour, and then I've got to be somewhere. Any questions?"

"Yes, sir, I have a question," Bernie said, removing her shades as she leaned over the console. "If I have to pee, do I need a court order? Or do I just not flush?"

Detective Lillevick straightened, looking a little wounded. "Geez," he said. He turned on his heel and pulled a penknife from his pocket and sliced the gate sticker in half. Then he squeezed through, and must have pressed a button on the controller, because the gate swung quietly inward. We waited for him to return to his car, where he restarted his engine and led us down the drive.

The house was pretty much as Terina Webb had described it: Old California in style, probably dating from the fifties. The landscaping was an attractive mix of tall eucalyptus and palm trees, with colorful splashes of flax and lavender and lantana. The front door was arched and ornamented in heavy iron hardware, which the detective, setting down his briefcase, proceeded to unlock.

"Where'd the key come from?"

He examined the house key before pocketing it. "We found it under a pot, out back by the pool."

The interior looked pristine, as though Joan had bought the house from its original owner, or maybe from the owner's estate. The walls were white plaster, and the floors were tiled in warm terra cotta. There were coved ceilings and a beehive fireplace with a heavy wooden mantel. Beyond the living room was a dining nook backlit by French sliders leading out to a kidney-shaped swimming pool.

The furniture was mostly heavy wood and leather, and the tables were all dusty. It was, I thought, a fairly masculine space. Even the artwork—large landscapes of mountains and meadows and drooping eucalyptus trees—seemed more in tune with a male sensibility.

Not that Pam minded. She moved as though through a dream, her head on a swivel and her fingers tracing the furniture. When she stopped short at the fireplace,

I followed her gaze to the mantel, where a framed photo rested amid carved tribal figurines.

She turned pleadingly to the detective, who nodded. She took the photo down carefully, and I moved to stand behind her. The color was faded, and the photo itself was a little fuzzy, as though it had been enlarged to fit the eight-by-ten silver frame. In it, three young girls posed in size order by the curved fender of an old pickup truck.

"Goddamn," Pamela whispered.

The detective checked his watch. "Were you looking for anything in particular?"

"Office?"

He led the way, through the dining nook and down a short hallway. Halfway to the kitchen was a bump-out in the wall into which a desk had been custom built. This had probably been a hutch or linen closet, and appeared to be the home's only modification. There was a black Aeron chair, plus three electrical outlets, a telephone jack, a small printer, and a still-blinking broadband modem box.

"No computers?"

Lillevick shook his head. "Or laptop or PDA."

I sat in the chair and opened the desk drawers. There were office supplies and printer paper and envelopes and stamps. I sank back in the chair.

"What about mail? Any bank statements or bills?"

"I thought you might want that. Come on."

He led Regan and me back to the dining nook, while Bernie and Pam wandered off to explore the bedrooms. He swung his briefcase onto the table and popped the latches and removed two bulging manila envelopes.

"These were in the house when we first searched

it," he said, handing me the larger bundle. "The other is what's come in since. We send an officer out to the mailbox every day."

I scraped a chair and sat, and Regan watched over my shoulder. Down the hallway, a toilet flushed.

"Am I under arrest?" Bernie's voice echoed, and both women giggled.

Disregarding the junk mail and flyers and clothing catalogues, of which there were several, I examined the first bundle. It contained two art magazines, a Sotheby's auction catalogue, the latest issues of *Vanity Fair* and *Vogue,* gas and telephone bills, and a Citi credit card statement. I returned everything to the envelope but the telephone bill and the Citi statement.

"My clients will probably have to deal with these."

The detective shrugged. "We've gone through every call and every charge. Nothing helpful."

There were voices outside. Pam and Bernie were circling the pool.

I opened the second of the detective's two envelopes. Inside were more of the same: magazines, catalogues, and bills…and a bank statement from the Montecito Bank and Trust branch on Coast Village Road.

"When did this arrive?"

"Yesterday."

The envelope had already been opened. I removed the statement inside.

It was a checking account in the name of Jordan Mardian. The balances were nominal, and the activity minimal. None of the previous month's checks was for more than three hundred dollars, and all were in odd amounts. There was no charge for a safe-deposit box.

"Household bills is what we figured," Lillevick said.

"We'll get a warrant for the checks and deposit slips, but I'm not holding my breath."

"What about the business mail?" Regan asked.

"The mailbox at her studio didn't burn, and the post office still delivers there. We pick it up every day. No bank statement yet. It could be they banked electronically. We're working on it."

From outside came a splashing sound. We all looked up to see Bernie and Pam, both stripped to their underwear, both of them doing the backstroke.

"Christ," the detective said.

TWENTY-ONE

THE COAST VILLAGE ROAD branch of Montecito Bank and Trust was back down by the freeway. I left Bernie in the car with the top down, drying her hair in the sun, while Pam and Regan went ahead to the next name on the list, which was the Santa Barbara Bank and Trust branch, on Anacapa Street downtown.

The manager, when I finally got to him, was a thin, nervous sort with reading glasses perched low on his nose. He leaned forward in his chair to reinspect the court order, then looked at me again before swiveling to his computer keyboard. He typed with two fingers. After a minute or so he found what he was after and frowned at the screen. His hands flapped like wounded doves as he spoke.

"I'm afraid there are no safe-deposit boxes associated with that account, Mr. MacTaggart. Nor is there any other account in Ms. Mardian's name, or in the names of Joan Marsden or Jordan Mardian Design. I'm sorry I can't be of further assistance."

His eyes flicked to the office door behind me. Longingly, I thought. I settled back in my chair.

"Did you know her? Jordan Mardian?"

"Know her? Well of course I— Wait. What are you suggesting?"

The doves, poised for flight, had moved to the edge of his desk. I nodded to his computer.

"Does that database include all your branches?"

"Yes, it most certainly does."

"You're quite certain of that?"

The doves settled as he peered over his glasses. I thanked him and gathered up my papers.

"DID YOU KNOW that Pam grew up in a trailer park?" Bernie said as we exited the freeway at State Street. "She never had a backyard or a swimming pool. Not even the blow-up kind. Or a pet. Not even a guinea pig. Doesn't that suck?"

"Not for the guinea pig."

"She said she plans to fence off the backyard and buy herself a pony and offer free rides to the neighborhood children."

"I'm sure she'll be a big hit with the homeowners' association."

My phone vibrated. The caller ID read M. SUAREZ.

"Camarillo State Hospital, Warden speaking."

Mayday laughed. "That bad?"

"I've witnessed worse. How goes it down there?"

"We're just leaving the coroner's office. They made Shelly identify the body, and she's still a little shaken. We're heading to the PAB next," she said, referring to the Police Administration Building. "Detective Alvarez wants to meet us in person."

"Don't let him push you around. And if he asks you where we got the coroner's report, tell him I found it while digging for bones. Tell him you find all sorts of things if you just dig a little."

"How about I tell him it's attorney work product?"

"Even better. I've already acquainted him with the

concept—and remind him it's supposed to be a public record."

"What about you, any luck so far?"

"One bank down and many yet to go."

"Okay, I'll talk to you later."

Regan and Pam were waiting for us on the sidewalk outside Santa Barbara Bank, talking with two guys on a green motorbike parked at the curb, one of whom cradled a camera with a telephoto lens.

"Shit."

All the other spots were taken, so I pulled the Benz abreast of a car parked just behind the bike. Regan saw me and trotted over to the passenger-side window.

"Any luck?"

"No. We can cross off all branches of Montecito Bank and Trust."

"Same for Santa Barbara Bank and Trust."

I nodded toward the bikers, one of whom was up and walking our way.

"Friends of yours?"

"They had the bank staked out. They followed us in and watched from the lobby. I think they're freelance photographers."

The guy with the camera stopped in the middle of the street, lifted the lens, and aimed it at my driver's-side window. I turned from Regan and gave him a full-face target. He clicked off a staccato burst as a horn honked and a car swerved in the street behind him. I waved him over.

He was young, early twenties, and wore green-and-black motorcycle leathers. His long hair was matted with sweat from the helmet he'd left on the bike. He looked a little like Thor, the God of Thunder.

"What's up?"

"How ya doin'?" he replied in an accent that definitely wasn't Norse. He hefted his camera. "Thanks for the shot."

"Will that do it, or are we dating now?"

He looked to his partner, still on the bike.

"Depends, I suppose."

"On what?"

He shrugged. "You know. Things."

I leaned over to retrieve a roll of bills from my pocket and peeled off five twenties.

"That bike can't use much gas."

"Oh, man," he said, eyeing the bills. "Haven't you heard? Nixon resigned, Dad. We can't even eat lunch on that."

The passenger door opened and Bernie stepped out of the Benz and started down the sidewalk toward the bike. Her boyfriend Lance, as I recalled, rode a Harley.

"First tell me what it is I'm paying for," I said. "You got friends at the other banks?"

He shook his head. "No friends in this game, Dad. Just competitors."

Bernie was chatting up the other biker now, admiring his machine. He was standing and pointing and describing its features.

"Tell me something. You ever been to San Marino?"

"San Marino?" Thor glanced back toward the bike. He straightened. "Hey!"

Bernie was walking quickly. The biker was cussing and backing his machine onto its kickstand as Thor moved to intercept Bernie, and as Regan moved to intercept Thor with her badge held up in his face.

"Hold it right there," she said to him as Bernie opened the passenger door and I put the Benz into gear.

"Go!" Bernie said as the Benz lurched forward, swerving to avoid Thor. The biker shouted something as we zoomed past, with Pam watching from the sidewalk openmouthed as we took the next corner with tires squealing.

Bernie twirled the motorbike's keys on her finger.

"Dipshit should have taken the hundred," she said, palming them and rattling them like dice before flinging them out the window.

WE MET, AS AGREED, at the Best Western in Carpinteria. It was almost five o'clock when Bernie and I arrived, and Pam and Regan were already seated in the lobby as we entered from the parking lot. They looked tired, and they looked discouraged.

I withdrew my license and credit card and set them on the counter. The woman took them and fiddled with her computer and eventually laid two check-in folders on the counter. "MacTaggart. One king and one double," she said.

"We'll need a third room. A king if you've got it."

She frowned at her monitor. "I'm afraid we're all booked tonight. It's the wine festival, you know."

I turned and beckoned Bernie with one finger.

"How about swapping the king for another double?"

The woman, still frowning, tapped at her keyboard.

"What's wrong?" Bernie asked.

"You booked only two rooms, that's what, and one with a king-sized bed."

"The king's yours. Nobody told me Regan was coming."

The woman shook her head. "I'm sorry, sir, but there's nothing we can do. We're fully booked."

"Hold on," Bernie said, her smile spreading. "Don't tell me you and Regan aren't..." She bumped her fists together.

WE ALL ATE dinner at a steakhouse called Sly's, where we compared notes and concluded we were roughly halfway through the list. The place was loud and jammed with tipsy wine-tasters, and my head had begun to throb.

Mayday called to confirm success with Chico Alvarez, at least as far as the jewelry was concerned, and Bernie explained the motel snafu to Regan, which the latter shrugged off with a smile. My headache was improving already.

A television hung over the bar, and I could see the screen from our table, reflected in the polished glass of a framed wall photo. It was a news channel, possibly CNN, and there was a yellow BREAKING NEWS banner splashed across the screen.

"Excuse me," I said, standing and making my way toward the bar, which was packed with ruddy-faced couples swirling and sniffing and blathering on about notes of dark plum and raspberry. The sound on the TV was low, but the triple split-screen image of Wolf Blitzer, David Gergen, and Terina Webb was still pretty jarring.

"Here, you should try this," a woman at the bar insisted, handing me her glass. "Can you taste the anise?"

"Could you turn that up for a second?" I asked the bartender, who found a remote and pointed it at the screen as I dutifully sniffed the woman's wineglass.

...this close to the election could be devastating to

the Archer campaign, Gergen was saying, *but I hasten to add that these are merely allegations at this point.*

Terina jumped in.

Wolf, my sources tell me that the violations are wide-spread and systemic, and that a formal complaint has already been lodged with the Federal Election Commission. The Burkett campaign has called a press event for tomorrow morning at which we're told a summary will be released that documents hundreds of illegal corporate contributions funneled through straw-man donors. If proven, federal indictments could very well follow.

"What is it?" Regan asked, appearing beside me.

I returned the woman's wineglass.

"Larry Archer," I told her, "just caught a whiff of anise."

REGAN TOSSED HER gym bag onto the bed. She unclipped her holster and unzipped the bag and tucked her gun inside, removing a toiletry case and what looked like an oversized T-shirt.

"Okay if I go first?" she asked, sidling past me toward the bathroom.

I sat on the bed. It was a standard-size room with a matching nightstands-and-armoire combo and little else. The carpet was shag, and the framed vineyard poster above the headboard was slightly off-kilter. The sliding glass behind the curtain faced onto a little land-scaped courtyard where, despite the late hour, I heard children's voices squealing.

It was, in short, a perfectly serviceable motel room, but a far cry from the sylvan bower of my seductive imagination.

The toilet flushed, and water ran in the bathroom.

To make matters worse, I'd packed no nightclothes—just a small tote bag in my briefcase with a toothbrush and deodorant and a single change of underwear.

The fan died, and the bathroom door opened. Regan's T-shirt read RIO HONDO POLICE ACADEMY. It came almost to her knees, but not quite. She carried her clothes in a bundle under her arm that included, I noticed, her bra. These she stuffed into the gym bag, arranging her gun atop the pile.

She sat on the bed beside me.

"Is this awkward?" she asked.

"Ever shot a man for snoring?"

"Never had to, but there's a first time for everything."

I excused myself to the bathroom, and just as I was uncapping the toothbrush, studying my face in the mirror, Regan tapped on the bathroom door.

"Your phone's ringing!" she said.

I stepped out to answer it. It was Mayday again on the caller ID.

"Hello?"

"We have a slight problem."

There was urgency in her voice, and Regan read it on my face.

"What's going on?"

"The police arrived ten minutes ago. Here, at your house. They have a search warrant."

"*What*? What are they looking for?"

She spoke to somebody there, and Sam barked, and I heard a voice that might have belonged to Chico Alvarez.

"They're looking for the Jordan Mardian murder weapon," Mayday said when she came back on the line, "and they think they've just found it."

TWENTY-TWO

THAT I WASN'T stopped for speeding was itself a kind of miracle, since I covered the distance from Santa Barbara to San Marino in world-record time.

I found the white Crown Victoria in my driveway, with a patrol unit parked in the street behind Mayday's Lexus. My garage door was open, and lights shone inside both the garage and the house. I parked behind the black-and-white and trotted up the walk.

Sam ran barking and skidding to a halt at my arrival, then did a U-turn back to the living room. There I found Mayday and Shelly on the couch in their nightclothes, with Madden and Alvarez sitting opposite. All were drinking coffee. Two uniformed LAPD officers were standing by the fireplace with folded arms. One of them started toward me as I entered.

"Mr. MacTaggart? We'll need you—"

"Hold on," Alvarez said wearily. He made a gesture toward the empty chair. "Sit down, asshole."

The search warrant and an inventory form lay on the coffee table next to Warren Burkett's belt, still in its Ziploc baggie. I read the warrant application as I sat.

"What anonymous letter?" I asked.

"We'll get to that," Alvarez said. "You want coffee?"

"If I wanted coffee, I'd get it myself. From my own coffeemaker in my own kitchen."

He showed his palms. "Okay, calm down."

"What's this bullshit about a murder weapon?"

I glanced at Mayday and Shelly. Shelly's hair was up in rollers the size of beer cans. She wore a faded robe over a pink flannel nightdress, while Mayday wore black silk pj's with little black slippers.

Alvarez looked to the fireplace and nodded. The uniform crossed to the kitchen, studying me as he went. I heard the front door open and close.

"We're gonna have to take a ride," Alvarez said. "Afraid that can't be helped."

"Am I under arrest?"

"Damn it!" he said, and Sam's ears perked. "I'm sick of this legal bullshit! We've got an open homicide here, and you may have the murder weapon in your garage."

"What are you talking about?"

It was Madden who answered, his tone conversational.

"We found the back door to your garage unlocked. Is that unusual?"

I shook my head. "There's nothing in there of any value, and it's not that kind of neighborhood."

The front door opened again, and the uniform returned. He was carrying an ax. It was an old-fashioned tool with a curved wooden handle and a tapering head of rusty iron. It was wrapped in a clear plastic sleeve, taped, and labeled. He held it out in both hands as Alvarez spoke.

"Recognize this?"

My mind flashed to my last meeting with Angela Archer. *I heard you got the ax.* Again I shook my head. "Whatever stuff is in that garage came with the house. I don't remember seeing any ax."

"You'll be interested to know that your prints aren't on it. Or anybody else's prints, for that matter."

We shared a look.

"Yeah," he said, setting down his mug, "but right now you have two choices. Either you come down in the front seat and give us a voluntary statement, or you come down in back and get booked. It's your call, counselor."

I SAT IN an interview room for the better part of an hour before Alvarez finally returned. He had a manila folder file under his arm and two foam cups that he held by the rims with his fingertips. Those he set down carefully, pushing one in my direction as the door snapped closed behind him.

"I warned you to keep your nose out of this case," he said as he sat.

"That you did."

"But you didn't listen."

"I have a new client."

"So I've heard."

He set the file folder on the table between us. He flipped it open. Inside was a single typewritten sheet in a clear plastic sleeve. He turned the folder around. The letter was undated.

The publicity hound so-called lawyer Jack Mac-Taggart is playing a double game and as a CON-CERNED CITIZEN I wish to report that he plans to blackmail somebody and make LOTS OF MONEY. I went to his house on Sycamore Lane in San Marino and he showed me a man's belt in a plastic bag that he said has INCRIMINATING

*FINGERPRINTS on it. He also has in his garage
an ax that he said is the MURDER WEAPON
used to kill that woman who fell off the bridge.
He told me he will soon be FILTHY RICH and
that he doesn't care who gets hurt. I feel it is my
duty to report these things to the police, but I do
not wish to become involved.*

"'Wish to report'? 'Do not wish to become involved'?"

"Yeah." Alvarez nodded. "I know. Educated."

I leaned back in my chair. "And you got a warrant
with *this*?"

Alvarez closed the file. "We could corroborate the
belt. That made the rest of it credible—which it was,
apparently."

"Where'd it come from?" I asked, nodding toward
the folder.

"Never mind that. Let's talk about your whereabouts
on Friday evening, October the eighteenth."

"Oh, bullshit."

He gave me his dead-eyed stare. He blew on his coffee and sipped. Then he looked up at the ceiling vent
and made a slicing motion with his finger.

"The letter turned up in an envelope late this afternoon." He checked his watch. "Make that yesterday afternoon. On the windshield of a patrol unit parked on
Broadway. It's been through Trace Analysis and Questioned Documents."

"And?"

"And nothing. It's clean."

"Gloves?"

He nodded.

"What about the ax?"

"FIU found what appears to be blood residue on the blunt end of the head. It's at Serology as we speak."

With the exception of Sam, my house had been empty since 8:30 in the morning, when I'd left for Mayday's condo. Whoever had done this had planted the ax first, then typed out the letter, and then delivered it. They'd had to have concocted the scheme quickly, soon after hearing the morning news, then wiped down the murder weapon, traveled to San Marino, and charmed their way past Sam. Then a quick trip downtown to find an empty police cruiser parked near the Civic Center.

They'd had, in short, quite the busy day.

"None of your neighbors saw any activity at the house until late afternoon, when the lady next door saw the Lexus pull up," Alvarez said, reading my thoughts. "Then again, she said she was gone most of the day. And your dog isn't talking."

"Whoever did this knew about the belt. That narrows things quite a bit." I gave him a meaningful look. "Or does it?"

"Try this on for size. The Mardian woman made trouble for your client. You ran her prints, so you knew who she was and where to find her. When her records burned up in the fire, you were there, and when that job was done, you got a nice fat paycheck. Then the murder weapon turns up in your garage, and now you're on some kind of a treasure hunt for her safe-deposit box. It fits pretty good, you ask me."

"It fits like a cheap suit. Joan Marsden's death didn't help Burkett; it hurt him. And I didn't know her identity until Saturday morning, after she was already dead. Officer Fife can corroborate that. I didn't know who Jordan Mardian was until you told me, and why would I kill her in Burkett's backyard? Why would I keep the murder weapon at my house? And why would I wipe off the prints but not the blood? Sorry, but you'd be laughed out of court with a case like that. Even Slew isn't that stupid."

He didn't respond.

"Speaking of stupid," I added, "how's he liking his pal Archer these days?"

Alvarez cleared his throat. "The district attorney wants you to know that he's appalled by recent developments in the campaign, and that the full weight of his office will be brought to bear in rooting out political corruption wherever he finds it."

"He make you memorize that?"

Alvarez sipped at his coffee again, then set it back on the table. "Okay, so you don't like my story. Tell me a better one."

"Who else knew about the belt? Besides Burkett and Harwood"—here I looked up at the video camera in the ceiling vent—"and you and Madden and Slewzyski?"

He didn't like the question, but to his credit, he didn't try to dodge it.

"Okay, so maybe the D.A. mentioned it to Archer. That opens the field, doesn't it?"

"It does, but let's not lose sight of the timing. The whole world knows I'm looking for a safe-deposit box that might lead to the killer. I thought if I made that public, the killer might try to stop me. He might yet, but first he did something I wasn't expecting. He tried to undermine my credibility, to make it look like I'm out to hang a frame. That was clever. He even gave up the murder weapon to do it. That tells me something."

"Like what?"

"Like maybe there really is a safe-deposit box, and he's afraid of what's inside."

Alvarez tapped the folder with a finger. "Where'd you hear about this box? I notice your court papers didn't say."

"Sorry, but that's attorney work product."

In the bad old days, this is when the rubber hose would've come out, but today, Chico Alvarez only sighed.

"The D.A.'s obtaining warrants for all the banks up in Santa Barbara. I don't think he likes the idea of you upstaging him on national TV. Matter of fact, I don't think he likes you at all."

"That's why you're a detective, Chico."

Alvarez tried not to smile. He looked over his shoulder and made a circular motion with his finger.

"Okay, Mr. MacTaggart. Let's start with your whereabouts on the afternoon of October the eighteenth…"

THE SUN WAS already up by the time I steered the Benz onto Sycamore Lane. I parked in the street behind Mayday's Lexus, which was itself parked behind two strange automobiles and a TV news van.

I never thought I'd be happy to see reporters outside my house.

They'd surrounded my car before I could get the door open, shouting questions and thrusting microphones into my face. I ignored them all, cutting across the lawn under the big sycamore tree. The questions formed an overlapping jumble that included catchwords like "murder weapon" and "safe-deposit box" and "search warrant." The last question, the one that rang in my ears as I closed the front door behind me, was "Did you kill Jordan Mardian?"

Mayday and Shelly were sitting out back eating pancakes. Mayday looked up as I appeared in the doorway, and Sam came wriggling over to greet me.

"Any of those left? I'm starving."

"Comin' right up," Shelly said, standing and bustling past me into the house. I crossed to the chair she'd vacated.

"They've been out there since sunrise," Mayday said, her look one of maternal concern. "I think they were expecting you to come out."

I set my phone on the table and touched the MAIL icon. There were forty-seven new messages.

"You should have let me come with you last night."

"You didn't miss much. Just Alvarez, checking the boxes. He did show me the letter, though. Whoever wrote it knew about the belt. Problem is, it seems like everybody knows about the belt."

"And the blood?"

"Serology came in just as I was leaving. It's the murder weapon all right."

She processed this, absently stroking Sam on the head.

"I promised Alvarez that if we find the safe-deposit box, he gets the first call."

"Are you in trouble?"

"I don't think so. Whoever did this overplayed his hand. The letter accused me of plotting a blackmail scheme. It was a good idea, hanging a cloud over whatever we might find"—I nodded toward the front of the house—"but tipping the press was a bridge too far. If Alvarez or Slew had any doubts before, they have to realize now it was all a setup. Someone's laying a nice thick mattress for whatever's in that box."

She didn't respond.

"What?"

"It's not helping your reputation any. Or the firm's."

"I know, and I'm sorry. How's the client handling it?"

Her eyes moved to the door. "She doesn't think you're involved, if that's what you mean. I explained to her that it was what we expected, the killer showing his hand. I think she thinks we live like this all the time, with cops and dead bodies and murder weapons and reporters. She can be flinty, but she's a little naïve."

Sam had wandered over to the garage. He sniffed at the yellow tape on the rear door and lifted a leg. My sentiments exactly.

"Look, Marta, I know that reputation is important, especially for a new law firm trying to make a name, but there are some things that take precedence over reputation. Like seeking truth and busting your ass to do justice, whatever the odds, whatever the stakes. I know that sounds corny, but that's how I roll, and that's how I'd like our firm to roll. Because if you let things like propriety and decorum and concern for reputation interfere with that core mission, then what's the point?"

She looked into the half distance. She smiled.

"What?"

"You sounded like Russ just then."

I lifted her hand and kissed it. "Have we heard from Santa Barbara yet?"

"I was going to call Regan"—she checked her watch—"but it's only seven-thirty."

My phone vibrated just as Shelly returned from the

house with a steaming plate of empty calories. I nudged the phone toward Mayday. "Speak of the devil."

I fed my face while Shelly and I listened to Mayday's end of the conversation. She ended it with "Okay, I'll let you know. I think he should be in bed, but he never listens to me."

"I listen to you. I should be in bed. Come to think of it, I should be in bed with Regan."

Mayday frowned her disapproval. "She wants to know if you're coming back up."

I pushed the plate away, clean.

"I might as well, if I can lose the fan club out front. With two teams working, we can cover the rest of the banks today and maybe beat Slew to the punch. Chico says he's out getting search warrants."

"What if you don't find the right bank?" Shelly wanted to know.

It was a good question. It was now Thursday morning, with only four business days left until the election. Even if we were to find the box today, getting into it by Tuesday would be problematic, and getting into it by Wednesday would be too late.

"Don't worry, we'll find it." I patted her shoulder. "Trust me, I'm a lawyer."

TWENTY-THREE

By 8:30 THE SCENE out front had expanded to seven cars and two news vans, with a dozen bleary-eyed reporters standing in clusters drinking coffee and checking their watches. There were no paparazzi bikes as yet, and none of the cars looked capable of tracking me all the way to Santa Barbara. Or to Wilshire Boulevard, for that matter, where the Burkett press conference was scheduled for nine o'clock.

"I'm going now," I told the ladies. "Where's my ax?"

"I'll take Sam to the office," Mayday said, watching the sidewalk through the kitchen window. "Today's Halloween, you know. I don't suppose you bought any candy?"

"Would you let your kids near the home of an ax murderer?"

"Good point. Call me when you get to Santa Barbara."

I donned a ball cap and shades, but not for the benefit of the reporters outside. For them I had a big smile and a "No comment," and I was into my car and gone before they could shoulder a video camera.

None of them tried to follow me.

I listened to news radio on the drive to L.A. The coverage was wall-to-wall campaign updates, with the late-breaking story of my so-called arrest bumping the Archer money-laundering scandal to second position.

There was no mention of the safe-deposit box, which suited me fine, since that message had already been delivered. All the stations I checked were standing by for live coverage of the Burkett press conference.

It was 9:15 when I finally found a parking space three blocks east of the Burkett campaign headquarters on Wilshire, and by then the event was under way. I'd heard the warm-up act on the radio, in the person of attorney Frederick J. Pollard of Plimpton, Simmons, and Stark, giving the assembled media a primer on campaign finance law. He was still going at it, with Burkett standing impatiently beside him, by the time I opened the big glass doors and slipped quietly into the room.

No heads turned, and nobody recognized me as I slouched against the side wall with my cap pulled low—nobody except Harwood, of course, who notices everything. The big man was standing by the door to the back office, and he gave me an imperceptible nod.

By the time Burkett took to the podium, the crowd was growing restless. He wasted no time in feeding them their sound bites, mentioning casino gambling, organized crime, money laundering, out-of-state influence, and "the pay-to-play culture of corruption so prevalent in Washington today." Unlike his new lawyer, he was brief and to the point, honoring the itinerant preacher's maxim that nobody gets religion after the first ten minutes.

At the conclusion of his prepared remarks, he gestured to a table up front on which were stacked copies of Max's report, which Burkett described as "a white paper highlighting some of the issues under discussion." He concluded by urging the media, which he called "the most powerful instrument of detection known to modern civilization," to undertake their own corroborative investigations.

Then he threw it open for questioning. The first question had nothing to do with his carefully orchestrated message, but pertained instead to a certain Sierra Madre attorney formerly in his employ. I slouched a little lower.

"Mr. MacTaggart is no longer representing me," Burkett said gravely. "I'm afraid I know nothing more than what's been reported, and I certainly hope those reports are wrong."

When the second and third questions proved to be in the same vein, Scott Tully lumbered to the podium with a hand raised and thanked everyone for attending, again drawing their attention to the table laden with neatly stacked documents. Reporters moved toward the table as Burkett retreated to the back office, and Harwood made a faint gesture with his head before following his boss through the door.

I was first out the front door, back on the sidewalk and around the corner before anyone noticed my presence. I counted doorways in the alley. I knocked loudly, and when a young staffer answered, I brushed past him before he could protest.

The room, buzzing with excitement, fell silent.

"Excuse me," I said, "isn't this the Kabbalah Center?"

"Get him out of here before the press sees him!" Tully commanded, and Harwood stepped forward with a hand on my chest, easing me backward toward the alley door.

The same staffer who'd opened the door now opened it again, and Harwood and I danced a Fred-and-Ginger into the alley while Burkett, whose face I was watching, looked as though he'd seen a ghost.

Maybe Jordan Mardian's ghost.

"You're not welcome here," Harwood said a little too loudly, slipping his free hand into his jacket and tucking an envelope into mine. Then he returned to the office, glanced once over his shoulder, and slammed the door with a bang.

I DROVE TO Santa Barbara with the LAPD forensics reports strewn in my lap, until a drifting honk-and-swerve near Oxnard convinced me to focus on matters at hand. What I'd seen to that point had only served to confirm the coroner's conclusions, both as to cause of death and absence of other contributing factors. I'd get a second opinion later from Mayday, the doctor's daughter and erstwhile premed major.

As I approached the Carpinteria exits, I again noticed a white Honda hatchback—the same Honda hatchback I'd seen thirty minutes earlier, back near Santa Paula. It was still behind me, still following three cars back. I checked my mirrors and glanced around, then made a fast two-lane change, feinting toward the off-ramp. The Honda did likewise.

I punched up Regan on her cell. They were just leaving Wells Fargo and heading to the Bank of the West branch on State Street. They'd already struck out at B of A, she told me, and the list was growing shorter.

I found a parking spot on Carrillo, and as I stepped from the Benz with my neck craning for the Honda, I heard instead the familiar revving of a powerful Japanese motorbike. It screeched to a wobbling halt beyond the spot where Regan's Toyota was parked. The two hunched riders lifted their visors and spoke to one another. Then the driver walked the bike backward as the passenger swung his backpack into the narrow space between them.

I was expecting to see a camera, but it was a tire iron that Thor produced and rested on top of the pack. He removed his helmet and shook his blond hair loose.

I approached from their blind side. Thor was off the bike now and carrying the heavy tool close against his leg. He stood beside Regan's windshield and scanned the empty sidewalk. Then he raised his arm overhead.

I caught his wrist at its apex and bent his arm backward as the iron clattered to the pavement.

"Owww! Fuck!"

I kept on bending, lowering him to his knees as I watched his buddy back the bike onto its kickstand, then come at me with a gloved hand balled and cocked. I beat him to the punch, shooting a left jab to his sternum that knocked him backward onto the pavement.

"You're breaking my arm!" Thor protested as the bank's glass doors opened and Bernie, Pam, and Regan spilled onto the sidewalk.

Regan drew her gun. She circled the car and paused, then half-rolled the driver, who was gasping like a beached manatee, with her foot. She picked up the tire iron and reholstered her weapon.

"Are you okay?" she asked me.

I hauled Thor to his feet and bent him facedown on the hood of the Toyota. On the sidewalk, pedestrians had stopped to watch.

"I'm fine, but your car had a near miss."

"Police! Nobody move!" came a sharp voice from behind us, and we all turned to see a pair of plainclothes officers with LAPD shields aloft—Slewzyski's process servers—cutting through the traffic on State. "Break it up! Step away from the car!"

I did as instructed, setting Thor free. The officers, both young and earnest, drew up short and appeared momentarily lost. Regan showed them her badge, and as one of them inspected it, the other squinted at me and said, "Hey, aren't you MacTaggart?"

"That's right, and this is Officer Fife from the Sierra Madre PD."

Thor stood rubbing his elbow. The motorbike's driver, still on the pavement, was now sitting upright. "You broke my ribs," he said.

"No, but you're lucky I didn't. Here."

I hauled him to his feet, and he stood leaning on the car in front of us. The cops, meanwhile, were stowing their shields and scratching their heads and refereeing the finger-pointing melee that quickly ensued. So I alone witnessed Bernie stroll casually toward the motorcycle, remove the keys from the ignition, and walk them over to the sewer grate at the gutter.

WE EXITED THE last bank on our list, American Riviera, at four o'clock sharp. The ocean breeze had risen, and masked children had sprouted like so many weeds on the downtown sidewalks, their plastic costumes flapping under the gaze of trailing adults. The L.A. cops had long since left to execute their warrants, plowing ground we'd already plowed, and a deflating sense of finality settled over our little group of four.

We looked at one another. Or, more accurately, the others all looked at me.

I shrugged.

"I'm still certain the box exists. The problem is, if it's not in Santa Barbara, it could be anywhere."

"Maybe another bank statement will show up in the mail," Regan suggested.

"Maybe." I checked my watch. "Meanwhile, I'm asleep on my feet. Shelly's at Marta's condo now, and so is Sam. Let's all meet there at six, and we can discuss Plan B."

"What's Plan B?" Bernie asked as she eased the Benz into southbound traffic on the 101 Freeway, just in time for rush hour. I settled deeper into the passenger seat with my eyes closed.

"I don't know. Let me sleep on it."

We rode in silence for another few minutes before she spoke again.

"The reason I ask is that Pam and I were up last night, you know, kind of girl-talking. Did you know that Lester, her husband, is a drywall contractor who hurt his back and hasn't worked for almost three years?"

"I did not know that."

"And how much could a drywaller make in the first place, even when he's working full time?"

"Probably not much."

"Exactly." The car swerved, and Bernie laid on the horn. "Asshole!"

I opened an eye. She'd tilted the mirror to check her makeup, and now she adjusted it again, slipping her lipstick into the purse in her lap. I checked the side-view mirror. Nary a motorbike nor a Honda in sight.

"Anyway, she said something that got me to thinking."

"How did that feel?"

"All right, never mind."

"Sorry. Go on, I'm listening."

Another long pause.

"She asked me if inheritance was community property."

"It isn't."

"That's what I told her. Then what she said was that if she inherited a bunch of money from her sister, she was gonna drop Lester like a bad habit, on account of him being a nonworking breed and her being sick of supporting the both of them. Which kind of surprised me, because I didn't think she worked. When I asked her about that, she got all quiet. Said she didn't mean working like a job-job, but just doing housework and stuff. Which didn't make any sense."

I grunted, and the German V8 purred, and the road hummed quietly beneath us. If Bernie spoke again, I couldn't swear to it, because I'd already drifted off to sleep.

WE ARRIVED AT Mayday's condo at 5:50 P.M., whereupon I collected Sam and we all made plans to rendezvous at El Cholo, a cloth-napkin Mexican joint in the Paseo Colorado shopping mall, across from the old Henley and Hargrove offices on Pasadena's East Colorado Boulevard.

Sam and I listened to more news radio on the drive home to San Marino. They were still gumming on the Burkett press conference, quoting now from Max's report and speculating on a forthcoming federal indictment. Next came an update on my so-called arrest, in which Slewzyski called me a "person of interest" while cautioning that the matter was "still under investigation."

"Asshole," I said aloud.

I checked my cell phone for voice messages. There were five in total, all from Terina Webb, each more urgent than the last, the final one informing me that Fox News had upped the ante to forty grand if she and I would appear together that evening.

Forty grand, I thought, was almost what Archer had offered for the identity of Joan Marsden's killer.

The lawns of San Marino were crawling with little kids in costume, moving door to door as their doting mothers waited down on the sidewalks, often with dogs or strollers or both. I'd heard it said that inner-city kids from East L.A. and South Central were bussed into San Marino to trick-or-treat, but I saw no evidence of that in my neighborhood. Maybe that had once been true, back before the Chinese influx had altered the city's demographics, or maybe it was just another urban legend.

As I took the curve onto Sycamore Lane, I slowed to check out the street ahead. There were no cars or vans visible in front of the house. Sam, recognizing his environs, sat up in the backseat. He eyed a little Spider-Man and growled.

"Everyone's a theater critic," I told him, swinging into the driveway.

Once inside, I took a can down from the pantry, opened it, and scooped dog food into Sam's dish. While he scarfed that down, I walked down the hallway, removing my jacket as I went.

Then I stopped—because the door to my bedroom was closed. I hadn't left it closed. I held my breath and listened, then reached for the knob.

Both men wore Halloween masks. A bulked-up Barack Obama was stretched out on my bed, his big arms folded behind his head, while the ghost-faced slasher from the *Scream* films rose from my easy chair with a hand in his jacket pocket, from which he produced not a butcher knife but a black, snub-nosed pistol.

His eyes behind the mask crinkled in an unseen smile that I recognized, even without the baseball bat.

TWENTY-FOUR

We exited the 405 Freeway and followed Sunset westward as it snaked its way through leafy residential neighborhoods on its journey down to the Palisades. The driver wore a generic red devil mask with stubby plastic horns. Obama sat behind him, with the ghost-faced slasher, armed and definitely dangerous, directly behind me.

None of the men spoke, other than to grouse about the traffic, until my phone rang in Ghost Face's pocket. He checked the caller ID.

"Who's Shoshanna Gold?"

"This chick I've been wanting to set you up with. Be sure to give her a call."

We'd descended into hedge fund and movie mogul territory, past the Riviera Country Club and almost to Will Rogers State Park, where we slowed and our headlights swung onto an unmarked country road.

Oak and eucalyptus trees crowded a narrow lane bordered by white plank fencing. A streambed appeared on our right. Farther on were taillights, and voices, and the slamming of car doors.

Ghost Face leaned forward behind me. "Okay, killer, here's how it goes. You and me go in the front and turn left. Walk slow and keep quiet. I'll have a gun on your back, and I'll use whichever end I need to use."

Mexican kids in short jackets and bow ties were

opening doors and helping guests from their cars. The guests wore costumes that ranged from simple rubber fright masks to elaborate French Regency gowns with beehive wigs and feathered masks on sticks. We rolled to a stop beside a short pedestrian bridge, where Ghost Face got out, brushed off the parking valet, and opened my door with one hand still in his pocket.

The security men on the far side of the bridge were no-neck brutes wearing dark suits and earbuds. They nodded to Ghost Face. One of them spoke into his shirt cuff.

"Hold on," Ghost Face said as I stepped onto the bridge. He reached back into the car and came out with the Barack Obama mask. "Put this on."

From a security standpoint, it was a beautiful setup. The stream served as a moat, with the gated entry bridge the single point of ingress. The home beyond the bridge was a classic haunted house in the French Second Empire style of an Edward Gorey illustration, with its limestone façade, white portico, and high mansard roof. It was, like much of the plagiarized architecture of urban Los Angeles, both grandiose and grotesque.

I felt the gun muzzle in my ribs. "Let's go."

Greeters in blue satin livery and white powdered wigs bowed in unison as they opened the huge double doors. Chamber music and flickering gaslight filled the foyer. We faced an elevated landing from which guests would descend a wide marble staircase to the main hall below, which was teeming with costumed revelers.

The hand on my shoulder steered me away from the staircase, down a hallway of leaded glass windows and Belgian tapestries, to a mahogany door at the far end. Ghost Face rapped twice, the muzzle still in my back, and when the door opened inward, he goosed me forward.

The man who greeted me was older, a Jewish uncle in a tailored suit with an open dress shirt and a matching pocket hankie. He wasn't big, but he wasn't a pushover. He had a pit boss's face: liver-spotted and jowly and wise to whatever it was you thought you had in mind.

"Come," he said, gesturing to a couch. "Sit."

The room was a library, or maybe an office. It was wood-paneled from floor to ceiling with built-in bookshelves. The books on the shelves were leather and had probably been bought by the yard, by the same interior decorator who'd thought that the stuffed pheasant, huge antique globe, and the faux Etruscan urn would all go nicely with the standing suit of armor.

"Drink?" the pit boss offered, opening the globe, which pivoted on hinges.

"Scotch, if you've got it."

I removed my mask and set it on the coffee table. A large wooden desk stood at the room's center, and behind it a thronelike chair upholstered in red-and-gold damask. A scarlet couch was at right angles to the desk. I turned a slow, appraising circle. I sat.

"That'll be all, Jimmy," the pit boss said to Ghost Face, who placed my phone on a table and disappeared back through the same door we'd entered. The pit boss set my drink down next to the mask.

"Barack Obama," he said, lifting his own glass. "Now, that's what I call scary."

He took a seat in the wing chair opposite.

"So," he said, tasting his drink. "We meet at last. I've heard a lot about you."

"I can't say the same."

"And that's how it will have to remain, I'm afraid, but I will tell you that I'm a lawyer and that I handle mostly corporate and regulatory problems for Mr. Archer."

"I guess that would make me a regulatory problem."

"No, my young friend. Like everyone else, you're either an asset or a liability. In your case, we're hoping for the former but fully prepared for the latter."

I considered this as I took a sip. It was excellent Scotch.

"Let me ask you something," he said, leaning forward, elbows on knees. His hound dog eyes were as sharp as the broadsword in the corner. He wore gold cufflinks, and his fingernails gleamed in the lamplight as he gestured with his glass. "What does a young hotshot like you earn in a shithole law office like yours? After overhead, I mean."

"That depends. Is Archer good for the reward?"

He chuckled. "You're a real comedian. Ballsy, too. I heard that about you."

"Look, you went to a lot of trouble to bring me out here, so why not cut the bullshit and tell me what's on your mind?"

He started to respond, but then a section of the bookcase opened, and two mismatched figures stepped into the room, the sounds of laughter and music trailing behind them.

Tony Gags wore a Roman toga and laurel wreath crown, his hairy arms bangled in thick leather cuffs. Behind him, Larry Archer sported a white dinner jacket, à la Humphrey Bogart in *Casablanca*.

"Tell me something, MacTaggart," Archer said as he took his place on the throne. "Do I look like a welsher to you?"

"You look like Hervé Villechaize to me."

Tony Gags marched over and grabbed my jacket and hauled me to my feet. He dug a short right into my kidney, crumpling me to the floor. Had I been a heavy bag, I'd have spilled my sand all over the carpet.

"Okay," Archer said. "Now everybody's even."

I couldn't breathe. Tony grabbed me again, lifted me up, and walked me back to the couch.

Archer composed his hands on the desk. "Jack Mac-Taggart. Born and raised in East L.A. Your father left home when you were seventeen, and your mother offed herself in the nuthouse a year later. You attended Cal State L.A. and Loyola Law School, where you graduated tops in your class."

He pointed to the globe, and the pit boss fixed him a drink.

"Four years as a deputy public defender, then private practice, then a short stint at Henley and Hargrove, where you got yourself into a jackpot. People died, as I recall."

He leaned back into his seat.

"You want to know something? We're not so different, you and me. I grew up in a tough neighborhood. So did Tony. So did Sal. And look at us all now."

Sal, Archer's consigliere, handed the drink to his boss.

"That's the great thing about this country, MacTaggart. Any punk kid with smarts and a little moxie can make for himself whatever life he wants. Just keep the government off his back and the tax man out of his pocket. That's my philosophy. Those are the cornerstones of my campaign."

I wheezed, "You really believe that bullshit?"

"The voters believe it. That's all that matters."

He sipped at his drink. Then he opened a drawer and removed a fat envelope and tossed it to Tony Gags.

"Okay," Archer continued. "To business. You and I both have a problem, MacTaggart, and lucky for you, we have the same problem."

Tony opened the flap and looked inside the envelope, then dropped it onto the coffee table next to my drink.

"Open it," Archer said.

I reached for the envelope with the hand that wasn't holding my spleen in place and shook the contents into my lap. There were four fat bundles of crisp new hundreds, totaling ten thousand dollars each.

"This cockroach who calls himself Ricky Rio is a dead man," Archer declared. "First he tries to frame me for his bullshit art heist, and now he's helping Burkett pin me with a campaign finance rap. At first I thought maybe you were in on it, but then the next thing I know you've been cashiered by Burkett and you're out looking for Rio yourself. Now you're in shit up to your sideburns. So, the way I see it, we have a common enemy, and the enemy of my enemy is my friend."

I tried to sit up straight. "What makes you think it was Rio behind the money-laundering report?"

He waved a hand. "Let's just say he had access that he shouldn't have had. That's been corrected. The problem now is that Rio's crawled into a hole, and we can't smoke him out." He looked at Tony Gags. "We've got his houses staked and his phones tapped, but he's a clever little cockroach."

I put the money back into the envelope. "What makes you think I'm out looking for Rio?"

"You were spotted at his house in Santa Barbara, for starters."

Archer nodded to Sal, and the old fixer pulled a little tape recorder out of the globe, walked it over, and set it on the coffee table. He hit the PLAY button.

What did you mean on Sunday when you said that Larry Archer is a killer?

You didn't come here to see me, did you?

I've seen you plenty. Now I'd like to talk to you. Who did he kill?

I heard Ricky talking to Mrs. Archer about her husband. About what would happen if he won the election—

"That's enough," Archer said, and the consigliere shut it off.

"My guests are waiting, MacTaggart, so let's cut to the chase. It was Rio who killed the Mardian woman. She was a hooker once, and Rio pimped her out. They were in it together from the beginning. How else did he get the painting? Then she must have put the arm on him, so he offed her. Her and that Russian doll up in Santa Barbara. That means it was Rio who set you up with the murder weapon. That way, even if you did find evidence against him, you'd look like some kind of shyster."

"You've got it all figured," I told him, gritting my teeth as I reached for my drink.

"Let's just say I didn't go to school to eat lunch." Again he eased back into his throne. "So. You find that safe-deposit box yet?"

I shook my head. "We've checked every bank in Santa Barbara."

"That's too bad. On the other hand, it does free up your time."

He finished his drink and stood.

"You're working for me now, counselor. Consider that a retainer. You find Rio, and there's another sixty grand in it for you. Only you turn him over to me, not to the cops."

"So he can get the same treatment as the Jaworsky kid?"

"Let's just say I owe him."

"Right, I get it. And you're not a welsher."

Archer smiled. Then he straightened his jacket and walked to the bookcase, where he reached a hand into the shelf. The false door sprang open, and music again filled the room.

"What if I can't find Rio?" I asked.

Tony Gags loomed over me. He pointed to the tape recorder. "You'll find him, and you'll find him by Tuesday. If not, I'll mail that fish-faced girlfriend of his to your house in small packages."

Tony crossed the room to where Archer still waited. "So long, asshole," Tony said. "You were never here."

As the bookcase closed behind them, the hallway door opened and Devil Face stepped into the room. I winced as I stood. Sal the consigliere placed the cash envelope and my cell phone into a brown legal file that he closed with an elastic band.

"Thank you for coming, Mr. MacTaggart." He handed me the file. Then he reached into his pocket and produced a plastic ARCHER FOR SENATE lapel button, which he pinned to my jacket.

"Do us all a favor." He patted me on the shoulder. "Be an asset. Liabilities don't fare well in this organization."

I'D READ WHERE boxers will sometimes piss blood after taking a hard shot to the kidney. I'm happy to report that I didn't, but only because I couldn't seem to piss at all. Still, I flushed the toilet and replaced my mask and carried my file back into the hallway, where Devil Face waited, eyeing the action at the front door.

"Let's go," he said, taking me by the arm.

A clutch of late arrivals stood air-kissing in the foyer. We tried to sidle past, but I felt another, firmer hand on my arm.

"Why, Mr. MacTaggart, is that you?"

Angela Archer wore a rhinestone-studded cowboy outfit, complete with white hat and red kerchief and black Lone Ranger mask. Her hair she wore in a thick dock-rope braid. She had pearl-handled cap guns slung low in a tan leather holster that matched her tooled calfskin boots. She pried me loose from the Devil—how's that for a metaphor?—and escorted me down the staircase.

"I saw you coming in," she said at the bottom, turning me and waltzing us both into the center of the crowded dance floor. "I've been waiting for you to come out."

We danced a wide circle, past the string quartet and a gaggle of laughing drunks and over to a far corner, where she broke it off and led me by the hand through a paneled doorway and into a brightly lit pantry area. Two waitresses in Playboy bunny costumes squeezed past us from the kitchen bearing hors d'oeuvre trays aloft.

"Are you all right?"

I lifted the Obama mask onto my head. "I'm okay, but your husband is fucking nuts."

"I hope you didn't antagonize him." She glanced at

the door to the living room. "He's been in a terrible rage. We've had a dozen cancellations, including the mayor and the governor. I've never seen him so—"

I reached for her hand. She flinched as I pulled back the shirt cuff, exposing the dark purple bruising that ran from elbow to wrist.

She yanked her hand free. "It's not as bad as it looks."

"That's good, because it looks like hell."

"He thinks I gave something to Ricky, and now he thinks I know where Ricky's hiding."

"Do you?"

She shook her head. "No."

"Would you tell me if you did?"

She stepped closer. "You know I would."

I knew nothing of the sort, but I let it slide. Again I reached for her hand.

"Has your brother seen this yet?"

"God, no. Tony would kill him."

"Good. That would solve two problems at once."

"You don't understand. It's more complicated than that."

"The hard decisions usually are."

She grabbed for the file then, and I let her take it. She opened it as she backed away, fumbled inside, and looked at me anew. It was the look she'd probably given her parents on that cold December night when they told her the truth about Santa.

"It's not what you think," I said, but she'd already dropped the file and drawn a cap gun from her holster.

She shot me in the heart.

TWENTY-FIVE

"ONLY FOUR DAYS until the election," I said again.

We were all assembled in my office, with Pam and Shelly in the client chairs and Mayday and Bernie on the couch to my left. The Marsden sisters' overnight bags were on the floor by the hallway door. Outside my window, the rush and lull of Friday morning traffic seeped beneath blinds drawn tight against the low morning sun.

"Can't we just call the cops?"

I looked at Pam. She wore one of Mayday's USC LAW T-shirts, plus the diamond earrings and the gold Cartier watch and the chunky charm bracelet I'd last seen on her dead sister's wrist. The shirt was two sizes too small, and she'd stretched it in ways it had never before been stretched.

"And tell them what, exactly? That I'd like to press charges for having been driven to a party and given forty thousand dollars?"

The envelope sat on the desk before me, as did the LAPD's forensics reports and several dozen pink message slips, all from various media. I gathered the messages, squared them into a stack, and dropped them into the wastebasket.

Mayday opened her laptop. "The overnight polls are showing Burkett up three, but the margin of error is five." She looked up from her screen. "And are you ready for this? Politico is reporting that an Internet write-in candidate might control enough votes to swing the election."

I laughed out loud. "If Max were smart, he'd cut a deal with the White House for a presidential pardon."

"If Max was smart," Bernie corrected, "he'd stay out of sight until Wednesday, or this Tony Gags might make him an offer he can't refuse."

Pam stood up, took the Nerf ball, and tossed it at the hoop. I opened Archer's envelope and shook the bundled bills onto my blotter.

"I'm wondering if we shouldn't contact Legs somehow. Get her to a safe place until this blows over."

"You mean until Tony decides to forgive and forget?"

Mayday had a point, as Mayday often does. Legs would never be safe unless one of two things happened: Either we found Rio by Tuesday and turned him over to Archer, or we found admissible evidence that Archer, and Tony, were behind at least one of the three unsolved murders.

I looked to Shelly, who hadn't spoken all morning. She sat with her hands in her lap, twisting and untwisting the braided strap on her handbag. She glanced up and caught me looking.

"Y'all really think this Tony person will kill this woman Legs?" she asked in a quiet voice.

"From everything I've heard, he's not the type to make idle threats."

She nodded, examining her palm. "And you think whatever's in that safe-deposit box will prove he killed Joanie?"

"I think he's as good a candidate as we've got."

She looked to the window. Bernie started to speak, but I stopped her with a finger.

"If you've got something on your mind, Shelly, now might be a good time to get it out."

Shelly half-turned in the chair, to where Pam stood watching her. Pam fingered the gold watch on her wrist. She shrugged.

"Yep, I reckon so." Shelly sighed, opening her purse. From it she withdrew an envelope. It had a glassine window in front and a ragged tear along its edge. She set it on my desk.

"It started around five years ago," she said. "Right after my divorce."

I unfolded the September bank statement of Michelle M. Johnson, from the Bank of America branch in Victorville, California. It was a checking account, and the balance was surprisingly large.

"I never knew for sure who was sendin' it, but I guess I did. I didn't tell Pammy at first, but when it just kept comin' every month, I started splittin' it with her, fifty-fifty." She looked again to her sister. "Lester bein' hurt and all."

The statement showed the sum of five thousand dollars entering the account by wire transfer on the last day of the month.

"I figured that's what Joanie would've wanted," Shelly continued. "I figured maybe she didn't have Pammy's address."

Mayday had stood and circled the desk, and was looking over my shoulder.

Shelly added, "I guess they ain't gonna be comin' no more, are they?"

The transfers originated from the OneWest Bank branch on Beverly Boulevard, in West Hollywood.

"She never contacted you?"

Shelly shook her head. "I figured she could of if she'd wanted to, but I reckon she didn't."

"Shelly! Why didn't you tell us this on Sunday?"

Shelly gave Mayday a weary look.

"Honey," she said, "I been lookin' out for Pamela all my life. You two I didn't know from Shinola."

THE BANK BUILDING was a concrete bunker at the bustling intersection of Beverly and San Vicente, just south of Tail O' the Pup and across from the gleaming towers of the Cedars-Sinai Medical Center. Shelly and I parked in an underground lot and caught the branch manager just as he was leaving the building for lunch. We were fobbed off on an assistant manager, whose desk in the open lobby anchored a bouquet of helium balloons.

The girl behind the desk read our court order, fiddled with her computer, and then excused herself. She disappeared into a back office, and when she returned it was in the company of a gray-haired matron who in a former life had been either a librarian or a prison guard. The woman lifted eyeglasses by a chain from her bosom and read the order twice over, studied my business card, nodded at Shelly, and bade us follow her into the back office from whence she'd emerged.

"You'll forgive our caution in these matters," she said to Shelly as she settled into the chair behind a tidy laminate desk on which reposed the nameplate CORNELIA REESE, CLIENT SERVICES. To me she added, "I'm sure you can appreciate that this is an unusual situation."

"Death?"

Cornelia Reese eyed me over her cheaters. "Special administration," she said, lifting the receiver on her telephone.

She punched up a number and spoke with someone who might have been an in-house lawyer for the bank. She read from the Letters of Special Administration we'd given to the girl out front. She *hmmm*'d and clucked and pursed her lips. She said thank you and hung up without saying good-bye.

"Key?" she asked.

"Is the box actually here?"

She looked puzzled. "Of course the box is here. What have we been discussing for the past twenty minutes?"

Shelly and I shared a look.

"I'm afraid there was no key among the decedent's personal effects," I told the woman, "and time is of the essence. How long would it take to drill the box?"

She all but flinched at the thought. "Oh, dear. A week. Possibly two."

"I'm afraid we don't have that long."

She folded her hands.

"Mr. MacTaggart. I'm aware of who you are, and I'm aware of the...notoriety attendant to Miss Mardian's death, but bank rules are bank rules, and certain protocols must be observed."

"If you know who I am, then you must have known we've been searching for this box for days. Why didn't you call us? Or call the police?"

"What reason, you mean, other than the California Financial Information Privacy Act? As I explained earlier to Mrs. Johnson—"

"Is there a way we can speed this up?" Shelly interrupted. "Like, maybe we pay some kinda fee or some-thin'?"

Cornelia Reese's look was not without sympathy. "Even if I wanted to help you, I'm afraid the earliest possible day would be Friday, one week from today. I'm terribly sorry."

Her eyes followed me as I stood to pace.

"Jordan—Miss Mardian—was a valued client," the women volunteered before I could speak. "I dealt with her on a regular basis."

"How regular?"

She replaced the eyeglasses, swiveled her chair, and punched up a screen on her computer.

"Seven, eight, nine in-person visits this year alone. Monthly, more or less."

"When was the last?"

"Friday, the eighteenth of October."

"The day she was killed."

She removed her glasses. "I didn't realize that."

"Did you open the box for her that day?"

"Yes, of course. I'm here Monday through Friday. Jordan generally came on Fridays."

"Her key—was it on a ring or a fob of some sort?"

"No." She shook her head emphatically. "She always had it loose, in her hand. That much I remember."

I returned to my seat.

"Where are the statements mailed for this account? We didn't find any at her house or office."

"It's an electronic account. There are no paper state-ments."

"Can't we at least see the box?" Shelly pleaded. "We've come a long way."

The woman started to tell us why that would be

against FDIC regulations, but then seemed to change her mind.

"Oh, very well. Come this way."

We followed her down a back hallway to an enormous walk-in vault the inside of which featured three gridded walls surrounding a central granite counter. It was like stepping into a submarine. The woman ran her finger horizontally, stopping halfway into the vault at a medium-sized compartment located at around shoulder height. Like the others, its flat metal surface was pimpled by twin brass keyholes.

"I don't suppose you have a crowbar I could borrow?"

Cornelia Reese did not smile. "I wish I could be of more help," she said before showing a hand and ushering us back into the hallway. We followed behind her until, halfway to her office, she stopped.

"There is one thing," she said, turning to face us. "It's probably nothing."

"What's that?"

"As you may know, Jordan was an elegant woman, always beautifully dressed. I thought it odd the first time I saw it, but you see odd things this close to Beverly Hills. I'd gotten so used to it, it slipped my mind completely."

"'It' being what, exactly?"

"Her key," she said, fingering her eyeglasses. "To the safe-deposit box. She'd had it plated in gold."

I MADE THE CALL as soon as the Benz topped out at street level, catching Mayday at the Only Place.

"Who's with you?" I asked her.

"Just Pam. Why? What happened?"

"Is she still wearing her sister's charm bracelet?"

"Yes."

"Good. Whatever you do, don't let that bracelet out of your sight."

Shelly's mouth hung open as I rang off and returned my phone to the console. I gave her a disapproving look.

"Is there something you'd like to tell me?"

She didn't answer. Then again, she didn't have to.

"When?"

Now she looked away, at the storefront windows scrolling past. I turned north from Santa Monica onto Highland, tires squealing, barely making the light.

She tightened the grip on her bag. "Yesterday," she finally said.

"And if you'd found a will in that box, what would you have done?"

She shook her head. "I don't know. Tore it up, I reckon, dependin' on what it said."

I nodded. "For whatever it's worth, I don't blame you. Although we wasted a lot of time that we didn't have to waste."

She shifted in the seat to face me. "And you think the key—"

"I think your sister was a very smart woman," I told her, weaving through traffic, driving faster than both prudence and the speed limit allowed. "Her goal was to hide records that people might want to find. Powerful people, with means and motive. Not to mention the police and the IRS, both of whom can obtain search warrants. And don't forget, these are records that would need to be updated on a periodic basis."

There was a traffic snarl at Sunset, but we squeezed around it, making our own lane along the curb.

"Storing those records in a safe-deposit box was smart. Using an out-of-town bank was even smarter. E-banking, to avoid a paper trail, was smarter still, but you still need to visit the bank, and that means having to carry a key. So the smartest move of all would be to hide the key in a place where, if you were ever followed and searched, it wouldn't likely be found."

"Is that what happened? They killed her for the key?"

"No," I told her. "I don't think so. I think whoever killed Joan didn't even know the box existed."

TWENTY-SIX

PAM AND MAYDAY hadn't returned from lunch by the time Shelly and I reached the office. I deposited Shelly in the conference room and dispatched Bernie for chow. At the center of my blotter were the LAPD forensics reports, portions of which Mayday had dog-eared and marked in yellow highlighter.

On the report from the Serology/DNA unit, Mayday had highlighted the sentence "CODIS match positive for fugitive Joan Marsden HIVAT on 5 February 1990," a reference to the fact that the Combined DNA Index System had positively matched Jordan Mardian's post mortem blood sample with that of an HIV antibody test performed on the prostitute Joan Marsden at the time of her 1990 arrest.

The report with the most highlighting, however, was from Trace Analysis. That's the unit within the LAPD criminalistics laboratory that identifies and analyzes things like hair, carpet fibers, and chemicals, including gunshot and explosives residues. The first highlighted language confirmed the absence of any accelerants, explosives, or clandestine chemicals on Jordan Mardian's person or clothing.

The second highlighted language appeared in the third paragraph, under the heading "Soil Residues." There Mayday had boxed a little chart, introduced by the sentence "Ammonium and high nitrifications were observed in the posterior smudges," a reference to the dirt stains found on the back of Jordan Mardian's sweater.

I took up the Nerf basketball. Then I put it down.

Around twenty minutes after she'd left, Bernie returned with our food, with both Pam and Mayday in tow. Shelly, looking sheepish, joined us from the conference room, and we all took seats in my office. The same seats, in fact, that we'd all occupied that morning.

"Regan called," Mayday said. "She's on her way over."

"Good." I gathered up the forensics reports and set them aside. "I have good news and bad news. Which would you like to hear first?"

"Come on," Bernie said. "Don't be a dick."

I ticked the points off on my fingers.

"First. The safe-deposit box has been located, at the OneWest Bank branch in West Hollywood. Second," and here I looked at Shelly, "without Joan's counterpart key, the box can't be opened, at least not for a week or two at the earliest. Third"—here I paused a beat for dramatic effect—"unless I'm badly mistaken, the key has been right under our noses all day."

I turned to Pam, who straightened in her seat. "What?" She followed my eyes to her wrist.

"May I see that?" I asked her, and she looked to her sister for approval before unhooking the clasp and laying the heavy charm bracelet in my palm.

All of the charms were gold. Some were plain, and others had inlays of gemstones or colored enamel. There was a heart and a teddy bear, a dolphin and a hummingbird, a playing card and a crescent moon, an elephant and a rocking horse—and yes, there was a key.

The key detached from the bracelet by means of a tiny clasp. The number stamped on its bow I recognized from the vault at OneWest Bank. I held it aloft by its blade.

"Fuck me," Bernie said.

The crash and the reception bell rang out simultaneously. We all jumped, but it was Bernie who was first into the hallway, with Mayday close on her heels.

The reception area was empty. I brushed past the others, through the glass door and down the staircase to the street, where, halfway up the block, a uniformed Regan Fife held a scrawny kid, one arm behind his back, face-first against a window. Both were breathing hard.

"He was in your lobby!" Regan called when she saw me coming. "When I walked in behind him, he knocked me down and bolted!"

She peeled the kid off the glass. He was small and disheveled in a ratty topcoat, and he had the furtive, darting eyes of a trapped animal. I bent to retrieve the porkpie hat that lay cocked on the sidewalk, then stepped closer to hand it to him.

"Hello, Mouse. Nice to see you again."

THE PACKAGE LAY sideways on the carpet beside Bernie's desk. I carried it into the conference room like a wounded bird and set it gently on the table.

"You can't hold me," Mouse protested. "I didn't do nothing illegal."

"I could be wrong, but I think assaulting a police officer is illegal. Of course, we could always call Tony Gags to get his opinion."

That shut him up. I took scissors from the credenza

and slit the paper tape on the package and parted the cotton batting.

The entire left side of the Etch-A-Sketch message was missing:

ME
OVE

"What did it say?" I asked Mouse.

He shook his head. "I don't know. It was already boxed when I got it."

"Got it where? Where's Ricky?"

"I don't know."

"Bullshit."

"I swear to God. It was on my doorstep, at the place where I'm staying. With a note that said I was to deliver it here, same as before."

"Where's your doorstep?" Regan asked him, but he looked away.

"Look, Mouse," I told him, "I know you're scared, and I know why you're scared, but we're all on the same team here. Nobody wants to take down Tony more than we do, believe me—and you can help us."

A guarded flicker of interest. "Help you how?"

"How much do you know about the missing painting? Or the Mardian woman?"

He shook his head again. "Nothing. Ricky had the painting, and he wanted to work it into the video. As a joke, he said. So we snuck it in and hung it in the other room during the setup. Then we took it down again. That's all I know."

"And the Mardian woman?"

"Nothing, I swear. After the show at MOCA, Ricky called us all together and said we had to split up for a while, to hide. He said that Angela's brother had killed this lady and that he'd kill all of us if we ever got caught. Said we shouldn't use our cell phones or try to contact each other until we heard from him. That none of us should tell the others where we're hiding, 'cause if one of us got caught, they'd try to beat it out of us. Christ." His voice caught, and his head dropped into his hand. "I thought he was just bein' paranoid, you know? And then I heard about K-Jaw."

I was on my feet and pacing. There was a play here, but it had to be perfect.

"Jack," Mayday said, tapping her wristwatch. "It's almost three."

I waved her off. "So Ricky knows everybody's whereabouts, but he's the only one, is that the deal?"

"Yeah. That was the plan, anyway."

"What about the girl, Legs?"

"What about her? She wasn't at the video shoot, so Ricky thought she'd be okay."

"How much do you trust her?"

"What do you mean?"

"I mean, is there a chance she'd give up Ricky? Like for money, or some political favor, like a green card?"

"No way, man. That chick worships Ricky."

I resumed my seat and opened the greasy bag Bernie had brought from the Only Place. I passed the salad to Shelly and slid the Big Cheese toward Mouse.

"Here," I told him. "I'm having a lunch special for all my new clients. You eat three of these, you get a gift certificate for an angioplasty."

I SPENT WHAT was left of the afternoon on the telephone—first with Chico Alvarez, then with Terina Webb, and finally with Cornelia Reese.

Mouse spent the afternoon in the conference room playing gin with Pam and Shelly, while Mayday sat on my sofa and listened, stone-faced, as I moved the pieces into place.

"Is that disapproval or boredom?" I asked her between phone calls.

She checked her watch again. "I take it we're not going to the bank?"

"That would be correct."

"I see. So after a week spent combing Southern California for the safe-deposit box, now that we've finally found it, we don't care anymore?"

"We care," I told her, "but it's not our highest priority."

"Right. Finding Jordan Mardian's killer is no longer a priority."

"I didn't say that."

My next call was to Angela Archer. She let it roll to voice mail, and I didn't leave a message. The message from Mayday, however, was delivered in eye daggers.

"What?" I asked.

"Okay, I'll bite. Why aren't we on our way to the bank right now?"

"Because we won't learn anything at the bank that we don't already know."

"Meaning?"

I took up the Etch-A-Sketch and shook it and played with the knobs.

"Meaning I already know who killed both Jordan Mardian and Catherine Orlov."

She sat bolt upright. "You do? How?"

I tilted the screen and showed her a smiley face.

"Because you told me."

INFORMATION IS A funny thing—where it comes from and what it tells you. I'd been fed all kinds of information in this case, starting with my very first meeting with Warren Burkett nearly three weeks before. Some of it was good information, and some of it wasn't. Sometimes, in the case of Chico Alvarez or Ricky Rio, the information was intended to lead. Other times, in the case of, say, Angela Archer, the information was intended to mislead. At the end of the day, however, it's not the information itself, or even its source, that really matters. What matters at the end of the day is motive. What people want and the lengths they'll go to get it.

Find the motive, Russ Dinsmoor had taught me, and you'll eventually find the truth.

We'd sent Pam and Shelly home, and I'd considered moving Mouse to Sycamore Lane, but figured he was better off where he'd been hiding, wherever that was. I just had to trust that we'd won his cooperation.

I'd spent Saturday morning in motion, dotting *I*s and crossing *T*s and above all, making sure I wasn't followed. As a consequence, I was a half hour late arriving at the office, where all the key players were assembled.

"Everything ready?" I asked Detective Alvarez, who sat at the head of the conference room table. He tilted his head to a heavy coil of climbing rope resting in a side chair.

"Mouse?"

Eric "Mouse" Moskowitz, like the detective, was dressed entirely in black, and it occurred to me that, unlike the detective, he looked completely at ease with everything we had planned. He gave me a thumbs-up.

"Why so remote?" asked Regan, who, in her black jeans and black windbreaker and black tactical boots, was bent over the topo map on the table. I looked at Alvarez before answering.

"We concluded that a remote location would be more credible, more manageable, and safer for the public. Plus, it's a location the girl knows."

"What if they don't show?"

"Don't worry, as long as we catch her at Rio's studio loft, they'll show. If not, we'll have all had a nice afternoon hike."

Detective Madden's cell phone chimed, and he stepped into the hallway. Alvarez, meanwhile, leaned forward to trace a finger on the map.

"There's a nighttime horseback ride from Sunset Ranch on the Hollywood side, right here, over to Burbank for dinner, then back again. The riders should return, load up their cars, and be out by ten. The lower parking lot"—he jabbed again—"closes at 10:30. Everyone should be off the trail by then. That means optimum time for the meet would be on or after twenty-three hundred hours, and we need to nail that down now."

I looked to Mouse. "Okay with you? That's eleven o'clock tonight."

He shrugged. Mouse was easy.

Madden returned to the room, handing me his phone. "Slewzyski."

"Okay, Mac," the D.A. said, "we've got a lot riding on this." Slewzyski, torn between his animosity toward me and his political need to abandon the sinking ship that was the Archer campaign, sounded almost civil.

"I don't have to tell you what happens if you fuck up this time."

"Thanks, Slew. You're a leader of men."

"You checked your track record lately? First it was the painting at Archer's cabin. Then it was some bullshit about a safe-deposit box."

"Look, Tom, if you're losing your nerve, I can still call the FBI. You can read all about it in tomorrow's newspaper."

"Okay, okay. Just remember that it's my ass on the line, not yours. If this thing goes sideways, I'm the guy who has to answer to Archer. In fact, you're lucky to still be involved at this point."

I winked at Mouse. "Except that my client insists."

"Just remember to sign those ride-along waivers!"

I hit the END button and returned the phone to Madden. Now all eyes in the room were on me.

"Okay, let's make the call."

We all turned to Mouse, who pulled a paint-spattered cell phone from his cargo pants and powered it on. We watched as he waited for the signal. Then he touched a speed-dial button.

"Legs? Hey, it's Mouse… Yeah, yeah, I know, how you doin'?… Yeah, me, too. You at the studio?… Good. Ricky called me this morning, and he wants to get the crew together tonight… Yeah, I know, it sucks. I read all about it… Eleven o'clock… Uh-huh… He wants to meet at the big sign… Yeah, no shit. He says if he's goin' out, he's goin' out in style… Yeah. You remember the spot?… Yeah, from Beechwood. It's a long hike, so start early, and bring your night gear. Oh, and Legs?"

Mouse looked to me at the far end of the table.

"Ricky said to tell you, this one's for K-Jaw."

TWENTY-SEVEN

WE TOOK FRANKLIN to Beechwood and turned north, with Regan and me in her Toyota leading a motley caravan of unmarked vehicles that included Alvarez and Mouse in a dirty Subaru, Mayday and Madden in an old Ford Taurus, and four LAPD SWAT officers in a white Econoline van. We were ten bodies in total, plus climbing gear, masks, face black, spray paint, weapons, ammo, vests, parabolic microphones, night-vision goggles, radios, and God-knows-what-else the SWAT guys had stashed up their ballistic nylon sleeves.

You'd have thought we were planning to reinvade Iraq, which, come to think of it, might have been a plank in the Archer for Senate campaign platform.

Slewzyski had made no secret of his displeasure with my presence on the mission, but he knew it was non-negotiable. I wasn't happy with Mayday's presence, but she'd made it clear that *that* wasn't negotiable. And nobody seemed too thrilled with Regan's presence except me, riding shotgun beside her, admiring her handsome profile.

Our destination was the holy grail of L.A. graffiti artists: the nine white letters forming the giant HOLLYWOOD sign. Stretching longer than a football field across the face of Mount Lee, high in the Hollywood Hills, the five-story letters beamed their siren song of celluloid glitz and glamor to all mankind. Erected in 1923 by then-*Los Angeles Times* publisher Harry Chandler to advertise a real estate development, the sign, which originally spelled HOLLYWOODLAND, became the property of the City of Los Angeles after the development went bust in the Great Depression. Rebuilt, minus the LAND, in 1949, and again in 1978, the iconic sign was today protected against vandalism by a complex system of state-of-the-art CCTV, motion sensor, and infrared cameras perimeter-mounted on eight-foot chain-link fencing.

According to Mayday, the system included two live cameras through which you could watch the sign 24/7 from the comfort of your home computer. It was, as Mouse had described it, the most visible five acres in all Los Angeles, making it the white whale to Ricky Rio's Ahab.

Our plan was to ascend the unpaved fire road leading from Beechwood Drive, normally closed to vehicular traffic, all the way to the top of Mount Lee. There the City's Central Communications Facility, an industrial-looking complex bristling with huge microwave and cellular radio towers, sits perched above the sign to the east. From there we would stash our vehicles, and then hike back to a low, wooded knoll directly above the sign.

According to Mouse, that was the spot to which Rio had once taken the crew on a day-long reconnaissance mission.

"Odd place for an ambush," Regan said, gazing up through the windshield. Our caravan had stopped at the Hollyridge Trail parking lot, half full at this hour, where we waited as Madden stepped from the Taurus to open the gate.

"Perfect spot," I corrected her. "The police can monitor the site in real time. Odds are that Tony's never been up here, so he has no clue about the cameras. Even if he does, that's okay too, because we'll be avoiding the cameras until dark, giving him a false sense of security."

The Subaru took the lead now, with Alvarez and Mouse inside, the old car bouncing through the gate past Madden. Once all the vehicles were through, Madden locked the gate behind him and replaced Mayday behind the wheel of the Taurus.

The views as we climbed grew ever more spectacular as the sun reddened and the lights of the city began speckling the panorama below us. We passed hikers in twos and fours, most heading down toward the parking lot. Some waved, while others called out to ask how we'd gotten our cars past the gate. At odd intervals, couples sat on rocks or lay propped on blankets overlooking the glittering sunset. Some drank wine, while others partook in a friendly communal smoke.

"Romantic," Regan said in a voice that turned my head.

"Been up here before?"

"No, but I've always wanted to."

Horse flop littered the roadway, and beer cans, and a broken foam cooler. Then the road turned sharply upward, winding around to a paved section at which we all turned right, still following the Subaru, and there the giant sign rose into view like an argent moon ascending.

"Wow," Regan said, and I burst into song.

"Hooray for Hollywood!"

"God." She covered an ear with one hand. "Ethel Merman just hit her head on the coffin."

The paved road wended around to the Valley side of the mountain, from which we had a fading, bird's-eye view of Forest Lawn and the Warner Bros. studio beyond. Then a long, sweeping curve to counter-clockwise put us directly above the sign, where, by prearrangement, we all doused our headlights.

We rolled past the security cameras in near darkness, looking down on the black void of Lake Hollywood and, farther off to the east, the lighted towers of downtown. When our caravan stopped at the CCF gate, Alvarez alighted from the Subaru and bent to work the lock.

We pulled in behind the main building, under the blink and hum of the huge radio towers. Night had all but fallen, and the SWAT guys, stern and silent, worked with LED headlamps, hauling gear from the back of their van. Mayday, Mouse, and I watched from the sidelines as vests were donned and faces blacked and equipment issued and checked. Laptops glowed and radios crackled. Velcro zipped. Weapons, including several sniper rifles, were locked, loaded, and shouldered. Although Regan stood among them in her black POLICE windbreaker, the SWAT guys pretty much pretended she wasn't there.

After an hour or so of preparations, Alvarez and Madden approached us where we stood with hands in pockets, rocking and gazing out through the perimeter fence at the blazing lights of the city. They carried four Kevlar vests and a pair of climbing harnesses.

Alvarez lifted a vest. "Waiver or no waiver, I want you three out of harm's way. You're to stick with Detective Madden at all times. No matter what happens, do not break cover or put yourselves in the line of fire."

To Regan, Alvarez added, "And we'll need you to surrender your service weapon."

"Like hell I will."

"Listen, Officer. I'm in charge here, and I'm not putting my men at risk of friendly fire from some rookie they haven't trained with."

"And I'm not surrendering my weapon to you or to anybody else, under any circumstances. Especially not in a potential lethal-force situation—and neither would you, Detective."

Alvarez turned to face me. "Damn it, MacTaggart! Let me remind you that we have one shot at this guy. One clean shot, without any interference or cover-your-ass political bullshit, and I will not jeopardize this operation with some rookie cop from Podunk waving her gun around."

"If you're worried about getting shot," I told him, nodding toward the SWAT team, "I'd be issuing paint balls to those guys."

Madden laid a restraining hand on his partner's shoulder.

"Look, Officer Fife. Just promise not to draw your weapon, okay? We have a tactical plan in place, and nobody wants to see anyone get hurt."

"Least of all me," she told him.

"Good. Then we're all on the same page."

Alvarez said nothing as Madden hefted a vest.

"Here, put these on. We roll in five minutes." He turned to Mouse. "Mr. Moskowitz? Try this on for size."

We all donned our vests, with Regan helping with the adjustments. Then, while the rest of us stood and watched, Mouse and Alvarez stepped into their climbing harnesses and buckled themselves in.

Alvarez hoisted his heavy pack and turned to face the others. "Let's deploy!"

A faint breeze rose up from the city below us, carrying traffic noise and canine sounds and the potpourri scent of dry chaparral. We walked in single file, around the building and through the entry gate and onto the darkened roadway, the black-clad SWAT officers paired in front and rear. We all waited while the gate slid closed behind us. Then the SWAT team leader raised a hand and touched a finger to his ear.

"The girl is on the trail," he said quietly.

At the leader's signal, we all took a knee. He shrugged out of his pack and continued forward, low and shuffling, disappearing into darkness.

The sign from our overhead angle was enormous, the fifty-foot letters visible in negative, their skeletal framework black against the twinkling lights of the city.

I checked my watch. It was after ten o'clock, the time by which the last of the lovers and stoners and casual hikers would have started back down to their cars.

The team leader returned, walking upright. "All clear ahead," he said, addressing himself to Alvarez, who gave us the signal to rise.

A short distance farther and we stood on a fenced section of roadway directly above the sign. Here the packs were dropped and unzipped, and the coil of climbing rope was handed off to Mouse, who slung it over his shoulder. Weapons were checked and goggles donned. One of the SWAT guys produced a bolt cutter from his pack and knelt at the base of the fence, the *click, click, click* of the tool's mechanical jaws ticking the countdown.

A half hour later, and everyone was in place.

We all waited. Mayday, Regan, and I waited with Madden, the four of us huddled downslope at the base of a giant *L*. Mouse and Alvarez, both in their balaclava face masks, waited at the *H*, with Mouse on the ground and Alvarez suspended in his climbing harness some forty feet above him. The four SWAT team members, hidden and silent, waited above us, beyond the fence and the road, manning their parabolic microphones and their deadly sniper rifles from atop the wooded knoll.

"Whose wacky idea was this, anyway?" I whispered to Regan, who dug an elbow to my ribs.

We waited some more. Then, just as I'd grown tired of waiting, we heard a voice.

"Mouse?"

Legs's mantis figure appeared at the bolt-cut opening in the fence above us. She was wearing her black Spandex catsuit and shouldering a heavy pack. She shielded her eyes against the distant glow of the city.

"Down here!"

She ducked through the opening, picking her way downslope to where Mouse stood on belay, the climbing rope encircling his waist. It was only a matter of seconds before we heard another, gruffer voice calling down from above.

"Police! You're trespassing on government property! Climb up now, with your hands in the air!"

A big guy dressed entirely in black stood at the fence, his gloved hands gripping the wire. After a moment, three other figures appeared behind him, all of them similarly attired.

None of them was a cop.

"I am coming!" Legs called out in panic as she clambered up the slope. "Please do not shoot me!"

A flashlight beam raked the hillside. It settled on Mouse where he stood, and then it followed the taut rope upward, settling on the dark figure suspended amid the high steel scaffolding.

"I can't let go of the rope!" Mouse called.

As she crawled up through the fence opening, Legs was grabbed and spun and shoved face-first into the chain link. One figure held her there while the other three ducked single file through the fence, where I could see that the last of them carried a black baseball bat.

Beside us, Madden rose to one knee, drawing his weapon.

The three goons followed their flashlight down the hill toward Mouse, their arms flailing for balance, each man oblivious to the gun sight trained on his back.

"Hey!" Mouse protested as one of them—Tony Gags—shoved him to the ground and stripped the rope from his waist.

"Stay here," Madden whispered, moving forward in a crouch.

Tony held the rope in his fist. "Ding dong!" He jerked and slacked and jerked again, making Alvarez rock in the beam of the flashlight. "Climb down, or I'll pull you down!"

Mouse rolled where he lay and delivered his line perfectly:

"Don't do it, Ricky! These are the guys who killed K-Jaw!"

"That's right, asshole!" Tony said. "Now it's your turn!"

Alvarez neither responded nor moved to descend.

"Hold this," Tony said, handing off the flashlight to

one of his goons. Then, with his free hand, he pointed something upward.

The flat *pop* of a rifle shot jerked Tony sideways. Legs screamed from the roadway, while Madden sprang forward, sprinting toward one of the goons.

Footsteps approached us at a dead run, and a bullet whizzed over my head. I dove sideways, smothering Mayday with my body. The runner tore past, angling downhill, and Regan took off after him.

"Regan, don't!"

Two of the SWAT guys burst through the fence and crashed down the hillside, joining the scrum below. Mayday and I waited for the dust to settle, then we stood and approached them cautiously, our hands in the air.

"It's MacTaggart! Don't shoot!"

Tony Gags lay on his side, wheezing like a punctured bagpipe, attended by one of the SWAT guys. The other was helping Madden put cuffs on the second goon, who lay facedown in the dirt. Mouse was on his feet now, lowering Alvarez from above. Everyone was breathing hard.

"Regan went after the runner," I told them.

Madden looked up. "I told you to stay put, damn it!"

Alvarez landed heavily, already unclipping the rope. "Status?"

"Through and through," the SWAT guy said, looking up from Tony. "His lung's collapsed. We'll need a medevac."

"Call it in. Then get—"

Two shots echoed from the darkness below. Then a third.

Alvarez was already running, his harness fittings clanking as he crashed through the brush like an es-

caped circus bear. I followed him, with agile footsteps—Mayday's—right behind me, all of us stumbling
forward until we came to a shelf where the land fell
away, the way down almost vertical.

"Stay here!" the detective commanded, his breathing labored. Then he jumped feetfirst, the rest of him
swallowed by the brush.

"Marta!" I called, but she was already gone, disappearing into the darkness after Alvarez.

"Shit!"

The slope was steeper than a playground slide, with
brambles and branches lashing my body. I heard somebody stumble and crash forward into the brush. By the
time I'd reached her, Mayday was up again and swip-
ing at her jeans. Her breath came in gulps.

"Look!" she said, pointing to a spot where two mismatched figures stood in dark silhouette.

We scrambled downward, slower now, dirt and peb-
bles clattering before us. Alvarez was winded, doubled
over. The runner was splayed facedown in the brush, his
hands cuffed behind him, while Regan stood with one
size-six tactical boot pressed into the small of his back.

Mayday shouldered past me, wrapping Regan in her
arms. They hugged for a long time. They kissed for
even longer.

I guess that settled the jurisdictional issue.

TWENTY-EIGHT

THE MOOD IN the room was two parts exhaustion and one part tension as we waited for Slew to return. The four SWAT officers were wedged side by side on the same leather sofa that Alvarez and Madden had occupied on my last visit, while the two detectives sat in the client chairs in front of the D.A.'s desk. Regan and Mayday, appropriately enough, occupied the love seat on the opposite wall.

I continued to pace.

"Will you sit the fuck down?" Alvarez snapped, twisting in his chair.

He'd been riding my ass for hours, from the helicopter ride to the Internal Affairs debriefing to the grilling we'd just endured from Slewzyski and his deputies. Now a hazy sun was rising on the glass towers of Los Angeles, where the smog wasn't nearly as heavy as the atmosphere in the room.

When the door burst open, Slewzyski blew into his office like a tornado. He was still wearing the track suit he'd thrown on when they'd roused him from bed at one o'clock in the morning. Behind him, a bleary-eyed assistant pushed a television monitor on a wheeled cart.

"I just spoke with the mayor," the D.A. announced, tossing a file folder and the morning newspaper onto his desk. He paused to give us each a scowl before dropping into his chair. "Need I say he wasn't pleased?"

The assistant busied himself connecting ports to wires and plugs to sockets, then handed a TV remote to his boss.

"Thank you, Tim. That will be all."

The D.A. waited until the door had closed again before speaking.

"Anthony Gagliano is out of surgery and in stable condition at Cedars. You'll be interested to know that the other three"—he opened the file and flipped a page—"James Palermo, Anthony Minnelli, and Peter Tesla have between them a total of five felony priors in three states, for crimes ranging from bookmaking to extortion to aggravated assault. Minnelli has two strikes here in California. That's the first good news I've had all morning."

"What about the gun?" Alvarez asked.

Slew closed the file and looked to the quartet on the couch.

"You mean the one in Gagliano's holster? Right next to the concealed weapon permit in his wallet? It was legally registered."

The D.A. lifted the remote and pointed it toward the monitor. The screen blinked to life, and a test pattern appeared.

"Metro Ops took the feed from the infrared camera and synced it with the audio from the parabolic mic. Here's the incident as it happened."

The test pattern gave way to a ghostly negative image of Mouse and Legs standing at the base of the scaffolding. We watched as they both turned to the sound of a voice.

Police! You're trespassing on government property! Climb up now, with your hands in the air!

I am coming! Please do not shoot me!

The camera must have been motion activated, since it followed Legs as she climbed, then swiveled back to Mouse.

I can't let go of the rope!

The camera jerked again as the three goons stumbled into the picture.

Hey!

Mouse was down, and Tony Gags had one hand on the rope, his flashlight pointed upward.

Ding dong! Climb down, or I'll pull you down!

Don't do it, Ricky! These are the guys who killed K-Jaw!

That's right, asshole! Now it's your turn! Hold this.

Tony handed off the flashlight. Then Slew pushed a button, and the image froze.

"That, gentlemen, is what a million-dollar lawsuit looks like."

On the video monitor, Tony stood with the rope in one hand and his other hand raised upward, his index finger extended.

"Geez, Tom." Alvarez squirmed in his chair. "So he didn't pull a gun. We still got the admission on Jaworsky, plus impersonating a police officer, battery on the Japanese chick, battery on the Moskowitz kid, and attempted murder on me."

Slew rested his forehead in a hand.

"Chico's right," I said, "and don't forget the wiretap, and the shots fired at Officer Fife."

The D.A. looked up.

"Thank you for the advice, MacTaggart. It's for listening to you that I have a civilian in the hospital, a million-dollar tort exposure, and what is at best an ambiguous admission on the Jaworsky murder. I have the mayor up my ass, Larry Archer waiting in the wings, and a dozen reporters downstairs calling for a statement. And I'm still no closer to closing the Mardian case or finding the missing goddamn painting. But you're right, I should look on the bright side. If I can beat the entrapment defense and the police brutality charge, I have four solid misdemeanors I can prosecute."

"Oh, grow some balls," I told him, moving to stand behind Alvarez. "The shooting was in-policy, and with the multiple wiretaps and the threats and the campaign finance counts, you've got the predicate acts for a major RICO prosecution. You flip Minnelli on his third strike, and you've got the Jaworsky murder."

Alvarez was nodding. "Yeah," he said, "that's right."

"Heck, with your sparkling personality," I said to Slew, "you'll ride this horse all the way to the attorney general's office."

Slewzyski glowered as he unfolded the newspaper. He snapped it open, clearing his throat to read:

"'Los Angeles attorney Jack MacTaggart announced on Saturday that he will publicly open the safe-deposit box of the late Jordan Mardian on Monday morning at nine o'clock. In an exclusive arrangement with Channel 9 *Action News,* the event will be broadcast live from the OneWest Bank branch on Beverly Boulevard in West Hollywood. Mardian, a prominent Santa Barbara art and antiques dealer, died in Pasadena on October 18 in what was originally thought to have been a suicide related to her involvement in the Goldilocks political scandal that has clouded Tuesday's U.S. Senate election. MacTaggart, who was originally hired to represent candidate Warren Burkett, was himself implicated in the scandal when an ax believed to be the Mardian murder weapon was discovered in the garage of his San Marino home. He has maintained his innocence, and claims that the contents of the safe-deposit box will reveal the real killer's identity.'"

The D.A. peered at me over the paper. "I can beat you to the bank with a search warrant."

"No, you can't. The best you can do is tie, and that's if you've got the key."

"Where'd you get the goddamn key?"

"Do I have the key?"

"Well, do you?"

"Sorry, Tom, that's attorney work product."

Slew rolled his eyes to the ceiling. "And to think, people call *me* a media whore. Compared to you, I'm Howard fucking Hughes." He refolded the paper and tossed it aside. "You'd better hope there's a signed confession in that box."

"Tune in and find out. I'm told we're expecting a thirty share."

The D.A. stood and turned his back to the room, his shape silhouetted by the twenty-story view. There was traffic now on the freeways, backlit by the lilac glow of the San Gabriels.

"Okay, here's how we'll play it," the D.A. said. "Anthony Gagliano was shot in the act of assaulting a police officer. The matter is under investigation, and details will be forthcoming as they are known. The fact that Mr. Gagliano is both the brother-in-law and a close personal confidant of Larry Archer, and the fact that he was armed and in the company of three known criminals at the time of the incident, should not reflect in any way on the candidate or on Tuesday's election."

I looked at Alvarez, who was already looking at me. He rolled his eyes.

"A pair of young graffiti artists were material witnesses to the incident," Slew continued. "They have been questioned and released, and their identities are being withheld pending completion of the investigation, which is expected to take several days."

The D.A. sighed.

"The incident was also witnessed by an off-duty Sierra Madre police officer who was able to render assistance to the officers on scene." Here Slew turned to the SWAT guys on the couch. "Her identity is being withheld pending her own departmental investigation."

He returned to his desk.

"What about me?" I asked him.

"You? You weren't there, MacTaggart. Or maybe you were, but I forgot to mention your name. I'm not your goddamned publicist."

He slumped into his swivel chair.

"That should hold things together until the election. After that, we'll have a better read on the situation. I'm guessing Archer's terminal at this point, but in this crazy campaign, you never know for sure." He shook his head in disgust. "Voters and jurors."

He tilted back in his chair and put his feet on the desk.

"Okay, that's it. You six, stay where you are. You three, go home and get some sleep. Officer Fife, nice work out there. MacTaggart, you're a serial fuck-up. I should have had my head examined for listening to you. I'd say don't talk to the press, but that would be like telling a dog not to chase the meat wagon."

I WAS DROWSING in the backseat of Regan's Toyota as we sailed northbound toward Pasadena on the uncharacteristically empty 110 Freeway.

"I thought you showed remarkable restraint," Mayday said over her shoulder, "considering they almost parted your hair."

"Don't forget, we're going to need Alvarez on Tuesday."

"How come?" Regan asked, twisting in the driver's seat.

I caught Mayday's eye in the mirror. "My, but you do keep a secret. I'll grant you that."

The women shared a look across the console.

"We were going to tell you, once things quieted down a little."

"That would have been thoughtful."

"Not that our personal lives are any of your business."

I showed them both a hand. "All right already, let's drop it. I'm happy for both of you. Really, I am."

"Thank you, Jack," Mayday said to the mirror. "That means a lot."

"So what's happening on Tuesday that we need Detective Alvarez?"

"I'll let Marta tell you all about it," I said to Regan, settling back and closing my eyes. "Ask her when her mouth isn't full."

I NAPPED UNTIL noon on Sunday, then watched a little football, then spent some quiet time in the garden. Reporters had gathered out front, and the doorbell rang a few times, but I managed to ignore them and the election and the events of the past twenty-four hours and spend some quality time with Sam, who knew nothing of Warren Burkett or Larry Archer, and who wouldn't have given a shit if he had.

I picked up the phone to call Angela, but I set it down without dialing. I pictured her at the hospital, her mascara running as she wept at her brother's bedside. Then again, maybe she was having her nails done. Either way, she was probably connected enough to know I'd been present at Tony's shooting, but what she, and her husband, would make of that fact was anybody's guess.

I imagined Ricky Rio, stretched out on a stained mattress in some darkened hideout with the blinds drawn, a radio playing quietly in the background, and I wondered whether the last Etch-A-Sketch message he'd sent via Mouse was intended to help or hinder. If he was in contact with Angela, and if Angela thought I'd gone onto her husband's payroll, then I was betting on the latter. And in that case I was better off for having missed it.

As for Warren Burkett, I imagined him preparing his victory speech, maybe outside on the stone patio of the stone mansion overlooking the stone pavement where, if he looked real hard, a bloodstain might still be visible. I hoped the sight of it didn't distract him.

I tried not to picture Mayday and Regan, whatever it was they were doing. I'd made an ass of myself there on both fronts, and now I had some yardage to make up. Regan in particular deserved my support, as her nighttime presence on Mount Lee had been my idea, however misguided its motive, and because her ostensible sick day had turned into a use-of-force incident that would soon be reported to her commanding officer.

On the whole I felt like a fighter in his dressing room an hour before the bell: trying to relax, trying to keep

busy, and most of all trying to keep his mind off what
was to come. Because if there's one thing I'd learned
as a trial lawyer, it's that investigation and preparation
will get you only so far.

At some point, you just have to put twelve in the box.

TWENTY-NINE

ELECTION DAY MINUS ONE.

Mayday reversed the route I'd followed with Shelly on Friday afternoon—Ventura Freeway to Forest Lawn Drive, Forest Lawn to Barham, and Barham to North Highland. The drive took us past the Disney, Warner Bros., and Universal film studios, not to mention Griffith Park and the Forest Lawn cemetery and the backside of Mount Lee. More important, it avoided the worst of the Monday morning rush-hour traffic.

"'Lonesome Dove'?" Mayday suggested, continuing the Etch-A-Sketch guessing game we'd been playing since we left Sierra Madre.

"'Bring me a treasure trove'?"

"'She has me to love'?"

"Don't rub it in."

She gave me a look.

"'Time to move'?"

"Never mind," I said, jabbing the POWER button on her stereo. "Whatever the message was, we're past the point of no return."

We listened to news radio, abuzz on all channels with teasers for the morning's big event, which the radio hosts likened to Geraldo Rivera's televised opening of Al Capone's vault.

"Poor Terina," Mayday said.

"Please. You're talking about a woman who'd film her own colonoscopy for a five share."

As we passed the entrance to the Hollywood Bowl, I glanced in the side-view mirror in time to see a white Honda hatchback changing lanes behind us.

"Pull over!"

Mayday did, and I jumped out, but the Honda braked hard and pulled a honking, swerving turn across three lanes of traffic, disappearing under the Hollywood Freeway overpass.

"What was it?" Mayday asked.

"My secret admirer."

"Any idea who?"

"I have a pretty good guess."

We took a test run past the OneWest Bank branch on Beverly. Although it wasn't yet eight o'clock, news vans were arrayed like circus elephants, nose to tail around the block, their microwave antennas extended. Reporters and camera operators crowded the sidewalk in front of the bank, while a pair of news helicopters circled noisily above.

"The sacrifices we make for democracy."

We turned into the campus of the Cedars-Sinai Medical Center and found our way to a parking structure near the intersection of George Burns Road and Gracie Allen Drive. As we walked back through the urban maze of hospital wings and office towers, I imagined Angela Archer watching us from a high window by her brother's bedside. I straightened my shoulders and punched up Terina Webb's number on my cell.

"Where are you?" she demanded before I could speak.

"One block away."

"Come around back. I've made arrangements."

We jaywalked Beverly Boulevard to Jerry's Famous Deli, then crossed North Sherbourne to the lot behind the bank. A private security car blocked the vehicular entrance, while a hulking Mike Tyson look-alike stood guard at the rear entrance to the building.

"Mr. MacTaggart?" He held the door for us. "Yes, sir, you come right on in."

The bank was empty of customers, but bustling nonetheless. Technicians were setting up lights and rolling equipment and taping cables to the lobby floor, while a producer with a clipboard babbled orders into a headset microphone. Through the front doors to the street I could see the other reporters, not from Channel 9 *Action News,* cupping their faces to the glass, while behind the tellers' counter, a clutch of girls stood whispering and giggling and sipping their morning coffee.

"Mr. MacTaggart!"

Cornelia Reese beckoned, and we stepped over cables and around equipment to where she stood outside the doorway marked CLIENT SERVICES. Down the back hallway, klieg lights with umbrella reflectors had already been placed at the entrance to the vault. Inside the little office, Terina Webb was half-seated on the front edge of the desk, reading a script while having her makeup applied.

"I don't know what I was thinking," the older woman said, eyeing the chaos in her lobby.

"You were thinking of Jordan Mardian," I reminded her, "flattened under a bridge."

Terina heard my voice and straightened, waving off the makeup woman. She shot a cuff to check her wrist-watch.

"You should have been in makeup half an hour ago."

"I did my makeup at home. What's the story here?"

Terina scrutinized my face as she described how the program would begin, with her standing in the lobby reciting a lengthy intro. Then a second camera would track her as she walked down the back hallway to the vault, where Cornelia Reese and I would be waiting.

"You remembered the key, I hope."

I dug the gilded charm from my pocket and held it out for her inspection. Mrs. Reese did the same with its brass counterpart.

"Okay," Terina said, again checking her watch. "We'll have a soundman waiting right about here with a boom—"

Tumult erupted at the front door, and Cornelia Reese hurried off to investigate. Voices were raised, and one of them I recognized.

"There you are!" the D.A. said as I poked my head into the lobby. He wore a cashmere topcoat over what looked like his best navy suit, and you could have shaved in the reflection from his polished black brogans. Behind him stood the same young assistant who'd been pushing the TV monitor on Sunday morning.

"Mrs. Reese, meet Thomas Slewzyski, our intrepid district attorney."

"Oh, no you don't." Terina bulled past us to confront the intruders. "We have a filming permit, and this is a closed set."

The kid handed his boss a folded paper.

"I have a warrant to search any safe-deposit box in the name of Jordan Mardian a.k.a Joan Marsden"— Slew held the document by the edge and let it fall open, just like in the movies—"and to take possession of any contents thereof that pertain in any way to her business, her activities, or her contacts."

The producer then inserted himself into the skirmish, and voices were raised anew. I glanced over at Mayday, who stood with folded arms and a smile.

"Wait a minute! Everybody calm down," I shouted over the hubbub, waiting a moment for quiet. "Terina, I'm sure Channel Nine News will want to do what it can to accommodate the district attorney."

"No more than four in the vault at any one time," Mrs. Reese reminded us.

"That's all right. If the district attorney joins us, and if the camera operator and the soundman both stand at the threshold, then we won't be breaking any rules."

That set Terina and the producer going again, and I backed out of the melee to stand with Mayday.

"I can't believe he actually showed up," she said.

"Never get caught between Tom Slewzyski and a TV camera."

FROM WHERE WE stood outside the vault, I heard the sound of Terina Webb's voice, although I couldn't make out her words. This lasted maybe five full minutes, during which Cornelia Reese fidgeted and the D.A. silently preened, and then the lobby began to brighten. Soon Terina was backing down the hallway toward us, still talking into her handheld microphone, her body in black silhouette and her hair a golden halo in the solar glare of the lights.

"…joined by attorney Jack MacTaggart and our special guest, District Attorney Thomas Slewzyski. Together they will open the safe-deposit box and reveal to you, in a Channel Nine *Action News* exclusive, the contents that are rumored to include a clue to the killer's identity."

Terina's free hand, open at the small of her back, was flapping wildly, waving us into the vault. We each stepped inside, sidling past the lights and reflectors, and stood together by the box. Terina backed in behind us, using the same hand to feel for the narrow center counter. She still faced the cameraman, who, along with a soundman holding a microphone on a pole, stopped short on the threshold.

"And now, the moment we've all been waiting for, as Mr. MacTaggart and a OneWest Bank representative use their keys to open the box of the late Jordan Mardian."

At last Terina turned to face us. Ms. Reese stepped to the box and inserted her key, and I did likewise, following her example. We twisted, and the keys turned, and the flush metal plate swung open on its hinges.

The metal box within was oblong in shape, half again larger than a shoebox. Ms. Reese removed it with great ceremony and placed it on the counter. She then excused herself silently, edging past the camera and out into the hallway. This allowed the cameraman to step into the vault as he leaned in for a close-up.

I could almost hear the music as it swelled to a dramatic crescendo in a million living rooms across the Southland.

The lid was hinged at its narrow end, and so lifted lengthwise. I stepped forward to open it, but Slew couldn't help himself, shouldering me, aside.

"Ready, Terina?"

"Ready, Mr. District Attorney."

I'd inched out of the shot by then, and I was almost to the door when Tom Slewzyski lifted the lid and peered inside the box. The camera tightened on the D.A. as he inverted the box and shook it once, sending a plastic lapel pin bouncing and skittering onto the granite countertop until it stopped spinning, and the cameraman stopped zooming, and the message ARCHER FOR SENATE filled every television screen in the City of Los Angeles.

THIRTY

ELECTION DAY.

I stopped to vote on my way in to the office, where
Mayday, Bernie, and I spent the rest of the morning
shuttling between our respective desks and the big television monitor in the conference room, which carried
continuous election coverage of what MSNBC was calling "the most bizarre and contentious senatorial contest
in recent memory."

The upshot of AL CAPONE REDUX—Tuesday morning's
Times headline—was a twenty-eight share for Channel
9 *Action News,* some angry finger-pointing by our es-
teemed district attorney, a harmonious "No comment"
from Mayday and me as we waded back to her car
through a sea of shouting reporters, and a sputtering
denial from the Archer for Senate campaign, which,
according to Terina Webb, had lapsed into a kind of
fatalistic bunker mentality.

The overnight polls showed Burkett with a solid
eight-point lead—the same soft cushion he'd enjoyed
as he sipped his Geisha House sake roughly three weeks
ago.

Regan dropped by at noon, out of uniform, to announce her administrative suspension from the Sierra
Madre Police Department, the result of what her commanding officer had termed "an appalling lapse in
professional judgment," and what her union rep was

calling actionable sexual-orientation discrimination.
I had to physically restrain Mayday from driving to
the Pasadena courthouse to seek an injunction. To as-
suage her anger, I heard myself offering to take on Regan's wrongful-termination case for free, if and when
it came to that.

The Archer campaign's "victory party headquarters" was at the Hyatt Regency Century Plaza Hotel,
in Century City, while Team Burkett was ensconced in
the more traditional Millennium Biltmore downtown.
It was to the latter that Mayday and I set out after dinner, in ball gown and black tie, feeling like Michaele
and Tareq Salahi, or maybe Owen Wilson and Vince
Vaughn—technically uninvited, but blithely undaunted
about crashing the party.

California voting locations were scheduled to close
at eight o'clock sharp, at which time, if history were any
guide, the winner of our Senate contest would promptly
be anointed on national television on the basis of exit-
polling data.

We rolled the Mercedes up to the Biltmore's Olive
Street entrance at five minutes to seven. The valets
were working double time, running and sweating and
tugging their caps in hasty salutation as the crème de
la crème of *tout* Los Angeles streamed from the sidewalk and through the marble lobby and up the gilded
staircase, making their way on whispering carpets to
the cavernous Biltmore Bowl, a banquet room legend-
ary for having hosted its share of notable L.A. soirées,
including eight Academy Awards ceremonies in the Old
Hollywood heyday of the 1930s and '40s.

The crush of bodies and the dizzying potpourri of
perfumes in the long and crowded hallway were al-

most claustrophobic, but they made our surreptitious entry—fortuitously timed to coincide with a flash-camera supernova attendant to Barbra Streisand's arrival—a proverbial piece of cake.

"Champagne?" I offered, lifting two glasses off the tray of a passing waiter.

We stood and sipped and watched the Who's Who of liberal Los Angeles nibble canapés and swap Occupy L.A. memories with their fellow travelers, the genteel spectacle set against piped-in music and a patriotic tricolor backdrop of bunting and balloons. Once our eyes had readjusted from the Streisand eclipse, we were able to spot a few lesser notables in the crowd—Ed Asner, and Rob Reiner, and a pneumatic strawberry blonde who might have been Scarlett Johansson—along with what seemed like every Democratic politician in the state.

"Quite a distinguished gathering," Mayday shouted over the hubbub.

"More so for your presence, m'lady."

"And yours, good sir."

We touched glasses.

At exactly 7:30, as per our arrangement, we made our way toward the dais, which consisted of a lectern centered on a low stage flanked by huge video monitors, all of it overhung by netted balloons and the largest BURKETT FOR SENATE poster known to man. There, Detectives Mike Madden and Chico Alvarez waited in their best business suits, fidgeting like meter readers at a nudist colony. Both men wore press credentials around their necks, presumably to explain the laptop computer case Madden had over his shoulder.

"Working undercover, I see."

"Christ, look at this." Alvarez elbowed his partner. "It's James fucking Bond."

I bowed. "And you remember Moneypenny."

Chico did a double-take at Mayday. Madden moved around him to stand between us.

"You got it?"

I patted my jacket.

"No bullshit this time?"

"Cross my heart and hope to die."

"Don't think that can't be arranged."

I checked my watch. The polls were closing in fifteen minutes. I looked around for a waiter.

"Where's the boss tonight?" I asked the detectives.

Alvarez grunted. "Century City, taking one for the team. We told him we had a lead on the painting we had to check out. He said to call him if anything came of it."

"And the warrant?"

Madden patted his jacket.

I saw Scott Tully then, making his way toward the stage, stopping to shake the hand and kiss the ass of every blue suit he passed. For him, tonight was both a coronation and a valedictory, and he was already on the make for his next campaign.

"Bottoms up," I told the detectives, raising my glass. "The time is nigh."

We rode the elevator in nervous silence, with Madden and Alvarez pocketing their press passes and hanging gold shields in their place. The old car lurched to a stop on nine, where, as the doors slid open, we were immediately confronted by a pair of private security guards blocking our path to the suite at the end of the hallway.

"Hold on, buddy," the first said to Alvarez, clapping

a hand to his chest. Then he noticed the shield. Madden held up the warrant as Alvarez reached out and plucked the little plastic bud from the security guy's ear and then spun him to the wall and kicked his feet apart, all while stripping the wire out of his shirt collar.

The other guard showed his hands in surrender.

We knocked once, but didn't wait for a response. Five heads turned in the living room, where CNN blared from a television set in an armoire. Warren and Bobbi Burkett sat side by side on the couch, while Maureen, their portly daughter, stood behind them, sipping champagne from a flute. Harwood sat quietly in a wing chair by the window. The fifth member of the inner sanctum, to my surprise, was none other than Max Drescher, who brightened with recognition as we entered from the hallway.

"Hello, Mr. MacTaggart! Hello, Marta! I didn't know you were going to be here!"

Burkett found his campaign smile as he rose from the sofa. He crossed the carpeted expanse.

"By all means, a pleasant surprise. Jack, good to see you again. Miss Suarez." He pumped our hands in turn, and when he came to the frowning detectives, the smile wilted as he wiped his hand on his jacket. "Come in, come in. The polls are closing in five minutes. I was just going over my speech."

The suite was huge and ornate and suffused in the golden glow of a dozen table lamps. A room service cart stood angled in one corner, its dirty plates haphazardly stacked. There were flowers everywhere, and fruit baskets, and a large crystal bowl in which wine bottles floated in a sea of melting ice. On the coffee table were papers and a red marker pen.

Madden disappeared into the bedroom. When he returned a moment later, he walked straight to where Harwood was sitting. The big man stood and held his arms out to be frisked.

But I was watching the women: Maureen, sipping her wine and munching cashews from a bowl on the sofa table; Bobbi Burkett, her eyes still glued to the television, as though to look away, even for an instant, might unmoor her from her surroundings.

"Who are you?" Alvarez asked Max, and I answered for him.

"Max Drescher. He was a third-party candidate. I'm guessing he threw his support to the mayor."

Max nodded. "Last night, on my Web site. Mr. Burkett has been very sympathetic to my proposals regarding IRS reform."

"I'll bet he has. Now, would you excuse us for a while, Max? Mr. Burkett and I have some important attorney-client matters to discuss with these gentlemen."

Before escorting Max to the door, Madden unslung the laptop from his shoulder and set it on the coffee table. The TV cut to a live shot of a CNN reporter in the Biltmore Bowl downstairs, a hand to his ear, engulfed by cheering Burkett supporters. Randy Newman's "I Love L.A." was blaring over the loudspeakers, and the crowd was growing restive.

It was Harwood who broke the silence.

"What exactly is going on here?"

"A murder investigation," I told him. "But you already knew that."

Mayday crouched in her gown and unzipped the laptop from its case and began unspooling the cables.

"What murder investigation?"

This was Maureen Burkett, speaking through a mouthful of nuts. She'd been poured into a size-Huge gown in sequined gold lamé, looking like four quarts in a twelve-ounce goblet.

"The investigation into who bashed Jordan Mardian in the head with the blunt end of an ax, then threw her body over an eight-foot suicide barrier on the Colorado Street Bridge, then drove up to Montecito to destroy her client records, where she murdered a woman named Catherine Orlov in the process."

"She?" Maureen calmly sipped her wine. "You're not suggesting a woman did all that."

Back in the CNN studio, an anchorman stood before a huge blue-and-red electoral map. As the words SPECIAL ANNOUNCEMENT scrolled across the screen, all heads in the room turned to the armoire.

...*with polls officially closing on the West Coast, CNN is now calling the hard-fought and controversial California senatorial contest for Democrat Warren Burkett, the former mayor of Los Angeles.*

A muffled roar rose up through the elevator shaft, and the floor actually vibrated under our feet. Bobbi Burkett laid a hand on her husband's shoulder.

"No, Maureen," I said, "not a woman. A woman couldn't have moved a hundred-and-ten-pound body like that. Or ditched Jordan Mardian's car at the airport. That would have required at least two women. Both large, and both fairly strong."

The door to the hallway burst open, and Scott Tully fell into the room, his breath coming in gulps.

"What the hell is going on up here?" he demanded. "Warren? Are you all right?"

Burkett turned on the couch to face me. "You have no proof of that. No motive. No evidence."

I picked up the remote and muted the TV set.

"Funny you mention motive, because that's the one thing that had me stumped. You see, I made the mistake of assuming that your side was trying to win this election. What I didn't realize for the longest time was that it was actually the other way around."

"*Not* trying to win?" Tully yelped. "Are you insane?"

I turned to face him.

"You of all people know that Mrs. Burkett didn't want her husband back in politics, back on the hustings. She wanted him home, and retired, and having their Sunday brunch together on their little patio overlooking the Arroyo. Certainly not on the road, or in Washington, surrounded by aides and interns and sleeping in strange hotels. How does the saying go? Jealousy is a green-eyed monster."

"How dare you!"

Bobbi Burkett had finally disengaged herself from the television.

"I'm sorry to be so blunt," I told her, "but you didn't exactly hide your feelings. And if you couldn't dissuade your husband from running, you thought you could at least stop him from winning. A sex scandal would do the trick. Without the actual sex, of course. Nothing too sordid. Embarrassing, perhaps, but it wouldn't have been the first time. You'd heard of a woman in Santa Barbara who could arrange something like that, and so you went and paid her a visit."

Burkett remained silent, his hands gripping his thighs, even as the TV showed a sea of supporters in the ballroom downstairs waving signs and chanting his name.

"What you didn't count on is that the woman you hired had a past, and that her past had a connection to the Archer campaign. And that Angela Archer wanted her husband to win this election about as much as you wanted your husband to win—which is to say, not at all."

Harwood stepped forward, his hand on a chairback. "You mean *both* wives, each working against her own husband?"

I nodded. "Jordan Mardian told Ricky Rio about her new client, and Rio hatched a scheme of his own. Phase one was an art heist, all choreographed by Rio. A small favor from Mardian, or maybe it was a double payday. We'll probably never know, but Rio got the painting, and Burkett got the publicity. Contracts were filled, and everyone went home happy."

"Everyone except Angela Archer."

"Angela and Ricky," I corrected Harwood. "They're an item, you see. Which brings us to phase two of Rio's plan, in which he volunteers to shoot a campaign video for Archer and then slips the stolen painting into the background. Then, before the ad goes public, he tips off Burkett's lawyer as to what to look out for."

"Tips off how?" Alvarez demanded.

"Not important. The point is, it works. The polls flip again, and now Burkett's back on top."

"So why is the Mardian woman killed?"

"I can't say for certain, but I can guess." I turned again to the couch. "There was a second meeting between Jordan Mardian and Mrs. Burkett, only this time at Burkett's house. Either Mrs. Burkett invited her, maybe to reload on her husband, or else Mardian saw another payday and tried to blackmail Mrs. Burkett. I'm guessing the latter, the way things played out."

Harwood was frowning. "How do you know the meeting was at Burkett's?"

"Organic compost. Those were the stains on Jordan Mardian's clothes. High in ammonium and nitrates, the kind a body might pick up if it were moved in the back of a pickup truck in which potting soil and bedding plants had recently been hauled."

I watched Harwood's face. He'd been to the Burkett house and had seen Maureen's gardening project. He, too, swung his gaze to the couch.

"Maureen and Bobbi?"

"There's a maid you'll want to question, but here's my version of how it went down. Jordan Mardian and Mrs. Burkett are having it out. Maureen walks in on the argument and clocks Mardian from behind. Then panic sets in. They can call the cops and expose the whole sordid business, or they can pull on their gardening gloves and carry the body out to the truck and wait a few hours until the streets are empty, then drive over to the bridge. Two strong women, straddling the truck bed and the guardrail. One on the wrists, one on the ankles. Two swings and a toss. Three minutes, max, then a quick trip to the airport. Nothing to tie them to the crime or to the deceased. Nothing, that is, unless Jordan Mardian kept records."

The telephone rang. We all looked at it.

"Archer," Tully said. "His concession call."

Nobody else moved, so I picked up the phone. Larry Archer sounded like a man who'd just swallowed a golf ball.

"Congratulations, Burkett. I'd say it was a fair fight, and that the best man won, but we both know that would be bullshit."

"Thanks, Larry, I'll give him the message, and if Tom Slewzyski's still over there, tell him to get his ass to the Biltmore."

"MacTaggart?"

"That's right. And don't worry, I'll credit the forty grand against the reward money, which means you only owe me ten. Just remember, Larry, nobody likes a welsher."

As I hung up the phone, I saw Mayday at the television set, angling it on the pullout shelf and plugging cords into the back. All other eyes in the room were on me.

"You know the rest of the story," I said. "Orlov gets it from behind, just like Mardian, and the records are destroyed in a fire."

"The proof, you mean." Burkett twisted on the couch. "You admit you have no proof."

"Ah, but that's where Ricky Rio's second message comes in."

Alvarez stiffened. "His second message?"

"That's right. The one about the safe-deposit box."

"Which was empty!" Burkett shouted.

"Which was empty on Monday." I withdrew a DVD from my jacket. "Saturday morning was a different story."

I handed the disk to Mayday, who slid it into the side tray of the open laptop. The TV blinked from CNN to a grainy split-screen image: Jordan Mardian's front porch on the left and a small office on the right, both viewed from overhead, both overlaid with a digital clock. As

Bobbi Burkett entered the left-hand frame to ring the front doorbell, Jordan Mardian rose from her chair and crossed out of the right-hand frame to greet her.

Here in the present, at the Biltmore in Los Angeles, Bobbi Burkett was weeping. She lowered her face into her hands, and as her sobs grew louder, her body began to shake.

It was her daughter, not her husband, who moved to comfort her.

"You're wrong about one thing," Maureen said, her hand on her mother's back. "There was no panic. No vapors, Mr. MacTaggart, or wringing of hands. Not on my part. You can't pay money to a blackmailer, isn't that what they always say? So you see, we had no choice in the matter. No choice at all, and I, for one, am not sorry in the least."

A pounding rattled the door. Tully, moving like a sleepwalker, crossed to open it, and we heard the muffled chanting from eight floors below. He addressed Burkett when he returned.

"It's time," he said.

All eyes turned to Chico Alvarez, who glanced at his partner before putting the question to me.

"So what did Burkett know, and when?"

"Everything, I suspect. But not until after the Orlov murder."

Alvarez thought for a minute, then nodded.

"All right, go ahead. It's not like you can run."

Burkett stood. He looked down at his wife, still hunched and weeping, and at the television in the armoire, which had returned to the raucous scene downstairs. Then he gathered up his speech and turned on his heel, following Tully to the door.

He stopped before he got there, turning again to face me.

"She tried to frame you," he said, nodding to his daughter.

"Does she drive a white Honda hatchback?"

He nodded.

"Then she probably thought about killing me."

"If you had the evidence on Saturday, why didn't you go public then? Or take it to the police? Why that charade at the bank on Monday?"

I looked at Mayday, then back to the newly-elected U.S. senator from California.

"Because I'm an American," I told him.

THIRTY-ONE

IT WAS AFTER midnight by the time we'd given our statements to the police, returned to the Biltmore for my car, and rolled to the curb outside Mayday's Pasadena condo. The lights were on inside, and I could see a figure, a petite shadow, step to the window and part the curtains.

Mayday and I faced each other in the idling Benz. She raised a hand, and I raised mine, and we slapped a high-five. Then she bent for her handbag, reached inside, and extracted a folded slip of paper that she placed on the console between us.

"You really should call her," she said. Then she stepped from the car, slammed the door, and climbed the front walk, hiking her dress and wobbling up the stairs in her heels.

I unfolded the note. In Mayday's neat little handwriting was a telephone number I didn't recognize, beneath a name that I did—that of my old girlfriend, Tara Flynn.

As I took the curve onto Sycamore Lane, a car coming toward me flashed its high beams once and then sped off into the night. It was a late-model Porsche, silver in color, and in our fleeting moment of equipoise, I saw Angela and Ricky, their faces underlit by a greenish glow from the dashboard.

I think they were laughing, but I wouldn't swear to it.

Sam greeted me in the foyer with a new bone in his mouth. A fire crackled in the living room fireplace, and on the coffee table before it, propped against a sweating bottle of Dom Perignon, was a familiar red-and-white children's toy. The message on the screen read:

ART
IRRITATES
LIFE

I looked at Sam, whose tail was wagging. "You might be the worst guard dog in the history of your species."

There'd been two dozen DVDs in Jordan Mardian's safe-deposit box; some with video, some with still photographs of people and paintings and objets d'art. We'd watched only a few, Mayday and I, and we'd trusted that Alvarez, along with his counterparts in the FBI and the Santa Barbara PD, would follow up on the rest.

Meaning that the Goldilocks Affair, while over for us, was still a long way from happily ever after.

What I didn't find in the box was a will, or a trust, which meant that Pam and Shelly, as Joan Marsden's next of kin, would inherit their sister's estate. I had a vision of Pam in her red Ferrari, roaring up the shaded Montecito driveway, a bale of hay in the passenger seat for her new backyard pony. It had all the makings of a reality TV show, and I made a mental note to call Terina Webb in the morning.

I removed my jacket and tugged at my bow tie and draped them both on the couch. I went to the stereo cabinet and flipped through my old CDs until I found the one I was after.

Green-eyed lady, lovely lady
Strolling slowly towards the sun

Green-eyed lady, ocean lady
Soothing every raging wave that comes

At about the time that Mike Madden and Chico Alvarez were handcuffing the Burkett women at the Biltmore, Tom Slewzyski had been clear across town, standing behind Larry Archer on a badly lit stage while the embattled billionaire made a short and bitter concession speech to a half-full hotel ballroom. As a consequence, Slew had been late to the real party, which by then had moved to the Police Administration Building downtown. Mayday and I had passed him in the lobby on our way out, and although we'd stopped to bid him a pleasant good evening, he'd strode past us stone-faced, neither slowing nor speaking a word.

While we'd missed Burkett's acceptance speech, the commentators were calling it one for the ages, a soaring discourse on government and society that was already kindling talk of a run for higher office. He'd said that his wife was "too overcome with emotion" to join him onstage, and he'd described himself as "an imperfect man, off to battle an imperfect system, in order to form a more perfect union."

On the subject of unions, I'd raised with Mayday the prospect of Regan Fife joining the firm as an in-house investigator, in the event she should lose her administrative appeal. We probably couldn't keep her busy, I'd warned, but she'd at least have a job and a paycheck while she planned her next move. It was right around Dodger Stadium that Mayday had unbuckled her seat belt and leaned across the console to kiss me on the cheek.

I returned to the kitchen and took a glass down from

the cupboard. Back in the living room, I lowered the stereo and opened the champagne and poured myself a long-overdue drink. I sat on the sofa and unfolded the slip of paper Mayday had given me, and I set it on the table.

I checked my watch. Then I picked up the telephone.

"Hello?"

Shoshanna Gold had been asleep.

"This is Jack MacTaggart. I hope this isn't an inconvenient time to be calling."

"What? What time is it?"

"Because if it is, I can always call back."

There was a rustling sound, and maybe the squeak of bedsprings.

"Is it about the painting?" she finally asked.

I looked up at the mantel—at the heavy gilt frame, and at the soft pastel colors dancing in the firelight.

"No, Shoshanna. It was never about the painting. But that's a long, long story."

* * * * *

ACKNOWLEDGMENTS

THANKS GO FIRST and foremost to my agent, Antonella Iannarino of the David Black Agency, and to my editor, Peter Joseph of Thomas Dunne Books, for their unwavering faith and support. Thanks also go out to Luke Thomas of the David Black Agency, to Hector DeJean of St. Martin's Press, to Jon Cassir of CAA, and to everybody at Minotaur Books who had a hand in making *Green-Eyed Lady* a reality. Special, personal thanks go out to Lynda Larsen, Katie Greaves, Susan House, Dan Greaves, Steve Madison, and to the myriad others—you know who you are—who either assisted with the manuscript or helped to sustain and encourage me along the way. Without all of you, I wouldn't have Jack.